BOOM!

At first I thought a smoke bomb had gone off onstage, but the way the band members leaped back told me it wasn't planned. They were all miked, and as the dust settled I heard their shouts and curses.

Stagehands and band members surged to the apron, so I couldn't yet see what was wrong. Bardot sprang back to the mic and yelled, with a catch in his voice, "A doctor! We need a doctor!"

A couple of overwhelmed security guards rushed to the front of the theater and tried in vain to calm the crowd.

I turned to Melissa. "Did you see—" But she was gone. Maybe she'd run up to the stage to check on her idol, though he seemed fine to me. So did all the other musicians. But someone else must be hurt.

Lalita jogged back up the aisle, cell phone clamped to her ear, calling for an ambulance. I followed her out to the lobby, and when she hung up, asked what had happened.

"Oh, Jesus, a big chunk of plaster fell and hit one of the cameramen. He's still alive, but he's out cold!" Her eyes were wide with horror. "I can't believe it... That proscenium is old, but it should have been secure!"

I knew what she must be thinking. If the cameraman was seriously hurt, the Friends of the Rialto would be liable. "It was probably the fault of the guy working up there. He must've jarred something loose."

"What guy?"

"Somebody was up there—a stagehand, I guess—just before that piece fell. Walking on top of the arch."

"Walking?" Lalita stared at me, then gave her head an emphatic shake. "Quinn, that arch is less than a foot wide. No one could stand up there. It's impossible!"

HEX, DEATH
&
ROCK 'N' ROLL

by E. F. Watkins

As always, I need to thank The Writers' Workshop of Northern NJ—Elisa Chalem, Dan Karlan, Susan Moshiashwili, Ed Rand, Jeremy Salter and Joanne Weck—who always bring various types of expertise to their insightful critiques. I received background on the logistics of a video shoot from Mario Costabile of Visual Energy Entertainment; on legal issues from Louis M. Masucci, Jr.; and on journalistic conflicts of interest from Anne-Marie Cottone. Finally, I need to thank my painstaking editor E. J. Gilmer, who catches any problems the rest of us have let slip through the cracks, and Amber Quill Press, which I feel will provide an especially supportive "home" for this particular Quinn Matthews adventure.

PROLOGUE

Midnight. Vernal Equinox.
Waxing moon—the best phase to bring something new into form

Candles in short, votive holders burned at each point of the altar's pentagram. Two red, for Passion and Purpose. Three black, for Vengeance, Judgment and Destruction.

Their wispy smoke perfumed the small, darkened chamber, countering the stink of corruption from just beyond its walls. Their shivering flames threw the only light.

The solitary practitioner—magickal name, The Raven—stood naked before the draped altar. Hands trembled as they laid out all the necessary objects for tonight's ritual.

Graveyard dirt, harvested at a local cemetery.

A few locks of human hair.

A new razor blade, still wrapped in crisp paper.

At the center of the altar, a small brass bowl inscribed with astrological symbols held several delicate, dried bones. Near this, The Raven placed a palm-sized stone, also from the graveyard.

Tonight's ceremony would be dangerous, but The Raven had prepared for it carefully. Previous attempts had been unsuccessful, possibly because they had been too timid. The Discord Spell, for example—which involved a loosening of knots in a string—had failed miserably.

Time for a bolder approach. More decisive.

More terminal.

This time, The Raven had done the correct preparation. A full twenty-four-hour fast. Also a ritual cleansing—inside and out.

And it seemed to be working. Tonight, the practitioner felt light, empty, an open conduit through which larger forces could travel, unobstructed, to cross the boundaries between worlds.

The other key element would be strength of purpose. The instructions for this ceremony stated it must be performed "with full commitment, no hesitation and no mercy."

A few weeks ago, The Raven might have shrunk from such an extreme approach. A recent outrage, though, had swept away any hesitation. Just the memory of that rejection brought back a hot flush of mingled shame and fury.

No mercy?

No problem!

Hands steadier now, The Raven picked up the sheet of parchment-like paper printed with the words of the ritual. At this hour, in this secret space, no one else heard them recited aloud:

"Spirit of darkness, hear my call
I summon you to do my will
What was taken from me must be restored
And the interloper must be destroyed
You will go where I cannot enter
To cause pain to my supplanter
You will keep watch where I cannot see
Bring fear and death to my enemy."

Into the brass bowl, on top of the small bones, went the graveyard dirt and the silken locks of hair, which glinted in the candlelight.

Next, the Raven unwrapped the razor blade. Passed it once through the sterilizing fire, then drew a fine line across a fingertip. The blade was so fresh, so sharp, it gave hardly any pain—in fact, almost a perverse satisfaction. A squeeze released a few drops of bright blood into the bowl to stain the other substances.

The stone, especially chosen, was just the right size and heft to pound all the ingredients in the bowl. It ground together bones, dirt, hair and blood. The brass rang with the forces of many blows, but this inner sanctum was close to soundproof. No one would hear.

The chant for the next part of the ceremony was adapted from a traditional voodoo curse:

"Bones of anger, bones of lust
Know that my revenge is just
With these bones I now do crush
Make my enemy turn to dust!"

The vision of this coming to pass was so satisfying, it was almost hard to stop mashing and grinding, even after the bones indeed had been powdered to mix with the dirt. Finally, the touch of a candle flame set whatever solid bits were left ablaze.

The next part of the ritual was the most important. The Raven held the flaming bowl outward, in both hands, while reciting the incantation.

"On my anger you may feed
Until you have done this deed
Now my purpose is your own
This night, my Servant is born!"

In the silence that followed, the practitioner placed the bowl back on the altar and waited for the contents to burn down. As they did, a thin trail of smoke spiraled upward from the ashes. The air of the chamber also took on a new vibration.

The spiral solidified into a pillar. Expanded into a smoky shadow with almost human contours.

The Raven staggered backward in fear, spine pressing against the locked door.

The smoke grew thick, suffocating—even worse than the stench of death that lay beyond the door. The flames of the five small candles began to sputter, as if smothered by the weight of the shadow...

Then snuffed out.

With a gasp, The Raven groped frantically in darkness for

the overhead chain. A sharp jerk brought the harsh glare of the electric bulb.

The shadow had gone.

But it *had* been there. As proof, the brass bowl now sat empty, scrubbed clean.

The ashy offerings of bone, hair and blood had transformed into something else. Something newly born into dark power.

The Raven sagged against the doorjamb of the claustrophobic chamber. Exhilaration mixed with terror. The ritual had worked—the Servant had been summoned.

But could it be controlled?

Memories boiled up again. Of humiliation, mockery. But countered this time by a new sense of excitement, even hope.

I'm not alone anymore! The Servant will do my bidding now and clear my path. It will destroy the rival who replaced me...

...and anyone else who stands in my way!

CHAPTER 1

"Of course, they say the theater's haunted."

Lalita Washington confided this with a gleam in her ebony eye, as a nice, additional tidbit for my newspaper story. She couldn't know that her announcement sent a painful jolt of adrenaline through my veins.

I forced a grin. "Aren't they all?"

"Exactly—what's an old theater without a ghost? Oops, be careful, Quinn!" Her warning came as we started down a plywood ramp that covered some missing steps.

Luckily, because I knew I'd be spending the afternoon crawling around a hundred-year-old theater undergoing renovation, I'd dressed down in corduroy pants and flats. I felt positively frumpy, though, next to Lalita, whose elegant black pants suit seemed to magically repel the plaster dust. She also never mussed the sleek bob that formed perfect parentheses around her pretty, exotic face. Probably in her mid-thirties— same as me—she made a striking spokeswoman for the nonprofit Friends of the Rialto.

"No one can agree on who the ghost is, though," she went on. "One story says it's a vaudeville comic who owed money to loan sharks and was shot in his dressing room. It could have been the stagehand in the nineteen-thirties who fell from the catwalk and broke his neck. Or the old man who came to the movies almost every day, back in the sixties, and finally passed away in his usual last-row seat."

I smiled again, even though I really didn't want to hear all these colorful stories. Once upon a time, I might have found them as entertaining as Lalita obviously did. I'd since come to realize that a ghost was no laughing matter. Over the past few months, in my job of writing about architecture and interior design, I'd tried hard to avoid any encounters with the spirit world.

So far, though, I didn't pick up any negative vibes from the Rialto—only the superficial creepiness of its faded glamour. I tried to imagine it in its heyday. Mentally, I filled in the gaps in the decorative plasterwork, restored the frieze of classical figures along the upper walls and replaced the missing bulbs in the ornate brass sconces. Right now, much of the twelve-thousand-square-foot space was shrouded in drop cloths and half-obscured by scaffolding. Whining and scraping noises reminded us that the carpenters and plasterers had begun work.

Gil O'Bannon, the *Sentinel's* lanky, silver-haired photographer, had climbed the lower rungs of one scaffold to get a shot of the huge ceiling medallion. He made his way back down and joined me and Lalita, just as she wrapped up her story.

"At any rate," she said, "for decades, people have been hearing voices and footsteps, or feeling a touch when no one was there."

"Who's been touching who?" Gil raised an eyebrow, obviously hoping for some whiff of scandal.

"I was just telling Quinn about the Rialto's ghost."

"Hah. You're talking to the right lady!" Then Gil saw my expression and shut his trap.

Too late. Lalita spun back to me with interest. "Really? Why?"

"I actually had an…issue like that at my house, when I first moved in," I admitted. "But it seems to be over now."

Gil added, "She told the ghosts to scram, and by golly, they did."

If only it had been that simple, I thought.

To my relief, Lalita treated the whole thing lightly. "Well, if we have any trouble like that around here, Quinn, we'll know who to call! Come on, let me show you the stage."

Gil wandered toward the theater's deep orchestra pit. Eyes focused upward, he tripped on something—maybe a scrap of old wood—and barely righted himself before he and his expensive camera both went over the edge.

Lalita caught her breath. "Watch your step, please!"

"My fault," he assured her. "I got distracted by this wonderful old archway." He pointed up at the stage's heavily carved proscenium.

"Isn't that something?" she enthused. "All hand-carved plaster. We'll clean it up, of course, and redo the gilding on all that detail work."

"You told me on the phone a lot of celebrities have performed here." I hoped to steer her back toward stories of live past occupants rather than dead ones.

"Al Jolson and Rudy Vallee in the early thirties. Later on, Frank Sinatra and Tony Bennett—both Jersey natives, y'know!"

"They came here? To Elizabeth?" Gil asked, impressed.

"It's always been a good sized-city," Lalita reminded him, "and performers used to try out their acts here before taking them across the river to Manhattan."

I scribbled feverishly in my spiral notepad. This kind of walk-and-talk interview was always hard work, but I'd never gotten the hang of doing it by tape recorder. Either my batteries would die halfway through or the mic would pick up so much ambient noise that it drowned out the one person I was trying to record.

Last Christmas, my successful executive cousin Michael had given me a high-tech pen with a chip that actually recorded while you wrote. I wished I'd thought to bring it today.

"It's a wonderful building," I said. "Too bad it was allowed to deteriorate so far."

"I know. It was a legit movie theater for many years, then it became a Triple-X house in the seventies and eighties. For the last decade or two, it's been closed more often than open, and the city almost tore it down. But we think it can be a great live venue again. We'll bring in Latin and other multicultural acts, hip-hop artists, blues and jazz. And there's still a movie screen, so during the week, we can show indie films."

"Gonna take a lot of work, though, innit?" noted Gil, a touch of his brogue creeping out. "And a lot of money."

"We got a five-hundred-thousand-dollar challenge grant that's been matched by some private donors. And just recently we got another nice boost. You've heard of Mad Love, the rock group?"

Gil shrugged—though a proud son of the Auld Sod, he'd barely heard of U2 until last year—but I piped right up. "Oh, sure!"

"They're shooting a video here Friday night." Lalita saw my look of confusion and laughed. "I know, the place is a mess, but that's what they want! They were looking for a movie house with kind of a run-down, Gothic atmosphere. Anyway, they're paying us a nice sum to use the place just the way it is."

With that explanation, I could envision it better. "Sounds great."

She cocked her head at me. "You a fan?"

"I do like their music, and I bought their last CD."

"I'll give you tickets, then." Swinging toward Gil, she added, "You, too."

"Oh, thanks, but..." He raised one hand in polite protest. "I'll wait for those jazz concerts."

"Well, Quinn will use them, won't you? It's no big deal; they're free."

"Really?" I didn't even try to buy concert tickets for well-known rock groups anymore, since the prices were usually beyond my meager income as a part-time journalist.

Lalita walked us both back toward the lobby, with Gil snapping more vignettes along the way. "They're performing the song as a kind of mini-concert, and they want a live audience. They gave tickets to all of us on staff. My husband's out of town, and I'll be running around all night keeping things under control, so our tickets should go to someone who can appreciate them."

"In that case, thanks!" I wondered if I could lure my boyfriend, Tony Gordon, away from work for the evening.

"Wear earplugs," Gil warned me. "I know a guy who lost his hearing when he went to a rock concert in a small theater like this."

Lalita shook her head. "They're not bringing their full sound system—they'll be dubbing the video later, anyway. But they do want shots of the audience screaming and getting into the music, so I guess it'll be loud enough."

I had to wonder how the ghost of the old vaudevillian was going to feel about that.

"Sorry, hon," Tony told me on the phone. "The decision on the Contreras bribery case is probably going to come down Friday afternoon. I'll be here late, knocking out the story on deadline."

"Ugh, I forgot about that." Although I appreciated the important work Tony did as the *Sentinel's* chief investigative reporter, his long hours and total preoccupation with his job tended to strain our relationship. I almost felt guilty right now, at four P.M., as he toiled away at the office, while I lounged on my bed with cell phone and laptop. Of course, it wasn't my fault that, in the last round of downsizing, the paper had cut me down to twenty-three hours a week and now let me do a lot of my work from home.

"Mad Love…" he mumbled. "I read something weird about them a little while back, but I can't remember what."

To save him some much-needed brain cells, I went on the Internet to see what I could dig up. "Let's see…about a year-and-a-half ago, their former lead guitarist got arrested for heroin possession, so they fired him. Imagine that!"

"Wow, a rock band with a zero-tolerance policy? What's the world coming to?"

I read on. "They hired a new guy just before the last tour. If he's the one playing on their latest CD, it was a smart move. The lead guitar on that is brilliant!"

"Interesting…but not the weird thing I read about," Tony said.

I scrolled down through a few more headings about Mad Love and opened another story. "Lead singer Alan Bardot came out as bisexual a couple of months ago, in a radio interview."

The article, from *Entertainment Weekly*, included a photo of the band in concert. As I'd already observed from their CD jacket, they were a good-looking group. But the singer still stood out, even though he was only medium-height, slim and a bit boyish.

(All fine with me—Tony looks a little like that, too.) Another, solo shot of Bardot showed him lounging on a red leather sofa, dark bangs rock-star messy above big, sea-green eyes. He wore a cat-that-swallowed-the-canary smile, one silver skull earring and a snug black T-shirt with white letters that read, "The One Your Mother Always Warned You About."

I laughed out loud, then had to explain what was so funny.

"Guy's got a sense of humor," Tony admitted. "But what I read was something about an accident. Did their plane almost crash, or something?"

"Here it is. 'Toward the end of their last tour, the band's plane had just taken off from a small airport in Ohio when one of the engines lost power. Luckily, the pilot was able to turn around and land safely at the same airport.'"

"That's it," Tony said. "I think something else happened, too—"

"An equipment truck went off the road, another malfunction of some kind, and the driver went to the hospital," I filled in. "The band started calling it their Hard Luck Tour."

"Huh. Sounds like more than that to me!"

Hearing interest in Tony's voice, I pressed my advantage. "If you come along tomorrow night, you might be able to ask them some nosy, reporter-type questions."

"Not possible, I'm afraid. I'll just have to leave that up to you."

"You might be sorry—this Bardot guy is pretty hot. If Lalita can get me backstage to meet him, who knows what could happen?"

To my annoyance, Tony just chuckled. "Why should I worry? You just told me he's gay."

"Bisexual."

"Whatever. Hey, why don't you ask Nancy to go with you? Didn't she tip you off about that theater restoration in the first place? And she covers music."

"Classical. She plays clarinet with a chamber music ensemble!"

"Maybe she's up for a change of pace. Anyhow, I got some calls to make, babe. Talk to you later."

I let him go and decided phoning Nancy Sabatino might not be a bad idea. She *had* kind of gotten me into this, because her lawyer husband Rob handled some contracts for the Friends of the Rialto, regarding the restoration.

I punched her cell number. Still holding my phone—I never sprang for one of those Bluetooth gizmos—I crossed to my closet and opened it.

Nancy also works for the *Sentinel* part-time, and I caught her in the supermarket picking up two salmon steaks for dinner. She was happy to hear I'd been invited to the video shoot, but as I'd expected, noisy Goth-rock wasn't her cup of arsenic.

"I'm a little self-conscious about going by myself," I admitted. "What if I'm the only person there over thirty?"

"Wish I could help you, Quinn." But her tone suggested she'd rather have a root canal without benefit of Novocain.

"Sure you do." With my free hand, I pawed through my fairly boring wardrobe of tailored shirts and blouses, ladylike pullovers, plain Dockers pants, dark-wash jeans, knee-length skirts and low-heeled shoes. "Given your lack of experience with rock concerts, I don't suppose you'll be able to help with my other problem, either."

"Which is?"

"What the heck do I wear?"

CHAPTER 2

As it turned out, I wore the tightest jeans I owned (not very), my "holiday" black sweater with rhinestones trimming a deep V-neck, bat-shaped Halloween earrings, high-heeled black boots and a fitted burgundy leather jacket. I even moussed my medium-length brown hair, trying for a wilder look. Still, if I wasn't the oldest person shivering on line that night at the Rialto, I definitely was the most conservative-looking.

The two-hundred-or-so young people with tattoos, piercings, pale skin and unnaturally dyed hair drew just a little attention from passers-by headed for shops down the block. The neighborhood regulars must have assumed the theater was holding another fundraiser. Most could not have known, though, that it featured a hot Goth-rock band with a platinum CD. Those of us with tickets had been asked to keep it quiet— Mad Love's security did not want the old theater besieged by fans and would-be groupies who might screw up the video shoot.

Still, word seemed to have leaked out to a few.

"Larkin," the skinny young woman in front of me told the security guard with the clipboard, for the second time. "L-a-r-k—"

"Not on the list," he repeated, with a beefy shrug.

"Oh, come *on.*" Though she looked well into her twenties, she stomped her vinyl-booted foot like a preschooler. "Melissa *Larkin?*"

"Sorry."

He didn't sound as if he felt too sorry for her, but I did. She obviously had gotten all done up this evening to see her favorite band in person—though, even for this crowd, she'd overdone it. She wore a T-shirt from the last Mad Love tour, white with grungy black scribbles around a shocked-looking red heart. She'd paired this with a fake leopard miniskirt and capped the outfit with a silver lamé jacket, ragged strawberry blonde hair and a ton of makeup. Even a fashion model would have had a hard time carrying it all off, and this young woman stood barely over five feet tall, with a long, sharp nose and not much chin.

Right now, her plain face crumpled on the verge of tears. I feared a cascade of black mascara, and besides, the folks in line behind us were getting testy.

Then I realized I had the solution to the problem within my grasp. I opened my wallet and pulled out the two tickets.

"It's okay," I told the guard. "She's with me."

He narrowed his eyes, no doubt suspecting this was an impulsive gesture on my part. "And you are?"

"Quinn Matthews."

I was on the list. Now, that was a bit of a rush.

Inside the lobby, Melissa Larkin shot me a look of abject gratitude. "That was awesome of you! Thanks so much."

I waved a hand. "The extra ticket would just have gone to waste, and you're obviously a true fan."

A young usher in a different Mad Love shirt showed us to our seats. They were assigned, probably because the video's director wanted to fill the front rows rather than the back or mezzanine. We got the last two seats in Row 10, with Melissa on the aisle. I realized I had committed myself to spending the evening next to her. Oh, well, at least now I had someone to talk to—though I had no plans to ask her for fashion tips.

She took a moment now to size me up more critically and blurted, "How did *you* get tickets?"

I explained about the article I was writing and filled her in on a little of the history of the Rialto, leaving out the bit about the supposed ghost. "I gather the band's new guitarist grew up around here," I added, "and that's where they got the idea to scout out this theater for the video."

A cool expression flitted across my companion's face, and

she shook her head. "I'm sure it was Alan's idea. He loves old amusement parks and theaters and horror movies from the thirties and forties. He collects original posters of all those movies with Boris Karloff and Bela Lugosi and Peter Lorre. He's got them all framed in his new apartment in Hoboken!"

So Bardot also had a place in Jersey. I wondered how Melissa knew all this. She talked as if she'd been there, but she could just as easily have read about it in a fan magazine or on the Internet.

"That's where he got the name for the band, too," she chattered on happily. "*Mad Love* was an old Peter Lorre movie about a pianist who lost his hands in an accident and ended up with the hands of a murderer instead!"

"Very cool." I smiled. This girl obviously was crushing hard on Alan Bardot. I hoped when he took to the stage she didn't make a total fool of herself. At least she was small—security could handle her with no problem.

So far, the stage had stood empty, with a black tarp over the whole floor, a movie screen in back, and amps piled to either side of an electronic keyboard and a drum kit. But once the audience was mostly seated, a tall, lean man came to the mic. He had grizzled hair pulled back in a ponytail and wore a T-shirt branded Starlight Videos.

"Hi, folks!" he said. "I'm Mike Warner, and I'll be directing the festivities tonight."

Everyone cheered, as well they might, given the free show.

"Just a quick rundown of what'll be happening. The guys are going to perform a new single, 'Vampire.' The movie screen"—he pointed behind him—"will show images relating to the song. The effect should be pretty cool, and the song itself is"—the director grinned—"kind of intense!"

I wondered what that meant. Four-letter words? Judging from the one Mad Love CD I'd bought, that didn't seem to be their style.

Warner continued, "At some points, we'll be turning the cameras on you folks, too, so show your enthusiasm! Wave, pump your fists, dance, whatever you want. Those of you down front, when Alan comes to the edge of the stage, you can reach up to him, just like at a real concert. We want to show a lot of audience excitement, 'cause it goes with the idea of the song... as you'll see. Anyhow, have a great time!"

We all clapped again as he walked off, and now I was getting psyched. It was like being part of the performance!

In college and right after, I'd played a little acoustic guitar, written a few songs and even performed at a couple of amateur nights. I'd soon realized I should stick to journalism, but I guess, in some tiny corner of my psyche, I still fantasized about being a rock star. Waving and dancing around in this video might be the closest I'd ever come.

"Damn," said Melissa, "I wish we were closer to the stage!"

I shrugged. "These are the seats they gave me. I guess the first few rows are VIPs, and I didn't rate."

She said nothing more, but faced front again with a pout. I felt like reminding her that, if not for my extra tenth-row ticket, she wouldn't be there at all.

Meanwhile, three video cameramen took up positions at left, right and center stage, and an operator on the ground raised another camera on a crane high above our heads. Lights played over the stage for a few minutes, overlapping green, red, blue, purple and gold, as a technician somewhere above the mezzanine tested the effects.

Then, except for the Exit signs, everything went dark.

Five silhouettes wandered casually onto the stage, and the cheers shook the old theater. One sat down behind the drums, a second at the keyboard, two strapped on guitars and the last one stepped up to the mic stand.

The keyboard, with the voice of an organ, began a simple but ominous riff in a minor key. The big movie screen in the background filled with a black-and-white test pattern, as from an old newsreel. Then came an archaic-looking title page with Gothic lettering that spelled out "Vampire."

Silvery light from the screen washed over the band members, just enough to make them visible, while still leaving a lot of shadow. Alan Bardot bent toward the mic and began to sing.

Smiling faces sometimes hide
Cobwebs and decay inside.
Loving secrets as I do
I have no feelings left for you...

Wow. Now I understood what the director had meant by "intense." The lyrics sounded even more chilling because Bardot delivered them in a soft, almost crooning tone. A little like Jim Morrison retooled for the twenty-first century.

At the same time, the video behind the band pictured a series of characters, real and fictional, associated with vampire legends. Vlad the Impaler. Countess Elizabeth Bathory. Actor Max Schreck in the silent movie *Nosferatu.* Bela Lugosi in *Dracula.* In between, I spotted a medieval pope who I think may have stirred up the Inquisition.

Alan traveled with the mic now, prowling to the right of the apron stage. Over a black T-shirt and pants, he wore a retro, iridescent purple jacket. The lights also glinted off what appeared to be purple streak in the front of his hair.

You avoid the midnight alley
Where you think the danger lies
But I also hunt by daylight
Chill you with my graveyard eyes.

The lead guitarist, Jeff Randall, also stalked forward, but at stage left. He upped the tension with an eerie, moaning chord that rose in pitch as Bardot hit the refrain:

Watch out when I start to draw you
Get you underneath my spell.
Don't you know, I have the answers?
Join me in my lonely hell!

The images on the screen, though still black-and-white, became moving clips from old newsreels. Adolph Hitler. Joseph

Stalin. Benito Mussolini. They stood on platforms or balconies, mouthing speeches and gesturing dramatically before adoring crowds.

Not a subtle concept, I thought, but a smart one. I wondered how many of Mad Love's younger fans would actually recognize all of these bloodthirsty dictators from history.

I glanced sideways at Melissa. She sat literally on the edge of her seat and leaned forward, enraptured. Her lips moved, too. I wondered how she knew the words to the song, if the band had not yet released it.

Bardot surrendered the spotlight for a moment while his lead guitarist took a solo. Randall stood several inches taller, with a more athletic build and longer, wavier hair. And boy, he could play—those scorching minor-key riffs raised the hair on my neck. Meanwhile, the drums, organ and rhythm guitar set up a hypnotic *bong-bong* rhythm underneath it all, almost like a death knell. I could feel the throb in my rib cage.

For the last verse, Bardot roamed the front of the stage and cranked up the volume, too.

Backbone stiff with moldy pride
Veins that flow formaldehyde
Nothing colder than my touch
Killing everything I clutch...

Color news clips now. Cultists Jim Jones and David Koresh. The big, projected faces washed over those of Bardot, Randall and the other band members. I suspected the video cameramen creeping about the stage were capturing that effect.

Watch out when I start to draw you
Get you underneath my spell...

Heard live, Bardot's voice impressed me. These days, studio equipment can make anybody sound good on a CD, but he clearly had the pipes. And like every good lead singer, he served as the lightning rod of the musical storm, using all his physical and vocal agility to interpret the macabre song. For something that probably would be re-dubbed for the video, anyway, it was a great performance.

The audience, especially in the front rows, needed no coaching. They were reaching for both Bardot and Randall, pumping their fists and having a blast.

Just then, the video showed a rally for Saddam Hussein, with his followers doing almost the same kind of thing. *Interesting.* If the song was a warning not to blindly worship leaders, were the rockers including themselves?

Can't you see, I have no answers!
Join me in my lonely heh-ell.

That wail from Bardot, and another crescendo from the lead guitar, brought the number to a dramatic finish.

The handpicked audience exploded into screams and cheers, and I joined them. I heard frantic clapping to my left and saw Melissa's cheeks actually glistened with tears. Well, it was a good number, but that seemed a little much! On the other hand, she probably would have reacted the same way if Alan had sung "Rudolph the Red-Nosed Reindeer."

In some ways, I couldn't blame her. Not only was the guy a heck of a performer, but, especially under that moody stage lighting, he *did* have killer cheekbones.

All the band members remained in their spots, and the director came out to confer with them. Then he leaned into the mic and announced, "Folks, we're gonna do another take. You okay with that?"

More cheers, of course. It might be only a one-song concert, but at least we'd be getting an encore.

The organ intro started again. Knowing this time how the number would play out, I could pay more attention to the technical aspects. As Bardot began to stalk across the stage, one of the cameramen followed him steadily from about five feet away. Another hung close to Randall, now and then detouring to focus on one of the other musicians. I could envision how those tight shots would look in the final video.

This time, during Randall's big solo, Bardot hovered nearer the guitarist to sway and nod along to the ominous, chiming rhythm. He stayed in that spot and faced the audience as he launched into the last verse.

Something—maybe the shifting light from the movie screen—drew my eye up to the stage's proscenium arch. It was dark by comparison, but I saw someone up there...just a hazy silhouette, dressed all in black, walking along the top. Could he be working a special effect or adjusting something?

The climax of the song pulled my attention back to the stage.

"Watch out when I start to draw you—"

BOOM!

At first, I thought a smoke bomb had gone off onstage. But the way the band members leaped back and the music stopped told me it wasn't planned. They were all miked, and as the dust settled, I heard their shouts and curses.

"Oh, my G—"

"What the f—"

A woman in front screamed, and chaos broke out.

Stagehands and band members surged to the apron, so at first I couldn't see what was wrong. Bardot sprang back to the mic and yelled, with a catch in his voice, "A doctor! We need a doctor!"

All of us in the audience were on our feet, milling around in confusion. A couple of overwhelmed security guards rushed to the front of the theater and tried in vain to calm the crowd.

I turned to Melissa. "Did you see—"

But she was gone. Maybe she'd run up to the stage to check on her idol, though he seemed fine to me. So did all the other musicians. But someone else must be hurt.

Lalita jogged back up the aisle, cell phone clamped to her ear, calling for an ambulance. I followed her out to the lobby, and when she hung up, I asked what had happened.

Her face had gone ashen. "Oh, Jesus, a big chunk of plaster fell and hit one of the cameramen. They think he's still alive, but he's out cold!" Her eyes were wide with horror. "I can't believe it... That proscenium is old, but it should have been secure!"

I knew what she must be thinking. If the cameraman was

seriously hurt, the Friends of the Rialto would be liable. "It was probably the fault of the guy working up there. He must've jarred something loose."

"What guy?"

"Somebody was up there—a stagehand, I guess—just before that piece fell. Walking on top of the arch."

"Walking?" Lalita stared at me, then gave her head an emphatic shake. "Quinn, that arch is less than a foot wide. No one could stand up there—it's impossible!"

CHAPTER 3

Shortly after Lalita dropped that bombshell on me, the paramedics arrived. She hurried off to escort them through the chaos and toward the stage.

Security herded the rest of us into the lobby, where we milled about in confusion. Obviously, the show was over, but no one told us we could leave the building, and I think most of us lingered in a state of shock.

I eavesdropped on the conversations around me—some voices hushed in horror, others raised in outrage.

"You'd think the theater would've made sure it was safe—"

"Amps were up too damn loud, must've jarred something loose—"

No one else mentioned seeing a shadowy figure prowling on the archway above the stage. So why had I? I'd just gotten fresh contact lenses a week ago, and my eyesight with them was twenty-twenty. Had the flickering of the movie screen caused some kind of illusion?

I spotted Art Soorikian, the *Sentinel*'s rock music writer, hunched in a corner talking on his cell phone. Probably calling the night desk with a much different story than the one he'd planning to deliver.

Two uniformed cops arrived and disappeared inside the theater, probably to examine the scene. Still, no one actually gave the rest of us permission to go home. I felt like I was in one of those manor house murder mysteries, where we all had to stay for questioning because any one of us might be a suspect.

There would be no need for that, of course, if it really had been an accident. But despite what Lalita had told me, I found that hard to believe.

I still did not see the colorful Melissa anywhere. She must have bolted early on, from the shock. Unless during the confusion she'd exploited the opportunity, actually made it backstage and gone home with somebody in the band.

Lalita finally returned to the lobby, looking harried and accompanied by one of the cops. She craned her neck to search the crowd...until she spotted me. Then she and the stocky Latino officer made a beeline in my direction.

That startled me. I've never been in trouble with the law, but even so, my stomach did a somersault. I tried to remember if I'd ever paid that pricey speeding ticket five years ago.

"You Quinn Matthews?" the cop asked.

"That's right."

"Ms. Washington says you saw somebody walking on that ledge over the stage, just before the piece fell."

Lalita must be desperate, I thought, if she'd passed on to the police a lead that she didn't even believe in. "I thought I did. A silhouetted figure, all in black. I figured it was a stagehand or a technician working on the show."

The cop scribbled something in a notebook. "My partner just went up on the crane to examine that area. The arch is pretty narrow, and he said there was no way for anybody to even climb up there."

"That's what Lalita told me, too."

"You were in the tenth row? Pretty close."

I nodded. "But far enough back to see the proscenium."

The technical term made him blink for a second, then he jotted some more notes. "We've talked to some other people in the audience and the guy working the projector. None of them saw what you saw. Could it have been something else—some trick of the lights?"

"Maybe."

"You got some other explanation?"

I knew what he was thinking. You come to a rock concert, you get a little high, you see things that aren't there. "You probably won't believe me."

"Try me."

After a deep breath to get up my nerve, I told him I was somewhat psychic. An understatement, after what I went through last spring and summer, but I wanted to sound low-key and credible. I could tell right away, though, that I was losing him.

"You think you saw a ghost?"

"Not necessarily, but...it might have been some kind of premonition. Maybe I sensed the plaster was going to fall, and I saw it in terms of a figure knocking it loose."

The cop narrowed his eyes at me, then shook his head in disbelief. Without even a thank-you, he shut his notebook and walked away.

Hey, he asked.

Lalita caught my elbow and apologized for sending him over. "I thought possibly what you saw might have meant something."

"That's okay," I told her. "I just wish it had. After all, if anyone did cause the accident, that person would be responsible, not the theater."

She smiled sadly. "Even if you did see something up there, though...pretty damn hard to arrest a ghost!"

"As soon as I said the word 'psychic,' his eyes glazed right over," I told Nancy. "I thought these days the police worked with people like me to help solve cases."

My blonde friend smiled. "Maybe not so much in Elizabeth, New Jersey."

We sat on the vintage mohair sofa in the living room of my Victorian money pit in Crane's Crossing, a nearby suburb. It was ten A.M., and I'd gotten little sleep. Nancy had dropped over after hearing about last night's fiasco from her husband Rob. This morning he already had gone off to huddle with the Friends of the Rialto and advise them on what they could expect legally.

Also part-time at the *Sentinel*, Nancy was theoretically working from home today. Long, lean and naturally elegant— even in her well-worn yoga duds—she sipped coffee and listened patiently while I recapped the previous night's events.

"I know I saw *something*," I told her. "Of course, I've seen apparitions before, right in this house."

"Lalita told you the theater had a ghost," Nancy reminded me. "Maybe he feels the same way about loud rock 'n' roll as I do… Sorry, I shouldn't joke."

I nodded grimly. The cameraman, Ted something, was still in the hospital in intensive care. I reminded Nancy that Gail Kleinholtz, the professional psychic who had mentored me after my first encounter with the spirit world, always said a ghost can't physically harm someone. "It can startle a person into hurting himself," I explained, "but I'm sure she'd say no ghost could drop a chunk of plaster on somebody to maim him."

"Then maybe it was like you told the cops. You just had a vision warning you something awful was going to happen."

I supposed that had to be the explanation. "Too bad I didn't have time to do anything about it."

Feeling a little brighter from the caffeine, I took both our mugs back to the kitchen for refills. Although I'd managed to restore most of my Queen Anne house to a pared-down version of turn-of-the-century style, the kitchen remained a depressing, mini-museum of the nineteen-fifties. The terrible layout made meal prep a headache and left no room for even a dishwasher. The next time I came into any real money, it needed a total renovation.

Yep. Right after I repaint the outside of the house…and fix that rotted part of the front porch…

By the time I came back to the living room, Nancy was on her cell phone. She mouthed the name *Rob* to me as she continued to listen, saying, "Uh-huh," and making sympathetic noises. I set our mugs on the old trunk I used for a coffee table and tried to intuit her husband's half of the conversation. Mind reading, however, does not seem to be among my psychic talents.

My obvious impatience finally had the desired effect when Nancy said into the phone, "You want to tell Quinn?" and passed it to me.

"Hi, Rob," I said. "What's going on?"

"Ahh, it's a big mess, as you can imagine. The guy's got a

bad concussion and he's still in a coma. That was some heavy piece that hit him, about twenty-five pounds. The cops checked it out, and it looks like it had been burned partway through."

"Burned?" Demons with little hammers played scales up and down my spine.

"Yeah. Maybe with one of those heat guns they use to remove paint. Anyhow, it might've been ready to crack at any time. The vibrations from the music may have jarred it so it finally broke loose."

"Could that have been done on purpose?" I asked.

"Who knows? They're questioning all the workers. If it was tampered with, it had to have been done hours before the show, while the scaffolding around the stage was still in place. The big question, though, would be why." Rob broke off for a second to talk to someone else on his end. "Anyway, this isn't my area, so I'm hooking them up with personal injury guy in my firm. He's a good lawyer…and I'm sorry to say, they're going to need one."

"Let me know if there's anything I can do to help."

"Sure," he said. "Oh, and Quinn…the camera on the crane was taking full shots of the stage right before the plaster fell. There really was nobody up on the arch."

As Rob clicked off, I began to see the mishap from a new angle.

"Nancy," I said, "maybe that's what my vision meant. Even if no one was on the proscenium at that moment, someone still could have done this on purpose—rigged that piece to fall during the performance."

"It's possible, I guess…"

"Mad Love had a string of suspicious accidents all through their last tour. I read about them online, and even Tony was saying it seemed to be a pattern."

Nancy shrugged. "If he thinks so, now's his chance to check it out."

True, I realized. Right after wrapping up his bribery case the night before, Tony had been assigned to follow up on the incident at the Rialto. He probably was at the *Sentinel* office right now working on the story.

Nancy had just stood up to leave when my house phone

rang. I heard a man's voice on the line, very serious. "Is this Quinn Matthews?"

"Yes?"

"You wrote the newspaper story on the Rialto Theater restoration, and you were at the video shoot there last night?"

"That's right." My mouth went dry—was *I* getting sued for something?

"This is Dan Sternberg, manager for Mad Love. Alan Bardot would like to speak with you. This afternoon, if possible."

CHAPTER 4

If I had Alan Bardot's money and lived in Hoboken, I'd have bought one of the town's turn-of-the-century brownstones. In other words, an urban counterpart of my Queen Anne. Of course, I then would have had to find a place to park or garage my car, a major issue for anyone who lives in or even visits the city.

I didn't have to deal with that problem this afternoon. I was being driven in a luxury Town Car.

Dan Sternberg had assured me, on the phone, that neither he nor his clients suspected me of having anything to do with the accident at the Rialto. They only wanted to speak to me, he explained, because word had gotten back to them about "what you *said* you saw last night."

That skeptical emphasis alerted me that Sternberg had serious doubts about my story. Still, he'd reassured me on the phone that no one suspected me of having anything to do with the accident at the theater. In fact, he said, he'd checked me out online and knew I wrote regularly for the *Sentinel* and some regional shelter magazines. In other words, I was more-or-less gainfully employed and not an obvious crackpot.

So it must be Alan himself who'd asked to meet with me. It made me a bit giddy to think of the thousands of adoring fans who would have killed to be in my place right now.

My driver cruised past several blocks of stunning brownstones, but did not stop at any of them. Finally I asked, "Where are we going, Ramon?" (During the half-hour it took for us to get here from Crane's Crossing, we'd gotten pretty chummy.)

"Maxwell Towers," he said. "Ever hear of it?"

"Yeah, I have." It was a big condo hi-rise on the Hudson River, built on the site of a former Maxwell House coffee plant. As it came into view, I appreciated that its brick-and-limestone exterior blended as well as possible, given the building's size, with the older neighborhood structures.

My Town Car pulled up to the curb between the two front bays. Ramon opened the car door for me and told me the apartment number. Cheerfully, he added, "I'll be down here whenever you're ready to leave."

Couldn't beat that for service.

The circular entrance foyer was a knockout, with a marble floor, sleek maple columns and a round skylight. The concierge at the front desk called up to announce me, and I suffered a fresh attack of nerves.

I rode up on the elevator alone, wondering meanwhile about Alan Bardot. I might like his music, but if he turned out to be the stereotypical spoiled, arrogant, foul-mouthed rock star, this could be a long and difficult afternoon.

The hallway leading to his apartment was so quiet at this time of day that I could hear my steps on the carpet, which heightened my sense of unreality. At least I didn't have to step over any lovesick groupies camped outside his door.

I pressed the bell and waited.

The door opened to reveal a leggy blonde, inches taller than me, who could have been a model—in a very Goth runway show. She wore chunky black boots with fishnets and a short black leather skirt. Her snug tank top showed Lugosi menacing a toothsome female victim and read "I'm batty for Bela." Her pierced nose and eyebrow and multiple earrings complemented the tattoos on both upper arms and her long, metallic-purple fingernails.

"Hi!" she said, with a wide, pretty smile (no visible tongue stud, anyway). "You must be Quinn. I'm Lark."

I shook her hand and managed to avoid being scratched. We further bonded when I commented on her shirt and told her I had a cat named Bela. Then she showed me into a living room that gave me temporary amnesia about everything else.

Deep windows to the right looked across the Hudson, where Manhattan sparkled in the midday sun, seeming just a stone's-throw away. But the room itself riveted my attention just as much. Each wall was a different, rich color—mustard gold, cayenne red, deep plum and poison green. The palette obviously was inspired by the lurid hues of the posters of classic horror movies, which hung everywhere in sleek, chrome frames.

When Melissa had described Alan's collection, I'd never pictured anything as classy and imaginative as this. Even the black-leather-and-chrome sofa and chairs, and the polished wooden tables and bar, looked like authentic pieces from the nineteen-thirties and forties.

"Wow!" I blurted out to Lark. "This place is amazing."

She grinned. "We had a great decorator. Dara something…"

"Smithson?"

"Right! You know her?"

"I know of her." Dara Smithson was one of New Jersey's superstar interior designers. She worked mainly on the homes of celebrities, sports icons and media moguls.

"Anyway," said Lark, "she and Alan had a blast doing this place."

From down the hall, probably behind a closed door, two male voices rose in a tense exchange.

"They'll be right out," Lark promised me, still with the sunny attitude that contradicted her grim appearance. "Can I get you something? Water, coffee?"

I'm sure booze would have been available, too, if I'd wanted it. "Water would be fine, thanks. Okay if I look around? I'm in love with this furniture."

"Oh, that's right—Stern said you write about decorating and stuff. Sure, knock yourself out!"

I roamed around the living room like an art lover in a museum, now and then stroking the "waterfall" contours or the burled veneer of a wooden piece. Next to Victorian, Art Moderne is my favorite style. I also knew pieces in this kind of mint condition had to cost a bundle.

Just as Lark handed me a chilled bottle of water, two men emerged from the hall.

I knew Sternberg at once from his businesslike stride. Medium-height, with a square jaw and thinning brown hair, he wore his tour T-shirt, jeans and corduroy jacket like a three-piece suit.

"Ms. Matthews." He shook my hand and introduced himself. "Sorry to keep you waiting."

The second man followed with a more relaxed air, perhaps because he was at home. Though I knew he was around thirty, Alan looked very slim and boyish in black jeans and a loose gray sweater. His dark hair was shorter than mine—just past his collar—and yes, that was a purple streak through his ragged forelock. Surprisingly, beyond the one skull earring, he didn't have any piercings or tattoos—none I could see at the moment, anyway.

He put out his hand with less attitude than his manager. "Alan Bardot. Thanks so much for coming."

Wow, those eyes were just as stunning as in the *EW* magazine photo. None of the shots I'd seen of him so far, though, had prepared me for that dazzling white grin.

We all sat, I on the sofa and Alan and his manager in the twin chairs. Without being asked, Lark brought Sternberg a mug of coffee and Bardot a bottled water, as if she knew what they expected. Then she perched on a barstool and discreetly faded into the background.

"You probably think this is all pretty strange," Alan began. "It got back to us, through the cops, that you thought you saw someone on the arch over the stage last night. Can you tell me more about that?"

Lucky thing I had a lot of practice by now in relating the whole story. Otherwise, I might have been struck dumb by those gorgeous cheekbones and long-lashed, turquoise eyes. But I also noticed Bardot's lids drooped a little and stubble dusted his pale jaw, as if maybe he'd slept as badly last night as I had.

When I got to the point of explaining that my "vision" might have been just a premonition, I heard a skeptical snort from the manager.

Alan sent him a sharp glance, then turned back to me and winked. "We call him 'Stern' for short, and you can probably see why! He didn't want me to meet with you. He thinks you're just a publicity hound trying to get attention, but you don't seem that way to me."

"Lord, no," I said. "In fact, ever since I developed these abilities, I've been trying to avoid situations that might trigger them."

I explained just a little of what I'd gone through to cleanse my haunted house.

Lark piped up from her barstool. "Awesome! You've really seen *ghosts*?"

Sternberg crossed his arms and glanced out the window impatiently. Bardot, on the other hand, gave me his undivided attention.

"Sounds like you're the real deal!" he said. "Maybe you can help us."

"How?"

He leaned a little farther across the chrome-and-glass coffee table and lowered his voice with a touch of melodrama. "We've been told Mad Love is under a curse."

"Alan—" Sternberg began to protest.

Without even looking around, Bardot raised a hand to silence him, making it clear who worked for whom.

He went on to explain, "On our last tour, we had way too many 'accidents.' One of our truck drivers broke his back in a crash...he's still getting physical therapy."

"I read about that," I admitted. "And the problem with the plane."

"The cops found signs of tampering in both those cases. Trouble is, they couldn't prove anything. Whoever is doing this is pretty slick."

I still wasn't sure how I fit into the picture. "Why do you say it's a curse?"

"Because there's been other stuff, too. Not as dangerous, but meant to freak us out. Hate mail, which isn't so unusual. But also sick little 'gifts,' and notes saying that somebody's put a hex on us." He looked genuinely spooked. "I don't believe in curses, but I do believe some people can see and sense things others can't. I was raised by an aunt who could predict when the phone would ring and who was calling, when somebody who felt fine ought to see a doctor, where to find lost things... stuff she had no way of knowing. And she was *always* right."

With a shake of his head, Stern interrupted. "Alan, you've gotta admit, that's a lot different from—"

I saw where this was headed and felt I had to warn them. "I've never been able to read minds or predict the future. The closest I've come has been picking up an object and getting some information about a person who owned or handled it in the past."

Bardot mulled over my statement. "That might be enough. The cops are still investigating those suspicious accidents from last year, and I'm sure they're checking out what happened at the theater last night, too. But they're looking for facts, hard evidence. It couldn't hurt to have someone on the case who's approaching it from...a different angle."

I hardly knew what to say. "I don't know if I'm the right person. I'm not a professional psychic!"

"Maybe not. But if you got that flash last night, maybe you're tuned into something."

Sternberg cleared his throat and pulled a folded paper from his jacket. "Before this goes any further—"

Bardot sighed. "Is that really necessary?"

"Alan, it's for your own protection. And the band's." Sternberg opened the sheet and slid it across the coffee table to me. "If you agree to do this, Ms. Matthews, we're asking you to sign this non-disclosure agreement. It states any information you learn about my clients will remain confidential."

That brought me up short. "Huh?"

"It's no big deal," Lark reassured me, from her perch by the bar. "I signed one when they hired me. It's SOP for all PAs."

The lady sure knew how to sling an acronym. "Standard Operating Procedure," I got. "PA" must be...personal assistant?

So that's what she was. I'd been thinking, Alan's girlfriend.

If I refused, they'd probably conclude I'd just been in this for the publicity all along. I glanced at the form. "I don't know... we're talking about possible crimes. If the police—"

"That's covered." Sternberg jabbed a finger toward the

paper. "We can't stop you from talking to them. But you do work for a newspaper—"

Alan chimed in, like the "good cop," to counteract his manager's brusque approach. "If you agree to do this, we'll have to give you information that we wouldn't want to end up in the tabloids—or on the Internet. Especially if it turns out *not* to have anything to do with the threats and the accidents."

That did put things in a better light. Still—

"I'll have to think it over," I said. "Talk to...to my lawyer."

"No problem," Alan said readily. Sternberg also nodded and stood, as if signaling I was free to go. Maybe he was hoping I'd be scared off and he wouldn't have to deal with me again.

I got up, too, while mulling a possible conflict-of-interest with my job at the *Sentinel*. "I guess as long as I don't accept payment—"

Alan walked me to the door and opened it for me. "Well, we can work something out along that line. Especially if you are able to help us. And I sure hope you can."

Still dazed by the whole proposition, I stepped out the door and onto something that crunched under my foot.

I jumped back, startled. My revulsion went beyond just the physical sensation. It also carried a weird jolt of toxic emotions.

Jealousy. Betrayal. Fury. The overload of psychic pain made my head swim.

When the feeling passed, I looked down and saw a stiff, dead crow.

Alan stared at the ghastly thing, too. He went pale and spat out the first four-letter word I'd heard from him that afternoon.

"See what I mean?"

CHAPTER 5

Tony jerked open my four-foot-tall aluminum stepladder and smacked it down a little too hard on the floor of my wrap-around porch. "I can't believe you're actually going to sign a non-disclosure agreement with those guys! If someone is stalking Mad Love, it's news. And you do work for a newspaper."

"Not in a *news* capacity," I reminded him. "At this point, I'm only part-time—practically a freelancer. And it's not as if I'm covering that story."

"But I am. Puts me in kind of an awkward spot, doesn't it? My girlfriend will be finding out stuff she'll have to keep from me!"

He did have a point. Because in my mind I already had agreed to keep Mad Love's secrets, I couldn't even tell Tony about stepping on the dead crow. This latest implied threat to the band somehow had been smuggled into Alan's high-security condo building—and deposited right at his front door—while he, Stern, Lark and I had sat talking inside the apartment. The idea that the stalker had come so close to all of us, undetected, made me almost as queasy as the memory of that small, brittle rib cage cracking beneath the sole of my shoe.

Unaware of my dark thoughts, Tony turned his attention back to the job at hand and scanned the ceiling of my porch. "Where did you say you saw this—Whoa!"

He spotted it on his own. An enormous hornet's nest stuck in a high corner, almost hidden by some gingerbread trim.

"That's a big mutha," he said.

"Told you. But don't worry, I gave it a once-over with some Raid ant spray. Besides, everything I read online said the hornets die off in the winter."

Since it was now late March, I figured it was the perfect time to get rid of the thing. Otherwise, with my luck, a whole new bunch would move in this summer.

Give Tony credit. He took me at my word and started up the stepladder, though first he did pull the hood of his windbreaker over his head. "What are you supposed to do if there's a trial and you get subpoenaed?"

I realized he was back to the topic of my NDA. "I'm supposed to tell the band first, so they can contest it." I hurried to add, "But Alan said they had no problem with my talking to the cops. They're just trying to keep gossip out of the tabloids."

"Sure." Tony's voice dripped skepticism. He'd reached the second-to-last step, but still couldn't get a grip on the nest, so he balanced on the top step, which you're not supposed to do. At five-foot-nine, he's only a couple of inches taller than I am, so this job was a stretch for him.

"Face it," he went on, "you're just flattered they asked you to act as their own personal psychic, like you're the Amazing Kreskin or..." He obviously was groping for a more credible, female equivalent.

"I think you mean Alison DuBois. Honestly, when they first asked me, I felt the same way you do. Like Alan was putting way too much faith in me and I couldn't live up to it." It frustrated me again that I couldn't tell him about the strong, almost homicidal vibe I had gotten from stepping on the dead crow. "But as Alan said, if I had such a clear premonition about the Rialto 'accident,' maybe I am plugged into the band's situation in some way. Maybe I really can help them."

Tony's voice echoed from the high corner. "I need to jimmy this loose. Hand me the broom."

I passed it to him. He was practically standing on tiptoe in his sneakers now on the top of the stepladder. That made me so nervous, I took hold of his ankles, which were about level with my waist.

"Stop that!" Tony complained. "You're gonna *make* me fall."

I let go, but stayed in catching position.

"Look at all the people Gail has helped," I went on. "She's worked with the cops to find kidnap and murder victims. If I do have this ability, maybe it's selfish of me to keep it to myself. If I can prevent anyone else from being hurt—"

"They gonna pay you?"

From his tone, I couldn't tell if he thought they should, or not. "They didn't exactly offer, and frankly, I'd be uncomfortable asking for money. I'm not a professional detective or even a professional psychic, and I don't aspire to be. On the other hand, Alan did say if I could give them anything useful, he could 'work something out.'"

Another scoff from the recesses of the ceiling. "I'll bet!"

I realized then that Tony's surly attitude might not be based entirely on his journalistic ethics. "I don't believe it—you're jealous over Alan Bardot! Get real. I'm old enough to be his... slightly older sister. Anyhow, I'm sure I'm the furthest thing from his type."

"The guy's bisexual. Everybody's his type."

"Very funny. I promise you, you have nothing to worry about. If I like him at all, it's only because he reminds me a little of you." I knew I should resist, but went ahead with the punch line anyway. "Except *he's* a rich, famous and totally hot rock star."

Tony wobbled the ladder and almost lost his footing, which made me feel guilty. "Nice. Next time you need somebody to pry a damned hornet's nest out of your porch ceiling, call Bardot!"

He tossed the thing down to me. I shrieked and barely reacted in time to catch it. Once I saw it up close, I was glad I hadn't just let it smash. For something made of chewed-up wood and hornet spit, it really was a very cool piece of engineering. The pulpy layers built up in a spiral design, kind of like the Guggenheim Museum.

I put my ear to the outside and heard no buzzing or rustling. "It *is* empty, right?"

"According to all your online experts." Tony hopped down from the ladder, yanked back his hood and brushed probably-imaginary cobwebs out of his dark hair. "You should keep it as a souvenir."

"Maybe I will. Thanks!" I set it down on my wicker coffee table, then hugged and kissed him for his trouble. "Since I haven't handed over the NDA to Sternberg yet, I will leak one bit of information. Alan said the accidents on their last tour, with the plane and the equipment truck, are being investigated as suspicious."

"That's no secret. I got that from the cops in Florida and Virginia. They still don't have any suspects, though. They even grilled the guy who got kicked out of the band a couple of years back, but he seemed to have an iron-clad alibi."

We sat down on the tan wicker loveseat, still bare of cushions because I took them inside in the winter. "Well, I'm trying to be helpful. How about returning the favor? Got any inside tips for me?"

He put his arm around my shoulders. "Only one so far. You know the band's new lead guitarist, Jeff Randall? I found out his father is Steven Randall, the mayor of North Burwick."

"No kidding! I heard he grew up in the area, but nothing about his father being a mayor."

Tony nodded. "Maybe that's deliberate. Steve Randall's known as a real conservative, family-values type. Could be he's not crazy about his son's choice of profession."

This sparked a new flash of insight on my part. "I'll bet that's one of the reasons they wanted me to sign the agreement. They've probably got skeletons in the closet, embarrassing stuff. With five guys in the band, that could amount to a lot of old drug busts, angry exes, trashed hotels, unpaid child support—"

"Or worse," Tony warned me. "If somebody actually does want one of them dead."

Considering this, I studied the intricate twists and turns of my new coffee table centerpiece more intently. If I agreed to work with Mad Love, I might be sticking my head into a whole other kind of hornet's nest.

I e-mailed Dan Sternberg and made an appointment to meet with "his client" again the next morning, which was Monday. Luckily, I didn't have to go into the Sentinel office that day until two.

I also found a response to an e-mail I'd sent that morning to Gail Kleinholtz. She lived in Manhattan and traveled frequently

on book tours and actual psychic investigations. I'd met her only
once, shortly after I'd resolved the issues with my ghosts. Tall
and substantial, she wore her graying blond hair in a braid and
favored loose, earth-toned clothing. I'd found her surprisingly
down-to-earth—granola crunchy, maybe, but far from spacey.

In my latest message to her, I'd explained my current
arrangement with Mad Love and asked whether I should accept
payment for any psychic help I might be able to render.

"I never accept payment when I help with a police
investigation," Gail wrote. "On the other hand, I do when I
counsel a private client. Use your own judgment as things
develop. I'm sure you won't exploit someone else's trouble for
your own gain."

She sounded more concerned about my description of the
mishap at the old theater. "As I've told you many times, true
ghosts—earthbound spirits of those who have died—don't have
the power to cause anyone physical harm. Poltergeist activity
can cause objects to fall and strike people, but that usually
occurs in a more confined space and is triggered by a particular,
troubled individual. This sounds to me like something else."

She agreed there was a chance the chunk of plaster fell on
its own, and the figure I saw could have been just a kind of
"embodied premonition." Still, even in an email, she didn't
sound certain enough to suit me.

"Your friend the singer may not believe in curses, but
unfortunately they do exist," Gail wrote. "The real thing is rare,
but can do a great deal of harm. If you decide to get involved in
this case, Quinn, don't hesitate to contact me at any time, day or
night. And be very, very careful."

CHAPTER 6

I drove myself to Hoboken the next day, and Bardot arranged for me to have guest parking. Standing once again at the door of his apartment, I tried not to remember the sickening crunch of that dead crow under my foot.

I swallowed hard and rang the bell.

Someone inside paused and looked through the peephole—no doubt also remembering the crow. I passed inspection, and the door opened.

I expected Lark again, but before me stood Jeff Randall, the super-talented lead guitarist. Standing six-foot-plus with broad, athletic shoulders, he actually looked as if he could have handled any intruder. His bronze-toned hair waved to his shoulders and he wore a gray sweat suit with the sleeves ripped off to bare gorgeous muscles. Up close, he gave the impression of a young pro footballer who'd lost his soul to rock 'n' roll.

He smiled, unnecessarily introduced himself and shook my hand. "You must be Quinn. C'mon in. Alan's on the phone."

Back in that great living room, I felt starstruck all over again. Okay, these guys weren't Jagger and Richards—yet—but hell, they were younger and cuter. In a few years, they might at least have a shot at being Bono and The Edge…albeit with Goth overtones.

And already I was on a first-name basis with both of them. This was crazy!

Alan stood by the windows, almost silhouetted by the late-morning sunshine. He gave me a wave, but then pivoted to face Manhattan, cell phone clamped to his ear, now and then mumbling some response.

Jeff seemed to take that as a sign we should leave him to talk in private. "You write about decorating? Lemme show you the game room."

This was a bit more what I might have expected for a rock star with a sense of the macabre. In addition to the requisite pool table, it featured vintage skee-ball, pinball, flipper and claw-crane machines. The charcoal-gray walls displayed old-fashioned funhouse props—shrieking and grinning faces of devils, demons, clowns, wild women and madmen, painted in garish colors that probably still glowed in the dark.

To one side of the big-screen TV stood a man-sized, turquoise T-rex with an arm sticking out of its mouth. On the other side, a skeleton in a Beatle wig wielded an electric guitar.

And, believe it or not, Dara the designer once again had managed to arrange it all in a fairly tasteful, sophisticated way.

"This is wonderful," I said. "Where did Alan get all of this stuff?"

"Oh, you'd be surprised what goes up for auction on line these days." Jeff chucked a chartreuse demon under the chin. "And a few months ago, when I heard one of the Jersey boardwalk 'dark rides' was being torn down, I told him to check it out. We salvaged a lot of stuff from there."

I could easily picture Jeff spending boyhood summers at the Jersey shore. His single dagger earring almost seemed at odds with his broad, open face and warm brown eyes.

When I admired a glass-encased gypsy fortuneteller, Jeff switched it on so she waved her hands slowly over her crystal ball. Then he threw me a startled look. "Oh, man, is this politically incorrect? I mean, is she offensive to psychics?"

I laughed. "Don't ask me. I haven't had a lot of practice being a 'psychic.' At least, not for hire."

Alan joined us then, with an apology. "That was Stern, giving me an update on the legal stuff…from Friday."

At this reminder of the accident at the theater, my stomach knotted. "I heard the cameraman's still in a coma."

"Yeah, and it's not looking great. Meanwhile, his family's suing the video company, which is suing us—"

"And in turn, you'll probably sue the Rialto," I finished.

"Didn't the Beatles have a song," Jeff asked, "the 'Sue Me, Sue You Blues'?"

"George Harrison." Alan sighed and looked regretful. "Unfortunately, that's how the lawyers play these games... Speaking of games"—he spread his arms proudly to encompass the room and asked me—"whaddya think?"

"It's wonderful. I always loved the old funhouses and arcades. Glad to see someone's preserving these things."

I recognized the red leather sectional from the *EW* magazine photo, and again, the sense of unreality made me a bit dizzy. Artifacts grouped on the wall above included the lobby poster for the nineteen-thirties movie *Mad Love*—a disembodied hand with a knife menaced Peter Lorre and his leading lady—and framed copies of the band's three CDs, including the latest one, *Night Tremors*, which had gone platinum.

Alan gestured toward the sofa. "Please, have a seat."

When I did, I noticed that the zebra-printed ottoman held the only element out of sync with the room—a big cardboard file box. The gray-white kind you fold together yourself and use to store a lot of paperwork. Something about this bland object disturbed me more than any of the creepy, fluorescent faces leering at us from the walls.

"What's in there?" I asked Jeff.

His smile dimmed and he gave the box a nervous glance, as if something might spring out of it. "Oh...you'll find out later. I'll let Alan handle that part."

From the retro bar across the room, Bardot offered me something to drink. Again, I stuck with bottled water.

"No Lark today?" I asked.

"She's home," he said. "Hubby has the flu."

"Yeah," Jeff cracked, "she's off today waiting hand and foot on another helpless guy."

"Hey, who's waiting on you?" Alan tossed a Coke bottle across the bar, and Jeff caught it easily.

I grinned along with them. I'd heard lead singers and lead guitarists tended to be competitive with each other, both having big egos, but that didn't seem the case here.

Alan returned with my water, popped a beer for himself,

then sat down between me and Jeff on the sectional. "Quinn, I know you're kind of uncomfortable about taking on our... problem at the same time that you work for the newspaper. So I've got a proposition for you."

I entertained a brief fantasy involving both him and his guitarist—which Tony would *not* have appreciated—but didn't have time to get my hopes up.

What Alan actually suggested was far less naughty, but almost as much of a dream come true. "Ever since I finished this apartment, *Celebrity Homes* has been after me to do a story on it," he said. "I put them off because we were touring, and then all these bad things started happening. Anyway, Stern read a couple of your articles online and said you're really good."

My heart beat faster, but I didn't want to jinx the moment by saying anything.

"If you can figure out who's stalking us and what's going on," Alan continued, "I'll tell the magazine they can have the story, but only if *you* write it. They've probably got one of their own people in mind, but if I make that the only condition, I think they'll go for it. Whadaya say?"

I almost bounced on the sofa with glee. Whenever I picked up *Celebrity Home*, I always salivated over the gorgeous houses and the high caliber of the photography and the writing. Never in a million years had I dared to imagine my byline on one of those stories! And while I didn't know what the writers were paid, it had to be many times what I usually earned from the regional magazines.

Maybe enough to finally update my awful nineteen-fifties kitchen.

"That would be fantastic," I told Alan. "I'd love to write about this place!"

"*If* you can help us," he reminded me, though with a smile.

Since we all seemed on such good terms, I tried a little more bargaining. "Just one other thing. The Friends of the Rialto have worked so hard to raise money to renovate that theater. They're trying to bring in live shows again and do something positive for their community. If I *can* prove that piece of plaster was deliberately rigged to fall, would you drop your suit against them?"

He leaned back against the red leather cushions and considered this. "I'd have to talk to Stern and our lawyers. But if someone from the outside sneaked in and messed with the stage on purpose, it'd be a crime, right? The theater people wouldn't be responsible."

He glanced at Jeff, who shrugged and nodded.

That satisfied me. I pulled the letter of agreement from my purse and handed it to Alan. We both had to reach around the ugly gray-white carton that still rested on the ottoman between us. I'd been trying to ignore it because it gave off a kind of low-grade psychic pulsation, like something radioactive.

Now that I'd handed over the signed NDA, Alan's tone grew dead serious. He told me, "I asked Jeff to join us today for a reason."

"Oh?"

"I figure, if that piece *was* rigged to fall, it wasn't supposed to hit the cameraman. Jeff and I are the only ones who perform at the front of the stage. It was meant for one of us."

The guitarist turned a little green, got up with his empty Coke bottle and headed for the bar. "If we're going to discuss this shit, I need something stronger."

I tried to be reassuring. "Somebody might just have wanted to disrupt the show—"

"I'm also going by the threats we've been getting," Alan said. "Some mentioned Jeff by name, some me. A few things came to here to my apartment, like that dead bird."

I nodded. "One reason I agreed to help you is that I did experience something last time, when I stepped on the crow." I tried to describe to him the ugly emotions I had channeled.

"Jealousy...betrayal..." Jeff, returning with a beer, chuckled darkly. "Well, that sure narrows it down!"

I felt rush of elation. Had I solved the case already? "It does?"

"I'm afraid he means 'not.'" Alan smiled sadly. "Any band that struggles as long as we have makes enemies. People who think we've let them down or screwed them over, even if it's not true."

I voiced a theory I'd been considering. "Like Barry Callahan, your first lead guitarist?"

"Good example. I'm sure Barry thinks *he* should've been playing on our last album, instead of Jeff. 'Course, if he'd been on it, the CD never would've gone platinum."

"I thought you fired him over the heroin bust."

"That was just the last straw. He was blowing off rehearsals and screwing up onstage. His problem was out of control, and he wouldn't get help. The rest of us like to have a good time, but none of us are into hard drugs. We were working our asses off trying to make it, and Barry was dragging us down." Maybe inspired by the memory, Alan crumpled his empty beer can between his hands. "The rest of us took a vote—three to one—and let him go. But he sure wasn't happy about it."

"So he's a suspect?" I asked.

"The cops talked to him a while back and couldn't find any link with the tour incidents. But he quit music and now he's in construction. Probably knows just how to chip away at a big piece of plaster." Alan frowned. "And one other thing. We had a private lab check out that dead bird. It overdosed—somebody fed it 'opiates,' whatever that means."

"Wow." At least, I thought, the poor thing probably hadn't suffered.

Jeff leaned against the wooden T-rex and set his beer on its flat, reptilian head. "There *are* other possibilities, Alan. Don't forget the good Reverend Ted Willis."

"The radio evangelist?" I asked.

"Yeah. You've heard his show?"

"Never, but I've heard about it."

Jeff filled me in. "Lately, he's been using Mad Love as a prime example of everything that's wrong with American pop culture. It's ludicrous—our music and our shows are tame compared to a lot of the stuff out there! But according to the Rev, 'Goth rock is Satanic and it'll turn your kids into devil worshippers.'"

"We don't suspect Willis himself, of course," Alan hurried to explain. "I'm sure he's smarter than he seems and just lays it on thick to get ratings. But he's got a lot of listeners, and some could be crackpots who really think the world would be better off without our band."

Suddenly, my task sounded like it was expanding to unreasonable dimensions. Was I supposed to check out all of this guy's thousands of listeners, in case one might a stalker? "I'm not sure I—"

"We're not asking the impossible, Quinn. Just do what you can." Alan pushed the file box across the ottoman toward me. "These are copies of all the threats or hate mail we're gotten over the past few months, including printouts of some texts and e-mails. The cops have seen all of 'em, and in some cases, they kept the originals."

I guessed that explained the toxic vibe. When I started to lift the lid, Alan rested his hand lightly on it to stop me. "You'll probably want to take 'em home. My aunt always did her best work alone, so she could concentrate."

Jeff stepped forward, looking alarmed. "Uh, do you really think—"

"She signed the agreement." Alan handed me the box, which had to weight ten pounds—or did it just feel that way to me?

For a guy with a purple forelock and the world's prettiest eyes, Bardot had a stare that meant business. "Don't let this box out of your possession, and don't talk about this stuff with anyone else. Anything in here ends up in the papers or on somebody's blog, there'll be no *Celebrity Home* and no deal for the Rialto. Got it?"

He didn't say it, but I imagined I could be the next one facing a lawsuit if I violated the NDA. "You can trust me."

"I am."

Behind him, Jeff didn't look so sure, but seemed willing to follow Alan's lead.

We were all headed for the door when Bardot's cell phone rang. He checked the number and stepped away to take the call. "'Sup, Stern?"

Jeff offered to carry the file box down to my car. I was glad to surrender it temporarily; I even wondered about the wisdom of bringing the poisonous thing into my house.

At the apartment door, Jeff told me quietly, "I sure hope

you're on the level. The cops don't seem to be getting anywhere. We're supposed to tour again this summer, and that's gonna be tough if we think somebody out there is trying to kill us."

We heard a groan from Alan, back at the bar with his phone. "Aw, shit...Oh, *man*..."

"That can't be good," mumbled the guitarist.

A few seconds later, Bardot hung up and turned back to us, looking pained. "The guy in the coma, the cameraman? He died."

A clamp of panic tightened around my throat. Instead of just the sabotage of a music video, I'd now be investigating a possible murder.

CHAPTER 7

At least when I brought the cardboard carton in from my car, the roof of my house did not cave in. I made some coffee, poured myself a mug and sat on my vintage living room sofa. Finally, I dared to lift the lid of Pandora's File Box.

The vibe did not get any more intense than it had been at Alan's apartment, and nothing screamed out immediately for my attention. Someone already had divided the contents into three manila file folders, and the headings intrigued me. One said "Religious," the second "Barry?" and the third "Miscellaneous."

The labels made me think of Sternberg. I'd seen Alan's right-slanted scrawl on a couple of the framed album covers at the apartment, and I doubted the same person could have produced this neat, almost vertical handwriting.

The "Religious" heading sounded especially provocative, so I pulled out that folder first.

Whoever had organized the material also had sorted it by date, and the first letter in this group had been sent the previous December, about the time Mad Love's last CD had hit the Web and the stores. There was a note on a file card in the same tidy black script:

Rev. Ted Willis has given out the addresses of Mad Love's recording company and Sternberg Management, on his radio show and Web site, and encouraged *people to write letters harassing the band.*

The first item in the folder was a photocopy of a letter and its envelope. It had been badly printed on lined notebook paper with holes along one edge, and read, *You loor kids to Hell! Sex, drugs and rock-n-roll says it all. Thank God we have men like Rev. Willis to speak the truth and open peoples eyes!*

Then there were printouts of e-mails. One quoted a line from a Mad Love song—on the album I actually owned—and completely misinterpreted it as promoting teen suicide. It wound up, *Your music drives kids to self-mutilation and madness.*

The radio interview in which Alan had come out as bisexual drew another spate of emails and text messages.

I can only pray your impressionable fans don't imitate your "lifestyle" of depravity, disease and decadence. (This woman actually signed her full name, and I at least had to give her points for alliteration.)

Another wrote, *People like you break up families and corrupt kids. Someone should do God's work and strike you down before you do any more damage.*

That semi-threat got my attention. Anyone that fanatical might be capable of sabotaging the band's bus or plane. I wondered if the cops had attempted to track down the author of that message, difficult though it might be.

I moved on to the folder marked "Barry?"

These notes had come in generic "security" envelopes with nothing typed on the front but Alan's name, which suggested they were dropped off personally. They were signed only with a rubber-stamp image of a black bird—much like the dead crow left outside Alan's apartment door.

The first few did not make any threats, but sent chills down my back in a different way.

I can be everything you need, so let's not throw away a good thing. I know they all laugh behind my back. They MADE you send me away. Heard you had some trouble last week with your plane. Maybe Fate's telling you that you made a bad mistake??

More recent letters amped up the drama:

I knew they poisoned your mind against me, but can't believe what I'm hearing—Jeff Randall? You're going to ruin everything, even your career! If you can't see that on your own, I'll have to make you see it. Do you believe in curses?

Attached to this message was a photo of all five Mad Love

members, probably printed out from their Web site, with crude drawings of knives aimed at Jeff and a thick black X over his face. A blindfold also had been drawn over Alan's eyes.

Whew, I thought, heavy stuff. And pretty close to another threat.

But the "Miscellaneous" file was even wilder.

Reverend Willis's fans seemed to watch their language— probably because they considered themselves good Christians— and the writer who signed with the bird stamp sounded anxious to get back into Alan's good graces. This bunch didn't have any such inhibitions. They let fly with the four-letter words, mostly on the subject of Alan's radio announcement. The hatred, homophobia and threats that scorched the photocopied pages turned my stomach.

How awful it must be to open up your mailbox or your e-mail and face that kind of abuse from total strangers. If it happened to me, I'd be working my "Delete" key overtime. Unfortunately, Alan had to save or print out all this crap and pass it on to the cops, just in case one of these crazies might be responsible for the problems plaguing the band.

Now I understood why both he and Jeff had seemed so rattled when I'd met with them earlier that day, and why Stern had insisted I signed the non-disclosure agreement. They all had trusted me with something very personal, and I felt obliged to deal with it responsibly.

I was thinking I'd read enough of this craziness for one afternoon, when I came across a relatively innocuous e-mail with the subject line, *Long Time No See*. I might have ignored it, but Stern had attached a note saying it came from an untraceable service.

Glad to see you've done so well for yourself! What's it been, 11 years? Seems like only yesterday you were hustling gigs back in L.A. Hope you haven't forgot who gave you your start in show biz! Just in case, I'll send you a little reminder, now and then.

I could almost hear the oily tone of voice behind the words. While I held the printout in my hand, a prickly sensation traveled up my arm and the print blurred before my eyes. Instead, I had a brief vision from the only trip I'd ever taken to

California. I was aloft in the plane, during the day. Below, I could see a deep ridge across the earth's surface, like crumpled and scorched brown paper—the Rocky Mountains. At the time, I'd been thrilled by this spectacle, but now it frightened me.

Alan needs to stay away from there. If he goes near the Rocky Mountains, he'll be in danger.

I rubbed my eyes and shook myself to snap out of the trance. The room around me, and the paper in my hand, came back into focus. But I felt sure the premonition meant something. I'd have to mention it to Bardot. Maybe it had something to do with the next tour. Could it be a warning of another accident, this time more serious?

For some reason, it had been triggered by that last, smarmy "Long Time No See" e-mail. Though that one contained no overt threats, or even foul language, it felt to me like the most sinister of all.

Nancy took another bite of the shrimp jambalaya and made an ecstatic face, bless her. "Quinn, this is excellent! You must have been cooking all day."

"Not me. I was out interviewing the owner of a lovely contemporary ranch house in Westfield. My crock pot was cooking all day."

Her tall, square-jawed husband Rob also looked impressed. "Really? You made this in a crock pot?"

I shrugged. "I can't trust my oven—any time I try to make something special for guests, it gets performance anxiety and conks out. My broiler's also pretty unreliable, and once you open the door, it takes three or four hard slams to close it again. So I'm pretty much limited to the burners, my countertop grill and my crock pot."

"Yeah, that whole kitchen has had it." Tony topped off all of our glasses with more Reisling. A quick search on the Internet that morning had told me it was good with Creole food.

We were celebrating Nancy's birthday. In the past, I'd always taken her out to dinner at a restaurant. But this year, settled for the first time in my own house, I felt like hosting a sit-down meal in my Victorian dining room with my antique mahogany table and chairs. I had set the table with a nice mix of old, flowered pieces of china I'd collected from thrift stores. I'd even used tapered candles in pastel blue, Nancy's favorite color.

She'd already put on the T-shirt I'd given her, with a cartoon of the instrument she played in her quartet and the words "They call me Mello Cello." On Nancy, it almost looked elegant.

She paused now between bites to announce, "Well, once Quinn cracks her big case, she'll be able to afford a whole new kitchen!"

Uh-oh. Birthday or not, I might have to cut off her drinks.

"Case?" Tony asked. "You mean, this thing for the band? I thought you weren't getting paid."

"I'm not, exactly." I explained Alan's offer to have me write about his apartment for *Celebrity Home.* "It might not come to anything. I probably won't even be able to help them."

Rob suddenly glanced toward the floor. "Hiya, Bela! Sorry, pal, no shrimp for you."

Nancy also looked beneath the table, and I knew my black-and-white "tuxedo" cat was making the rounds. "That's funny...I thought you had him shut up in your office, Quinn. When I went upstairs before, the door was closed."

"Oh, I just did that because the office is such a mess," I lied and hoped for a change of subject.

Tony raised an eyebrow, as if to suggest that my home office was *always* a mess and I'd never been concerned about it before. "Haven't got one of your new clients stashed up there, have you?"

I laughed. "Of course not. Just some confidential background material."

"Related to what happened at the theater?"

I tried to warn him off with a look. "I can't talk about it. I signed an agreement, remember?"

"And you closed the door...why? So I wouldn't snoop?"

"No sense putting temptation in your path." I treated it as a joke. "Really, Tony, they're just letters from obsessed fans, the kind every celebrity gets. They may have nothing to do with the accidents. Alan just doesn't want them splashed all over the press." I stood up. "Anyone want seconds? Or are we ready for the cake?"

I put on coffee and brought out a chocolate cake with fudge icing, since Nancy is a hard-core chocaholic. She blew out the candles—just the numbers "3" and "5"—and for a few minutes that created a welcome diversion. But her husband *is* a lawyer, and I shouldn't have been surprised when he eventually brought the subject back around to the material hidden behind the closed door upstairs.

"Y'know, Quinn," he began tactfully, "one of the guys at my firm, Ralph Meeker, is defending the Friends of the Rialto. If there are letters that might help their cause, he should have access to them."

I raise my hands in truce. "Supposedly, the cops have seen all this evidence and investigated where they thought it was necessary. If Ralph wants to, he can talk to them."

Nancy patted dark icing from her lips. "I thought you wanted to help save the theater."

"And that's exactly what I'm trying to do! I'm on their side, all the way. But the cops and the lawyers"—I glanced at Tony—"and the reporters will have to do their thing, and I have to do mine."

She, at least, seemed to accept that explanation. "Did it help, seeing the material? Did you get any kind of vibe off it?"

"There was something," I admitted. "I don't know what it means yet. I'll have a few more questions when I see the guys tomorrow."

Tony looked up sharply from his cake. "You're going back to Hoboken?"

"No, Newark this time. I'm meeting them at an abandoned jail."

All three of my guests stared, as if waiting for the punch line.

"I'm serious! The band's doing a photo session there. It's not that far from Elizabeth, so I'm going to stop by on my way back from the office." I cut another forkful from my slice of cake. "I got a text from Alan tonight, just before you guys came."

Tony shook his head, fuming. "That's great! I can't even get Mad Love's manager to return my phone calls, and meanwhile, this Bardot guy is texting you behind my back?"

Hoping to calm him down, I put a hand on his arm and

batted my eyelashes. "Darling, you make it sound so...sordid!"

Nancy giggled, and even Rob fought back a smile.

"It's not funny," Tony insisted.

"The jealousy part is," I told him. "Look, I'm not sneaking off to some rendezvous. It's a photo shoot in a decrepit old jail. The whole band is going to be there. And their manager and a camera crew. I'll be lucky if I can talk with Alan alone for fifteen minutes." Bardot did say he had something new to show me, something the cops hadn't seen yet, but I wasn't going to tell Tony that and make things even worse.

He finished his coffee and slapped down his napkin. "Well, since I've got to dig up information *you* already know, I'd better get an early start tomorrow. Sorry to cut the party short, Nance—happy birthday."

I jumped up, too. "Tony, honestly—"

But he silenced me with a wave, stalked out my front door and shut it firmly behind him. While I stood frozen with shock in the hallway, I heard his car pull away from the curb.

I couldn't believe it.

Regarding our on-and-off relationship, it looked as if I'd just pushed the "off" button, big time. But so had Tony. How dare he ruin Nancy's celebration over something so petty?

"Blew things a little out of proportion, didn't he?" the birthday girl observed.

"I'm so sorry," I told her. "I don't know what got into him. He can't possibly think there's anything going on between me and Alan Bardot!"

"The guy did text you," she reminded me, dryly.

"Behind Tony's back," Rob added, in the same tone.

Yeah, that was a good line. It's not as if Tony and I were living together or even engaged. Sometimes I wasn't sure exactly what we were.

"And I notice you haven't said *you* aren't attracted to Alan," Nancy pointed out, to stir the pot a little more.

"Ha! Me and about six million other crazy fans. That's not the issue here. I've made a professional commitment. Tony, of all people, should understand that. But no—his work is important, mine's always frivolous."

Nancy had heard me gripe this way before, but Rob cleared his throat, as if embarrassed. "The two of you are just stressed out right now, being on opposite sides of the fence. Give Tony time to cool down. He'll get over it."

I took a break to get the Sabatinos refills on their coffee. Alone in the kitchen, I reached for the wall phone—I still had my uncle's land line—to dial Tony's cell.

But no, it *would* be better to give him time to cool down. Anyway, I needed to do the same. This childish jealousy of his was starting to piss me off.

I realized, though, that Tony was right about one thing. I did feel divided in my loyalties, between him and the band. Normally, I would have rooted for him to get every juicy detail he needed for his investigative story, but I did *not* want him to get hold of those letters and emails. He'd be more responsible about using them than a tabloid reporter, but still… That incendiary material should stay under wraps unless, and until, it turned out to have some bearing on the string of suspicious "accidents."

When I returned with coffee, Nancy raised a new concern. "You said you're meeting these guys tomorrow at an abandoned jail? You're not afraid?"

"Naw. From what Alan said, it used to be a bad place, but the cops have kicked out all the druggies and cleaned it up so it's safe. Besides, I'm sure Mad Love will have plenty of their own security people around."

"That's good, but that's not what I meant. People die in jails, Quinn—sometimes violently." Her silvery eyes loomed big and round in the candlelight as she made a wavy motion with her hand through the air. "Ghosts!"

CHAPTER 8

While stopped in my car at a red light, about a block from the old county jail, I started to wonder if Nancy was right. Maybe I should have agreed to meet the band anyplace but here. On this overcast afternoon, the faded-red-brick hulk from the eighteen-hundreds that loomed behind walls topped with razor wire was seriously creepy.

At least I wasn't worried about being hassled by any live criminals. An occupied police car blocked the drive at an angle sure to keep out the riffraff. Otherwise, the only sign of activity was a few nondescript vehicles parked inside the gates, including an unmarked white truck and a shiny black van.

No limo. Nothing to tip off the locals that a semi-famous rock band might be doing a photo shoot inside.

I pulled up to the gate and, as advised by Alan, showed the cop my press credentials. He let me through, and once more I enjoyed the thrill of having better access than the most determined groupie. Even though having access to *this* place might be a mixed blessing.

I parked next to the van and stepped out into the chilly afternoon that was technically a week into spring, but didn't feel like it. Buttoning up the neck of my hooded wool car coat, I hoped it would keep me warm enough. I pressed the door buzzer, and a uniformed security guard checked my ID again before letting me pass. The sound of the weighty steel door clanging shut behind me triggered an automatic sense of panic that I might never breathe freely again. I could only imagine what it felt like to somebody who actually had been convicted of a crime.

Inside the reception area, things got a bit surreal. A boxy desk, where they once must have processed the prisoners, held three pizzas with various toppings in open boxes. A few hip-looking characters were helping themselves. They included a couple of massive, tattooed guys who, if not for their "Security" T-shirts, might have looked right at home behind the bars of the establishment.

I flashed my press card again and asked where I'd find Mad Love.

One of the bruisers, whose single hoop earring made him look like a surlier Mr. Clean, pointed down a long, rusted corridor. "They're shootin' in the main cell block." His words evoked disturbing images of a prison riot. "Your tetanus up to date?"

Not sure he was kidding, I forged ahead.

Even though the passages obviously had been swept of really hazardous debris prior to the band's visit, a brownish grit still clung to the margins. Along the ceilings of the walkways and the walls and bars of the empty cells, old pea-green paint gave way to the rust that seemed to be eating its way through the place.

I picked up a lingering, sour scent of dead things. Just stray animals...I hoped.

Afternoon light filtered in a haze from broken skylights. I passed cells vacant, except for painful-looking metal bed frames and filthy holes once covered by metal toilets. Out of the silence, voices seemed to jabber or hiss at me, clutching at the fringes of my consciousness.

I stepped up my pace, my stomach clenching. Maybe Nancy had been right—maybe I shouldn't have come here. This was exactly the kind of thing I'd been dreading, and avoiding, over the seven months since I'd managed to "cleanse" my own house of tormented spirits. As I hurried past the cells, I struggled to block out the lingering misery of those warehoused prisoners. To open up even the smallest channel in my psyche, I suspected, would invite a host of waking nightmares—maybe more than my sanity could handle.

A flitting shadow on the skylight level stopped me in my tracks.

Was someone up there? The movement had seemed almost too quick to be human.

A bird, then. Or maybe even a cat, prowling the rafters. With these broken windows, anything could get in.

But a bird or a cat wouldn't explain the weird chill that spread through me, from my marrow outward.

I walked on, faster.

Other corridors of cells branched off from the main one, but I homed in on the general commotion up ahead. Someone was playing a rock CD—possibly the one Mad Love had not yet officially released—and I could hear mixed voices and occasional laughter.

Finally, I reached the center of activity, ablaze with several floodlights on tall stands and a couple of those umbrella-shaped reflectors used by photographers. Among the dozen or so people on the fringes, I first recognized Lark. Wearing platform gladiator sandals and with her ice-blond hair piled high, she looked taller than most of the men present.

Stern could have modeled for an L.L. Bean catalogue in his navy turtleneck, down vest and dark jeans. He watched the proceedings with arms folded across his chest, but when he saw me he actually sort-of smiled and nodded hello.

Beyond, the five members of Mad Love posed in front of a half-open cell door. It may have been solitary confinement, because even the gaps between the bars were sheeted with metal. No instruments today—the guys just stood around in brooding poses, with Bardot and Randall a bit more to the front.

Most wore jeans and boots mixed with retro elements that made them look vaguely gangsterish, but in the nineteen-thirties rather than the hip-hop sense. A dark shirt with a loud tie here, a tweed vest there, old suspenders. Bardot sported a vintage blue-black suit jacket with wide lapels, over a black T and skinny black jeans. Randall had topped his flowing locks with an Al Capone-style fedora.

A lean, angular photographer with short spikes of red hair, who turned out to be female, called out occasional suggestions as she moved around the band, trying different angles. A teenaged boy with similar coloring, who might have been her son, made adjustments with the lights. It reminded me a bit of the interior design shoots I did with the *Sentinel* photographers, except the armchair usually didn't try to make the sofa crack up for the camera.

I hung on the fringes and happily watched the process. At least those big lights made it warmer in this chamber than elsewhere in the jail. My chill started to ease, and I unbuttoned my car coat.

Finally, the redhead called a break while she set up in another area of the jail. Lark and a young guy, who may have been another assistant, fetched bottled water for the band. I thought I'd have to fight my way in, but Alan spotted me and waved me over.

"C'mon and meet everybody," he said.

I'd done my homework on some rock websites, so I already knew them all by name.

Donny Morelli, the compact, well-muscled drummer, greeted me with a wide smile, but a challenging glint in his dark eyes. "Ah, the psychic!"

Pat Jacy, the keyboard player, whose center-parted black hair spoke to his Native American heritage, met my gaze seriously. He shook my hand silently, as if open-minded and willing to give me the benefit of the doubt.

Jack Raynor, the bass guitarist, stood tallest of the bunch, with blond hair that brushed his shoulders and a large, sharply cut features. To my shock, he gave me an obvious once-over and a wolfish grin. Maybe I was the first woman he'd seen in a while who wasn't wearing a spandex miniskirt, a leather corset and a nose ring?

Alan stepped forward, as if to rescue me. "If you don't mind, guys, Ms. Matthews and I have business to discuss. In private." He scanned our surroundings and noticed the half-open cell door. "Quinn, care to join me in solitary?"

Donny hooted. "Smooth line, Bardot."

Pat nudged Jeff. "Sure you don't want to go along to chaperone?"

"Oh, I trust Quinn," he deadpanned.

Still, I hesitated. Even though the broken ceiling let plenty of light into the old cell, the only seat appeared to be one of those slotted metal bed frames. When *had* I gotten my last tetanus shot?

Alan commandeered two folding directors' chairs and set them up in the cell. He told the others, "Call me when they're ready to shoot us again."

More unsettling imagery.

He pulled the iron door shut and sat down across from me. Today he looked more like a rock star, guy-liner making his aqua eyes huge and spooky, iridescent jacket setting off his purple forelock. He reached into a pocket and lowered his voice.

"Got another note this morning. Even the cops haven't seen it yet." He held out a zip-top sandwich bag. "I need to protect it in case there are fingerprints. Don't know if you can tell anything about it this way, but…"

The anonymous, computer-printed message was flattened and readable. It said: *What will it take to convince you? You crushed my dreams; now I'll crush yours.*

I took the bag in my hands and concentrated. Tried to sense something beyond the typed words. Sure enough, I got another wave of hurt, betrayal and outrage. "I think this came from the same person who left the crow."

Alan nodded soberly. "That would make sense. I found this in my mailbox at the condo, no envelope. So whoever this person is, he's got access to my building."

"Guess you don't have a security camera by your mailboxes."

"Nope. Not in the halls or the elevators, either. It been suggested, but people feel it would be an invasion of privacy." He shrugged. "There are cameras by the various entrances, but with more than four hundred residents… And who knows, this guy might even live in the building!"

"That's a scary thought," I said.

Bardot slipped the bagged note into his pocket again, got up and faced the gangrenous cell wall. "Stern's been wanting to get me a bodyguard. That's fine when we do an appearance or a concert, but hell, just to walk around town? I grew up in East L.A. I've always been able to take care of myself—I don't want a babysitter." He shook his head. "Besides, what if they go after Jeff or one of the other guys? We can't guard everybody twenty-four-seven."

The sooner we could narrow down the suspects, I reflected, the sooner the band could feel safe. "About the other messages..."

He sat again, looking keen. "Yeah?"

"It seemed to me as if some of them—especially the ones stamped with the bird—got nastier after Jeff joined you. Especially after he recorded with the band and got good reviews."

"That's the main reason why I suspect Barry. And something else I thought of...that business with the birds? Barry had a thing about ravens."

"Oh?"

"He was into Celtic myths, and once he wrote this song about a raven goddess that he wanted us to record." Alan's mouth twisted at the memory. "'Song of the Raven.' I mean, do ravens even sing? Don't they just caw, like crows?" We both laughed. "But Barry thought it was genius, and he was really pissed when we wouldn't use it."

"So you think these messages and the dead bird—"

Alan shrugged. "In one of our new songs, I had a line about a raven flying past the moon. Seems like right after that, I started getting these messages stamped with the bird. Could be Barry thought I stole his great idea."

"What's he doing with himself these days?"

"Working for his dad's construction company, I think, in New York state. Suffern, maybe?"

Sounded like quite a comedown from the life of a rock guitarist on the fast track to stardom. I pulled my little spiral notepad from my purse and made some notes. "The other group of messages, the religious ones—they really cranked up after that radio interview you did a couple of months ago."

"Yeah." Alan sighed and got up again, hands in his jacket pockets. "Looking back, I hope that wasn't a mistake. Stern didn't want me to do it, but—"

"You mean, come out as bisexual?"

"He was afraid it would turn off some of our fans. But, damn, it's the twenty-first century! I don't think anybody cares that much. Except the Reverend Willis crowd—and they're not exactly our target audience, anyway."

By now, I'd heard a recording online of the interview. Alan had worked the information smoothly into some half-humorous banter about being lonely on the road. "Still, I guess these days it can be dangerous to let fans know too much about your personal life."

Bardot stared at the peeling wall again and a muscle twitched in his cheek. "Yeah, well...I did it for a reason."

A sharp knock on the old steel door made me jump. Jeff yelled in, "We're starting again."

Alan pivoted toward the door, but I held up a finger. "One more thing?"

He paused, then called out to Jeff, "Go on. I'll catch up."

"Okay. We'll be in the north wing. Don't get lost...or you could be stuck in here for *life*."

Alan grinned.

I waited until Jeff had gone, then reminded Bardot, "About the e-mail messages...there was one from 'an old friend' who gave you your start in show business."

"There was? Oh...Stern must've put that in by accident. That's nothing."

"The writer said he—or she—was going to send you something. A reminder of the past. Did you ever get anything like that?"

Despite his pale makeup, I thought Alan colored a little. "Yeah, actually, I did. A CD I recorded with my first band. *Very* embarrassing." He started toward the cell door again, as if eager to end the conversation.

I persisted. "That message gave me a bad feeling, too. Almost as bad as the 'raven' stuff." I told him about the vision I'd had. "I feel like you need to stay away from the Rocky Mountains. Are you supposed to fly over them on your next tour?"

This warning obviously startled Bardot—he swung back toward me in shock. But just as quickly, he suppressed his reaction and told me, "Nowhere near, I'm happy to say. We're doing just the East Coast."

That relieved my worries a little. "Anyway, I can't help

sensing the person who sent that email might be dangerous to you."

He slid the iron cell door open with a half-smile and a shake of his head. "Sorry to disappoint you, Quinn. That really was just an old friend."

I didn't believe him. And I wondered how he expected me to solve this case if he was going to keep secrets from me.

We found the photo crew and the rest of the band re-assembled in a corridor with steep tiers of cells on both sides. I could understand why the photographer had chosen this spot, because the day's milky light seeped through the bars from all directions to create a particularly eerie mood. She posed the members of Mad Love and made small adjustments in their outfits.

Alan playfully grabbed Jeff's fedora from his hand and slapped it on his head. "Showtime, Randall!"

The guitarist laughed and sent him a quick, fond glance that caught my attention. I remembered the guys' jokes about Jeff not trusting me alone with Alan, and wondered if I'd stumbled onto another secret.

The teenaged assistant carefully positioned the lights again, and the redheaded photographer resumed shooting. I hung to one side with Stern and Lark, watching the spectacle from about thirty feet away.

I listened, meanwhile, to the band's new CD and thought about Barry Callahan. The raven symbolism did sound as if it pointed to him. I might be able to get a vibe if I talked to him in person, but would it be safe to—

A prickle up the back of my neck interrupted my thoughts. Made me glance left.

A shadow, like the one I thought I'd seen before, rippled across the prison bars along the upper level. It stopped by a big light, hanging from an eight-foot pole with a tripod base that shone down on Alan and Jeff.

A dark appendage—I couldn't call it an arm—reached from between the bars.

Gave the light a shove.

"Look out!" I screamed.

Alan spun. Saw the thing falling and yanked Jeff out of the way. The pole and light hit the cement floor with a stunning crash. The big bulb shattered, glass splinters flying.

Curses rang out all around.

Stern darted forward to check on the band. "Everybody okay?"

They all nodded.

Meanwhile, the photographer lambasted her assistant. "Well, you *must* have set it crooked. How else could it fall like that? Not like there's any breeze in here!"

"I-I don't know." He looked on the verge of tears.

I really wanted to tell him, his mother and everyone else that it wasn't his fault. But I didn't think they were ready for my story about the shadowy specter...which had vanished.

A couple of the security guys came running from the front of the building. Looking pale even in his stage makeup, Alan barked at them, "Check this whole place. Make sure nobody's lurking around up there!"

Though the guards did as they were told, Randall squinted upward and commented, "Don't see how there could be. Just a narrow girder along the wall there—no place to really stand."

Just like at the Rialto, I thought, feeling ill.

"Thank God Quinn yelled out when she did!" Lark threw me a grateful smile. "I guess the rest of us were too busy watching you guys. Either that, or it was another of her premonitions."

"Could be," said Stern. Stepping aside while a crew member swept up the shattered glass, he dropped his voice and aimed his last comment just at me. "Seemed like you called out right *before* the light fell."

CHAPTER 9

As soon as I got home that afternoon, I called Gail Kleinholtz. Normally we communicated by e-mail, but she'd told me I could always phone in case of an emergency.

I thought this qualified.

Luckily, I caught her at home. I gave her a quick rundown of the mishap at the jail, noting its similarity to the accident at the theater.

"You told me a ghost can never physically hurt anybody," I reminded her, getting a bit shrill. "This thing injured a man the first time around—a guy who later died!—and today it tried to brain one of the band members with a heavy light stand."

She paused before asking, "You're sure, Quinn, that it couldn't have been a real person? Maybe he hid behind the bars and pushed the light with something."

"I told Stern, Alan and Jeff what I saw. Their security guys ran right up and checked the second tier of cells. But just like at the theater, the exact spot where I saw the figure was inaccessible. No one could have been standing there." Just remembering that made me shudder. "Besides, the photographer was snapping the whole time, and her pictures showed no sign of anyone near the light. It looked as if it just toppled for no reason...except a couple of shots *did* show a bright flare in the upper corner."

"Umm," said Gail.

I knew what she must be thinking. That kind of "vortex" on a photograph supposedly indicated a ghostly presence.

"I don't get it, though," I went on. "I can see an old theater having a ghost and an old jail having one, but the same ghost haunting both? Alan has gotten messages implying the band is cursed. Is there any kind of ghost that follows a particular person around, trying to do him in?"

"Not exactly," Gail said, slowly. "Not a ghost."

I didn't like her cautious tone. I'd had enough trouble last year learning to deal with lingering spirits of dead people. Was she going to lay some new kind of supernatural creature on me?

"I was concerned when you first told me about the accident at the theater," she added. "But these things are so rare—"

"*What* things?"

She sighed. "Some people do believe that a skilled practitioner can create a 'thought-form entity' to do his or her bidding. In Tibet it's called a *tulpa*. Some indigenous tribes in Australia and America also believe a shaman can project an ethereal version of himself to harm his enemies. Among Western occultists, a skilled magician or coven supposedly can create such a being, too. They call it a servitor."

I was glad to be sitting on my solid old sofa, because the living room started to whirl around me. "Are you talking about...some kind of demon?"

Gail's tone turned soothing. "I don't believe in demons, Quinn, or the Devil. A servitor is more like an ethereal double of a living person. And since the creator *is* still alive, he or she can direct it to do real harm. You've heard of a poltergeist? A destructive energy that's linked to a troubled person, usually an adolescent?"

I had.

"Well, this is similar, only more...personified. It's a projection of the creator's powerful emotions, his single-minded desire."

"Would it look like that person?" I asked, confused. "Because this was only vaguely human, no particular features. At first I thought it was just a shadow."

"The creator may prefer it that way, maybe because he doesn't want to be recognized. He hasn't got the courage to come after his victim in person, so he's created this formless being to do the dirty work for him. It can even go where he isn't allowed to go...or physically can't go."

I thought of the tight security around the jail that day. If the band's enemy was someone known to them, he surely wouldn't have wanted to show himself, even in spirit form. "That's incredible, Gail. As in, pretty darn hard to swallow."

"It's a stretch, I know," she admitted. "I've never encountered a *tulpa,* myself, but I do know a missionary priest who said he dealt with one in Nepal. It was following a tribesman there to carry out some kind of vendetta. The priest got rid of it through a regular Roman Catholic exorcism."

I tried to imagine the members of Mad Love sitting still for that!

Gail went on to explain that supposedly a servitor could be created through a ritual, similar to a voodoo curse. And as in voodoo, the fear of the victim seemed to strengthen the entity's power to harm him.

Bela sprang on the cushion next to me, and I almost dropped the phone. The living room's shadows had started to lengthen by now and suddenly felt menacing.

Just because I had a hard time believing all this didn't mean I wasn't spooked.

Not so long ago, I'd confronted real ghosts in my house. They'd moved objects; invaded my consciousness to make me relive traumatic moments from their lives; taken shape as real people one minute and vanished the next. Those experiences had made a serious dent in my prior skepticism.

And now I'd seen this vengeful "shadow" at work. Twice.

I got up and paced around my living room with the cordless phone, turning on more lights. "Gail, if it's just a projection by a human being, can it make a mistake? It seems to be targeting someone in the band, but at the theater it injured a cameraman, instead."

"I can't say for sure, of course. But if its creator is a novice and has trouble focusing completely, I guess he could make a mistake...and so would the servitor."

That sounded almost hopeful. "I still find it hard to imagine a 'thought-form' could disable the band's airplane engine or wreck their equipment truck."

Gail actually chuckled; I guess when you're a professional psychic, you develop a macabre sense of humor. "Yes, that sounds far-fetched to me, too. Though, who knows? If the creator is skilled as a mechanic..." Her voice trailed off, letting that idea hang.

I sat down on the sofa next to Bela again and stroked his glossy back. When I had ghosts in the house, he'd been my early-warning system because he'd usually freak out in their presence. The fact that he sat purring contentedly now was reassuring. "Okay, Gail. Worst-case scenario, it is a supernatural entity. Can Alan and the band do anything to protect themselves? Short of calling in Father Karras from *The Exorcist?*"

"Possibly." She sounded more hopeful. "You got my latest book, didn't you? Chapter Seven has instructions on how to raise a psychic shield. There are several methods from different traditions, one probably as good as the next. The practices are meant to protect a person from any kind of psychic attack."

I hadn't studied the book in detail, and again I tried to picture the members of Mad Love going for such a New Age solution.

Well, Alan, maybe. After all, he'd dragged me into all this.

I asked her, "Could it be stopped if we found the person who's creating it and...and talked with him? Got him to drop his vendetta?"

"That would be the best solution, whether the threat is supernatural or not. Certainly, they need to find out who's behind these incidents, and soon."

"I know," I said. "If this guy is targeting either Alan or Jeff, so far he's missed his mark. But judging from how close that light came today, his aim could be getting better."

After I hung up with Gail, I considered my next move.

The most obvious one would be to track down Barry Callahan and try to determine if he was causing all this trouble—by paranormal means or otherwise. Alan had said Barry was into Celtic mysticism. Maybe he'd progressed from that into the darker form of witchcraft Gail had described.

Could I locate his family's construction firm?

I wondered if by now Tony had checked out this lead. After all, if the plaster chunk at the theater had been deliberately rigged to fall, Barry would be a prime suspect. I'd been following Tony's stories in the paper, though, and so far, none had included any quotes from the former lead guitarist.

Tony. I hadn't spoken to him since the night before, when he'd stalked out of my dinner party for Nancy. I supposed we were at a standoff now, each waiting for the other to call and apologize.

Tony always could come up with ingenious ways to find people.

I looked at the phone in my hand. Considered calling him and trying to smooth things over by trading tips. After all, my NDA probably didn't forbid me to pass on factual information, such as where Barry Callahan might be working these days.

But, no, I couldn't involve Tony in this. I couldn't tell him about the accident today at the jail, and I sure as hell couldn't go into Gail's theory about the "servitor."

Plus, if he knew I planned to talk to Barry in person, he'd go ballistic. At the very least, he'd probably insist on coming along to protect me...which would screw up everything. I wanted to play it cool around Barry to see what kind of vibe I got from him. I couldn't do that with Tony along in full investigative reporter mode.

Well, I wasn't half bad at research, myself.

I sat down with my laptop computer. About ten minutes later, I'd turned up Callahan & Son Contractors in Rockland County, New York. I'd also come across an online news story that said they were renovating an old factory in Harrison, New Jersey for high-end condos.

A nice stroke of luck. The job site wasn't even too far away.

I hatched a plan, one that I figured should keep me safe even if Barry *was* behind the vendetta against Mad Love.

But before I drove to the job site, I'd reread Gail's book and try raising one of her "psychic shields." Just in case.

CHAPTER 10

I was standing on the flat roof of a factory in Harrison, New Jersey with Barry Callahan—former lead guitarist, heroine addict and all-around wild man with Mad Love. It was two o'clock on a cloudless April afternoon, and I could see all the way across the industrial landscape and the Passaic River to the Newark skyline.

Meanwhile, Barry talked to me about permeable pavers.

"This whole area back here"—his gesture took in a stretch of reddish soil now churned up by construction vehicles—"will be parking for sixty cars, but instead of asphalt, it'll be these special pavers. Y'know how when the rainwater runs off to the street, it pollutes the water system? This way, it's absorbed into the ground naturally."

He sounded totally into this admirable project and thoroughly sane. No sign so far of a psycho-killer who'd been stalking his former band. The only thing with which he seemed obsessed was this factory undergoing renovation as a "green," upscale condo complex.

I'd shaken his hand when we met and picked up no sinister vibes. Just to be safe, though, I kept my distance from the edge of the roof. I've got a touch of vertigo, anyway.

"Up here," Barry went on, "we'll have twenty solar panels providing energy for the whole building. On a good day, they'll produce more than necessary and send energy back to the municipal grid."

"That's great!" I jotted a few notes in my steno pad.

I'd called the Callahans' office earlier that day to make sure Barry would be at the construction site. When I first showed up,

I'd introduced myself as a freelance writer who specialized in interior design and architecture. All that was true, of course, and gave him no reason to connect me in any way with his old band.

Still, he'd acted a bit wary until I showed him a couple of magazine articles with my byline. I said I'd been on another assignment in the area, heard about Callahan's project and thought I'd swing by for a look.

The renovation of this building would not be completed for several more months, though, so I'd be under no pressure to show him a story any time soon.

Barry strolled to the rear of the roof and pointed down again. "See that big excavation? That's for the geothermal heating and cooling wells. When that system's up and running, these condos will have virtually free heat and AC year-round. The well covers will be sodded over for a kids' play area."

"Very nice!" I commented, sincerely.

He headed back to where the staircase hatch stood propped open, and I followed him down the narrow industrial steps. Meanwhile, the whining of power saws and anvil chorus of hammering grew louder.

I started to feel just a little guilty about my undercover role. Barry even looked a hundred-eighty-degrees different than he had on the band's first album cover. There, he'd sported a blond Prince Valiant haircut complete with shaggy bangs, a surly expression and a leather vest that bared arms full of tattoos. Today, his hair was short as a Marine's, he'd grown a downy moustache, and most of the tattoos were covered by a loose Kelly-green T-shirt with the name and shamrock logo for Callahan & Son.

He gave off a faint whiff of perspiration from honest toil in the noonday sun. He'd even provided me with my own hard hat, though I guess he had to if he didn't want to risk a lawsuit.

Back inside the building, I spotted workmen sanding the old floors and commented on it.

"Yeah," said Barry, "we kept the original shell of the building, just cleaning up the bricks, and we're saving and refinishing the original floors, too. Using all low-VOC finishes—you know about VOCs?"

He wasn't catching me off-guard with that one. "Volatile organic compounds. All those nasty pollutants in old-school paints and varnishes."

Barry nodded slowly, still giving me a sideways look.

I paused in my note taking and smiled. "Why do I get the feeling you don't think I'm legit?"

"Sorry." He sent his gaze out across the cavernous expanse where his workmen were sanding floors or raising partitions. "Guess I've just had a bad time in the past with reporters."

"Really? Why—" I feigned surprise. "Y'know, I thought I recognized your name from somewhere. You were in a band, right? Mad Love?"

He wrinkled his short nose as if smelling sewer gas. "For a little while, yeah."

"I have the first album." I pretended to scrutinize him and chuckled. "Took me a while, though, to make the connection."

"Well, maybe that's a good thing." He led the way to the old freight elevator. "C'mon, I'll show you something really cool."

He sounded so offhanded, I thought nothing of getting into the grimy elevator with him. I started to have second thoughts, though, when it continued down and down. I realized we were headed for the basement.

This turned out to be a dim, cavernous space, empty at the moment of any workers. Barry pointed out the Styrofoam-like insulation between the beams and explained its energy-efficient properties. All I could think was how well it would muffle sound if he really were a psycho and I got on his bad side.

Only one person knew where I was today—my "client," Alan. And being a good forty-five minutes away, he wasn't in a real good position to help me.

At least I spotted no unexplained shadows flitting about. That made me braver. It would be a wasted trip if I got no information at all from Barry about his conflicts with the band.

"This'll be the heartbeat of the building down here," Barry announced proudly, pointing to a hole about ten feet across in the middle of the room. "Our geothermal pump."

He explained in detail, with some pantomime, how the lines from the exterior wells would enter the pump, circulating water and refrigerant to control the temperature of the building. I wrote quickly to keep up, even though I'd probably never use the information.

"Well," I said, a bit breathless, "this certainly looks like an exciting project. You'll have to let me know when it's close to finished, so I can pitch the story to a magazine. Maybe give you some more positive publicity than you've had in the past."

"That would be nice," he said, with no expression.

I decided to take advantage of our isolation to ask a few more personal questions. "Music press gave you a hard time, did they?"

He made a derisive sputter with his mouth. "You could say that. Made out like I was some stoned loser who couldn't even keep his fingers on the guitar strings... Well, I know where *that* came from. That was Alan. Him and Stern, our manager."

"Oh, really?"

"Jack, Donny and me, we all come from upstate New York. Me and Donny, the drummer, had a band in high school. Later we met Pat, whose parents left him an old farm outside Warwick. We'd all crash there and rehearse in the barn. Jack came in as bass guitar, but we went through a couple of singers before Alan showed up. He answered an online ad...and took over."

I sensed this might be a long, bitter story. Noticing some unopened insulation boxes, stacked a couple of feet high, I sat down on them.

"We were just screwing around, playing local gigs and working at day jobs, but Bardot was ambitious. He got everybody psyched about writing more of our own material, making a CD, getting a manager... He'd been in a couple of bands before and had contacts."

"Looks like it worked," I offered, playing devil's advocate.

"Yeah, but pretty soon it got like the army. I mean, you're in a band, you want to kick back and have some fun, right? But Stern, Alan and sometimes even Pat got on our case about rehearsing, always rehearsing. And getting to gigs real early for sound checks...and nitpicky stuff about the arrangements... Got to be worse than a straight job!"

Silently, I imagined the other guys pushing Barry for excellence instead of mediocrity, but kept that to myself.

"Still," I said, "with the band on the way up, and fame just around the corner, it must've been rough to have them let you go like that."

"What do you think?" Barry snorted his disgust, then cocked one blond eyebrow at me. "You seem awful interested in all this stuff. You sure you're only here to write about the building?"

I shrugged innocently. "I showed you my articles."

"You could still be sniffing around for some tabloid. Not that I'd blame you—they pay good money."

"So I've heard. How come you never sold them your story?"

He also sat down on the cartons, too, not far from me. "A lawyer told me I was better off keeping my mouth shut. Still, I thought about it, plenty. 'Specially the last week or so."

"Why's that?"

"Aaah, the band's been having these funny 'accidents' and the cops've been questioning *me*. Like I'm carrying some big grudge against them! An' the papers have been calling... One guy from some Jersey rag left me, like, half-a-dozen messages. On our office phone that we use for business! My dad blew his top."

Uh-oh, I thought. That sounded like the work of my almost-significant-other. I could picture Tony blowing his top, too, if he knew the guy who'd been dodging his calls was giving me an in-person interview.

"Guess it would be a way of getting your side of things in print," I prodded.

Barry shook his head with a smirk. "Boy, I could tell them some stories. Y'know how they made this big deal about the guy who replaced me, like they just found him through another ad? I got my theories about that!"

"Oh?"

"He and Bardot got a thing going on. Why y'think all of a sudden Bardot made that little confession on the radio? 'Bisexual,' my ass. Only reason he ever dated chicks was so fans wouldn't know he was gay—Stern wanted him to keep it on the down-low. Anyhow, I'm betting he's known Randall a while. Probably had him warming up on the sidelines and found the first excuse he could to fire me."

I'd already had my suspicions about Jeff and Alan, but I couldn't share Barry's belief that the new guitarist had slept his way into his job. I'd heard both of them play, and had no doubt Jeff was hired for his talent.

Taking my lead from all the "good cop" performances I'd see on TV, I said, "That must make you pretty mad."

"Oh, I *could* be mad about a lot o' things." Barry lurched up again and stalked a few paces across the basement, his expression turning inward. "Like the fact that one o' their big hit songs from the last album was an idea Bardot ripped off from me. Told *me* it sucked, but once I'm out of the band, he puts his own twist on it and gets a big hit."

I figured Barry must be talking about the "raven" song, and thought how different his take on the situation sounded from Alan's.

"And my two best *pals*," he went on, growing more heated, "guys I grew up with, did they defend me? Hell, no. Wave dollar signs in front of their faces and they sold me out, too, in a heartbeat!"

He kicked a scrap of metal pipe across the room into the yawning pit, with an echoing clang that made me jump. I wondered again just how safe I was down here with him and figured I'd better show sympathy again, quickly. "That sounds awful. I'd hardly blame you if you did want to get back at them."

"Huh! Yeah, sometimes I think that way." Hands stuffed in his jeans pockets, he lingered at the edge of pit where the massive pump would soon reside and stared into its depths. "My dad tells me, life's too short for that. And with the crazy hours, the girls, the booze and drugs—it was too much temptation for me. My dad saw that. He kept asking me to give it up and come work for him." Barry swung back toward me and puffed out his chest in the company T-shirt. "After all these years, I finally did. Now I've kicked the hard stuff, I keep normal hours and I'm doing work I can be proud of."

"That's terrific." I hoped he meant it all.

He started back toward the elevator, and once more I trailed in his wake.

"Nah, I don't give a shit about getting back at those guys," he insisted, as we stepped into the cage and started to ascend. "'Cause you know what? Sooner or later, people like that get what's coming to them. When I heard about those weird accidents, I just thought, maybe they're all finally getting what they deserve."

CHAPTER 11

Back in my car, I took a second to text Alan on my phone: *Spoke to Barry and survived. Be home around 3. Call u then.*

The simple message left me feeling weird on several levels. I'm sure Barry would have been furious if he knew I was sitting in his parking lot reporting back to Alan about him—he might even have thrown me into that basement pit and poured some wet cement on top. I also remembered how irritated Tony had become when he'd found out I had this semi-secret communication going with Bardot.

Not that Tony had anything to worry about! I guess that part bothered me a little, too. I'd always told myself Bardot was far ou of my league, but if was Barry said was true, I had even less chance than I thought. Alan was totally playing for the other team.

Well, in my line of work I'd met plenty of hunky-but-gay male interior designers, so it wasn't my first disappointment along that line. Even if my crush might be more hopeless than I'd always expected, I'd continue to do my best to help Alan solve his professional problems.

Not only did I still have the prospect of an article in *Celebrity Homes* to look forward to, there was the even more important issue of saving the Rialto Theater. Unless I could prove the cameraman's death had been a criminal action by someone from the outside, the suit-countersuit drama would continue to play out and probably undermine the theater's restoration.

I started up my PT Cruiser and drove back across the Harrison Avenue Bridge toward Newark. Heading home, I reflected that I might have made progress in my investigation, but not the kind I'd hoped for. Barry Callahan had been everybody's best suspect, and now I had my doubts. Of course, I was new at this kind of psychic sleuthing—my chief experience up to now had been with ghosts, not flesh-and-blood bad guys. And no matter what Barry said, he did seem to be harboring a nasty grudge against Mad Love.

But if I could pick up such vivid impressions from a dead bird or a Xerox of a letter, surely I would have gotten some kind of flash when I shook the hand of the man who had delivered them! So, if Barry was as innocent as he claimed, what other prospects did we have?

Had we all been wrong about the saboteur's motive? If even I could feel a bit of jealousy over Alan—never having had a relationship with him, and with no encouragement on his part— what about someone who'd been involved with him in the past? The agonized letters saying things like "I can be everything you need" could easily refer to a personal breakup rather than a professional one.

But where to start looking for suspects? Among old girlfriends? Boyfriends? As Jeff had joked, it still didn't narrow the field too much.

And then there was the Reverend Willis crowd…

As I cruised along McCarter Highway, skirting the industrial fringes of Newark, it occurred to me that the timing might be right for me to pick up the minister's radio show. He broadcasted twice a week from one to four P.M., and since the station was in central Jersey, I should be just within range.

I'd already studied up a bit on the radio station. It played only Christian rock, and apparently, the featured artists were vetted for their lifestyles as well as their lyrics. I guess that was why the station was happy to give Reverend Willis three hours in the afternoon to rail against less acceptable kinds of entertainment.

From what I'd read, he also criticized contemporary TV shows and movies, often reading hidden meanings into them that sounded far-fetched to me. But his biggest beef always was with mainstream pop and rock music.

And as I tuned in today, close to the end of his show, I found Willis hard at it again.

"—many of our children are walking around these days with iPods glued to their heads. In the old days, at least a parent could hear what his children were listening to. Now, if your child downloads music from the Internet, you have no idea. You may wonder why suddenly your little boy or girl is talking back to you, using bad language, staying out after curfew, experimenting with drugs and alcohol and sex... But if you heard the music they've been listening to, you wouldn't be surprised at all!

"Let me read you just a few lyrics from one my *favorite* bands, Mad Love." He launched in a stilted recitation:

"'Shady sister, leave your presents
Rainbow of delights
Take me higher than the stars
And fill my empty nights
But I see when I come down
You are nowhere to be found.'"

My mouth fell open and I nearly missed my exit to I-78. I immediately recognized the song from Mad Love's last album. Not only did the lyrics strike me as pretty harmless, but I'll bet if a Christian-rock band had recorded them they would have been taken as a wholesome warning.

But Willis carried on in shocked tones about how this was obviously a one-night stand with a groupie, and that "presents, rainbow of delights" and "take me higher" referred to sex and drugs.

Probably true, I had to admit. But the song sounded rueful to me, as if the writer regretted having been taken in by this potion-peddling sorceress. Anyhow, what about all the rap groups out there who talked about beating up "ho's" and shooting cops? All the female pop idols moaning and squealing their way through really suggestive lyrics? The right-wing heavy metal groups decked out in "SS" armbands and swastikas?

"Take me higher than the stars and fill my empty nights"? *This* got Willis all riled up?

"So, my friends, pay attention to the ideas this music is

planting in your children's heads," he finished. "The rock star culture they admire so much promotes drug addiction, occultism, promiscuity, homosexuality and even suicide..."

Hard to believe someone was still preaching this way in the twenty-first century, I thought. From what I'd heard, conservative ministers had been saying all the same things from their pulpits since Elvis first swiveled his hips and the Rolling Stones sang "Sympathy for the Devil." But was anyone living in the New York metro area today actually buying this?

Apparently, yes. Following a commercial, Willis took calls from parents who thanked him for his courageous stand against the "corporate conspiracy" to make millions from the destruction of their children's souls. Some testified they had thrown out their teens' CDs and DVDs and would no longer let them download anything without supervision. One kid said he had felt himself "tempted to immorality" by his favorite band and now listened only to uplifting Christian rock.

By the time I pulled into my driveway, the program had wound up. These folks were entitled to believe and even boycott whatever they wanted to, but painting certain artists as minions of Satan was going a bit too far.

And why, of all groups, single out Mad Love? I couldn't help thinking there was something odd about that.

I walked in my front door, as expected, just about three o'clock. I immediately sat down in the living room with my laptop to record my conversation with Barry in as much detail as I could remember.

After about fifteen minutes, my cell phone rang, and I recognized Alan's number. Guess he couldn't wait to find out what I might have learned from my undercover assignment.

"Glad you survived the interview," he said, with a chuckle. "Okay, Mata Hari, what have you got for us?"

Damn, my heart actually fluttered. Well, he did have a damned sexy voice—after all, it had gotten him where he was today. "I don't know if this is good news or bad news, but I don't think Barry's your man."

"No? How come?"

I explained the lack of negative impressions on my part. "I

can't swear he didn't have anything to do with the sabotage of the truck or plane. But the raven business? The intense anger and jealousy? Even shaking his hand and spending over an hour in his company, I didn't get any of that."

"Hmm," said Alan. During a brief silence, I wondered if he doubted my conclusion, maybe even my qualifications.

"That's not to say he doesn't still have some hard feelings about being fired," I went on. I told him about Barry's minor temper tantrum in the factory basement, and his theory that he'd only been let go to make room for Jeff to join the band.

Alan laughed, with a hard edge. "Oh, man, the drugs really have made him paranoid!"

"You're not involved with Jeff?"

He hesitated, maybe remembering I'd signed the NDA. "That part is true," he said quietly, "but it had *nothing* do with our firing Barry. The band made that decision first, then advertised for a new guitarist. I'd never set eyes on Jeff before he came to audition."

"Could there be someone out there who knows about the two of you and has a more personal vendetta? Were you seeing anybody else when Jeff came into the picture?"

Again, Alan paused before answered, as if that seemed to him a long time ago. "Just Valery."

Ah, yes, I'd heard about her. The model. I didn't even know her last name because she went mainly by her first.

I still had the laptop in front of me, and with just a couple of keystrokes, pulled up an image of Valery. Tall and skinny, of course, with long, wavy, golden-red hair that made her look like a pre-Raphaelite waif. It went well with the multi-layered, New-Bohemian outfit she modeled in the photo.

Alan added, "I promise you—despite whatever Barry said— my relationship with her was *not* just for show. But we didn't make any big commitments, either."

Tactfully, I asked, "When it ended, was she upset?"

"It was pretty mutual, but if anything, she dumped me." Alan sounded amused rather than resentful. "Val was always a popular girl. Found herself a software tycoon—he could probably buy and sell me. Last I heard, they were still together."

"So she's got no reason to sit around sticking pins into a doll with your face on it…or Jeff's?"

"I can't picture that, no." I heard a smile in his voice, but then he sobered. "Though, while Valery and I were hanging out, *she* got some particularly nasty hate mail. I gather it's not so unusual for models. Most girls idolize them and ask for beauty and diet tips, but Valery told me others get insanely jealous of them and can be really abusive."

Interesting, I thought. This "assignment" sure was giving me an inside view of the drawbacks of being a celebrity. And Valery wasn't even putting out any controversial body of work, except…her body.

"She'd learned to just shrug off that kind of stuff," Alan went on. "The only reason she even told me about those particular notes was because they mentioned me. We'd only been out together in public a couple of times, but this person ranted that she wasn't good enough for me, wasn't 'my type' and could never make me happy. The tone *was* kind of like the notes I've been getting about Jeff."

"Were they on paper, like the ones with the raven stamp?" I asked. "Would Valery still have any of them?"

"Nah, they were emails. She didn't bother to track them down or print them out, and I'm sure she deleted them a long time ago. Probably no way to tell if they had any connection with what's going on now."

Another promising lead turned dead end. "Then all we have left is the religious right." I told him what I'd heard earlier that day on the Reverend Willis show.

"Jesus!" said Alan. "No pun intended…I guess he didn't bother to read the rest of the lyrics. That was probably the most *anti*-drug, *anti*-promiscuity song I ever wrote."

"He's gunning for you guys, that's for sure. And by this time, he may have gotten a lot of people whipped up against you. But that station broadcasts to a pretty wide area. If one of his listeners has decided the world would be better off without Mad Love, I don't know how we'll ever find him!"

"Could be tough," Alan agreed. "But that's the other thing I wanted to talk to you about. Stern and Jeff and I have got an idea to lure our mysterious enemy out into the open—and you definitely should be a part of it."

CHAPTER 12

"Sonia, if it's no problem, I'd like next week off."
The features editor peered up at me quizzically from beneath straight, black, Cleopatra bangs that grazed the tops of her eyeglass frames. She favored quirky glasses, and these, in candy-apple red, were new since my last visit to the *Sentinel's* office.

"I know it's short notice," I added, "but I can work ahead. I just turned in the spring-decor story, and by the end of this week I'll give you the one on the family living in the converted grist mill. I'm going out there tomorrow."

"Okay." Sonia nodded slowly. "Got ze photos yet for zpring decor?"

"Gil took 'em yesterday, and I just sent 'em to you." I nodded toward her computer screen, where the e-mails were stacking up, mine at the top.

Sonia opened up the photographer's gallery, scanned the assortment and nodded. "Have a nice vacation, zen," she said, in her faintly Slavic accent. "Doing anyzing fun?"

"Honestly, I'm working on a freelance project that's turned out to be more involved than I expected."

"Aw." She wrinkled her long, narrow nose in sympathy. "A shame you have to work, even on your time off."

"Well, it may be worth it in the long run." Sonia would not object to my taking time off to pursue a freelance story, I knew, as long as it didn't turn up in any publication that directly competed with the *Sentinel*.

I threaded my way back through aisles of desks and busy

reporters to my own humble workstation. A small cubicle with few frills, it was one of half a dozen set aside for us floaters.

I started to shut down my computer, but paused when I spotted an e-mail from Tony:

You free? Meet me in the lunchroom. Got news.

Gee, I thought, we must be back on speaking terms. I'd heard nothing from him in the three days since he'd stalked out of my birthday party for Nancy. I had half a mind to ignore his message and leave as I'd planned.

The other, more forgiving half of my mind won out, though. The idea that my assignment for Mad Love might endanger my relationship with Tony had scared me, and I welcomed this sign of detente. Also, I couldn't resist the tantalizing prospect of "news." No doubt, it involved what I'd come to think of as the Mad Love case.

I found Tony pouring coffee from one of the perpetually simmering lunchroom carafes. He still used the mug I'd bought for him a couple of years ago, with his favorite slogan, "The Truth Is Out There." It dated back to that old sci-fi TV series, *The X-Files*; I'd found the mug in a second-hand shop.

He made eye contact with me, but kept quiet while another reporter contemplated the meager fare in the vending machine. After the guy finally left with a bag of potato chips, Tony confided, "You'll never guess who called me this morning."

Since I didn't have my own mug at the office, I plucked a Styrofoam cup from a stack near the coffeemaker. "Hmm... Angelina Jolie? That would explain why you were too preoccupied to return *my* call."

He grimaced. "I know I acted like a jerk Sunday. I was just frustrated because you seemed to be making more headway on the Mad Love story than I was. But today, out of the blue, I got a call from their old guitarist, Barry Callahan!"

We sat with our coffees at one of the small, Formica-topped tables, and I squeezed my Styrofoam cup so tightly that the brew rose perilously close to the brim. "I thought he was dodging you."

"Has been, for weeks. But he said he'd thought it over and wanted to air his side of things."

I wondered if my conversation with Barry had helped bring about this change of heart. If so, I was glad, for Tony's sake. "Bet his lawyer is thrilled about that."

Tony shrugged, never one to question a scoop. "Anyway, he gave me a half-hour phone interview. Of course, he swears he had nothing to do with any of the suspicious incidents."

"Of course he does." Reluctantly, I emptied the contents of two tiny artificial-milk packets into my coffee. One of the perks of working from home most of the time was access to real dairy products.

"But he still sounds sore over being dumped just before the band made it big," Tony continued. *"And* he understands machinery and building construction. So I don't think he can be totally ruled out."

"He had alibis for the first two events, and they did happen in other states."

"He could've hired out one of his guys."

"Quite possible. Personally, though, I've moved on to other suspects, such as the Reverend Willis fan club. Have you ever actually listened to that show?"

We compared notes, comfortably sparking off each other as we had so often in the past. Meanwhile, other staffers came and went from the lunchroom. A couple of the older, male editors sat for a while at a corner table and argued about what the Yankees should do to pull out of their current slump.

Tony and I had to shift our chairs a little closer to carry on our own conversation. I savored the faint tang of his familiar after-shave. It had been a while since I'd smelled it at close quarters.

He apologized, again, for his rudeness the night of Nancy's birthday.

"Well, you were right about one thing," I admitted. "I do think investigating Mad Love's problems while I'm also working for the paper puts me in a dicey position."

"So...what? You're giving up the case?"

His expression and tone were so hopeful, I almost hated to disappoint him. "No, but I've put in for a week of vacation. That way, I can follow up on any leads with no other demands on my time and with a clear conscience."

Tony leaned back in his seat, a twist to his mouth. "You really think you can wrap it up in a week?"

"Probably not. If it takes a little longer, though, I can ask for a couple more days off without pay. They've been encouraging us to take furlough time."

"Can you afford that?"

I smiled. "I can if I solve the case and get the exclusive on Alan's groovy Hoboken apartment."

Tony's brows met above his dark-rimmed glasses, as they seemed to whenever I cozily referred to Bardot by his first name. "I wish I could believe the deal with the magazine story was all you wanted from that guy."

I squeezed his arm in its slightly rumpled, pale blue shirtsleeve. "Believe me, you have no reason to be jealous of Alan Bardot. He's gay."

"*Bi*sexual," Tony countered, using the same argument I had not so long ago.

"Whatever, he's—" I stopped myself. "He's sleeping with his lead guitarist" definitely sounded like something that would violate the terms of my NDA. "He's in a relationship," I finished.

"You don't say?" Tony looked relieved...and also a bit too curious.

"More than that, I *don't* say," I told him firmly.

"Okay. Understood. Anyway, I'll get a chance to question him personally on Friday." He drained his coffee with a satisfied air. "Your pals are holding a press conference in the city to announce their new album and tour."

This time I did hate to burst his bubble, but he'd soon find out, anyhow. "I know. I'm going, too."

"You are? As press?"

I shook my head. "They called the conference partly to lure more suspects out of the woodwork. They asked me to blend into the crowd and see if I spot anyone behaving oddly, or get any weird vibes."

"Anyone behaving oddly? In a crowd of reporters and rock music types? That'll keep you busy!" Tony looked just a bit deflated to hear I still had the inside track. "It's in midtown on a weekday afternoon. How are you getting in?" He knew I refused to drive into Manhattan under such high-traffic conditions.

"I can take the train from Crane's Crossing."

He snorted at this. "Don't be silly. Ride in with me."

The offer was tempting. It would save me train and cab fare, and Tony generally kept his head much better than I did when jostled on all sides by New York taxis. Still, I hesitated. "I don't know. That gives you an awful lot of time to try to pry confidential information out of me."

"I promise not to do that. But let's face it, if we go to the press conference together, I might pick up on something you miss and vice versa. They do say two heads are better than one."

That was the closest thing to a romantic suggestion I'd heard from him in ages. I finally agreed, with one more caveat. "Just remember, by Friday afternoon, I'll officially be on vacation, so I'll be working the room for Mad Love, not the *Sentinel*."

Never one to back down from a challenge, he toasted me with his *X-Files* mug. "Then, may the best sleuth win."

CHAPTER 13

On my way home from work that day, I decided to swing by the Rialto. I hadn't been back there since the night of the video shoot and the accident, two weeks ago.

Since then, I'd left a couple of phone messages for Lalita that went unreturned, which didn't surprise me too much. She must be frantic, dealing with the fallout from the cameraman's death. I wondered, though, if it had affected the work on the theater.

Pulling in to the curb at the end of the block, I saw a couple of contractors' vans parked in front. That was encouraging. I walked up the street and stepped carefully through the entrance—still rough plywood instead of the etched-glass doors planned for the future. I'd gone only a few steps when a paunchy guy in a hardhat asked gruffly if he could help me.

Of course. The Friends wouldn't be taking any chances with security these days.

I flashed my press card and introduced myself as the reporter who'd written the *Sentinel* story a couple of weeks back. "I just want to see how the restoration is coming along."

The man scratched his short beard and told me strictly to wait where I was. He pulled out a cell phone and faced the nearest corner to make a call.

Meanwhile, I listened to echoes from inside the theater of hammers and drills—I was hearing those a lot these days. Here, they mingled with salsa music from a box radio.

After about fifteen minutes, the elusive Lalita strode through the front doorway. She must have just popped over from her office at the accounting firm because she wore heels, a burgundy print shirtdress and a navy blazer. Her frown suggested she was not so happy to see me this time around.

"What's up?" she asked, in a crisp tone. "I've got a heavy schedule today."

"Just stopped by to see how things are going," I said, with a smile. "I see you're at least continuing with the renovations."

She shook her head. "Just keeping up with the most necessary repairs, that's all. Fixing a roof leak over the mezzanine and some issues with the electrical system. Can't afford to squander our money on anything else...now that we might be sued."

I read the bitterness in her voice and expression and tried to reassure her. "Let's hope it's all settled soon, and the theater is absolved of any negligence."

She leaned back against the framework of an unfinished ticket counter and folded her arms tightly over her chest. "Don't know how likely that is."

"Maybe more likely than you think."

"Really?" She raised one delicate black eyebrow at my implication. "I guess I made a big mistake, telling the cop what you said you saw, the night of the accident. I hear now you're working with Mad Love's people on this."

So, that explained the chilly reception. "I am, but I'm also trying to help you guys! If I discover someone is out to cause trouble for the band and may have rigged the piece of plaster to fall, it becomes a police matter. Probably, the Rialto will be off the hook."

"Long as they don't try to say we should have tried harder to prevent it, or something," Lalita pointed out, with a sniff. She checked her watch as if anxious to get back to her office.

"Sorry," I said. "Am I keeping you from something important?"

"Just the usual. Ever since the accident, I've been fielding phone calls from investors, demanding to know the Rialto's legal situation and threatening to pull their backing. I've got no answers for them, and they're getting damned impatient. Pretty soon, they're going to take their money elsewhere."

"Lalita, believe me, I don't want that to happen any more than you do. Look, can we just sit down somewhere and talk?"

Grudgingly, she agreed. We settled in the last row of

the theater's old, velour-upholstered seats, all destined for replacement. More comfortable, though, than standing in the lobby. And still private, since the construction work was taking place at a distance.

"I heard the plaster over the stage was cut through in some way," I said.

She nodded once. "The cops said it looked *burned* through, like with a blowtorch. To me, that proves it was fishy. None of our workers had any reason to use a blowtorch around that archway."

"I guess they questioned everybody in the crew."

"Of course. Doesn't mean one of the guys might not be lying to cover up a stupid mistake—" She stopped abruptly and faced away, as if suddenly wondering if she shouldn't admit such a thing to me.

"Don't worry, I'm not a lawyer! And you're right, you can't be sure everyone they questioned told the truth. But is there also a chance someone from the outside got into the theater before the show and cut partway through the plaster?"

"Couldn't have been too long before the band's performance, or some other loud noise or vibration would have jarred it loose in the meantime. We took down the scaffolding near the arch several hours beforehand. But up to then, I guess someone could've used it to reach that spot."

"Did you have a security system for the building?"

She shrugged. "We couldn't afford anything elaborate. The doors were padlocked at night, and we never saw any sign they were disturbed. Unless someone picked a lock, then closed it again when he left."

"You weren't concerned about vandalism?"

"Not really. Most people in the neighborhood supported our renovation project, and they kept an eye out for us. We didn't even have much of a problem with graffiti."

I considered all this for a minute. "Can we take a walk down there?"

"To the stage?" She sounded impatient again.

"If you need to get back to your office, I can go myself."

"No, I should stay with you." She glanced around, as if

making sure we wouldn't be in the way of any workers. "Okay, if it doesn't take too long."

The two of us headed down the theater aisle, as I stayed receptive to any available vibrations. When I passed the middle row where I'd sat during the performance, I tried to remember everything I could about that night. The buzz of the crowd around me; the cameras on cranes soaring over the stage; the shifting, colored lights.

It would be so easy to tell myself the shadow I saw had been just an optical illusion. If I had not seen it again at the jail, just before another accident nearly injured Jeff.

I gazed up at the plaster arch, now repaired.

A "servitor"? Now that I stood here again in the middle of the day, surrounded by mundane construction noises and the smell of sawdust, Gail's theory seemed harder than ever to believe.

And there was no way I could suggest such an explanation to Lalita. She was an accountant, for God's sake.

"It just kills me," she said now, at my back, "to think this place might go half-finished, even fall into ruin again. Already, we've had to push back the first few shows we had set for this summer, terrific acts that may never be able to fit us into their schedules again. If we lose our funding over this..."

She let that idea hang in the air, and I heard anguish in her voice. This project had given the neighborhood fresh hope. It had to succeed.

"Lalita, who knew Mad Love would be performing here that night? You were keeping it hush-hush, weren't you?"

"Yeah, that's another weird thing. Besides the band and their people, there was the video crew, of course. Everyone in the audience was invited—friends, family, press." When she got to the last category, she nodded in my direction.

I recalled checking in with the guard at the door, who had seemed very strict about making sure everyone had a ticket. Then I had a rueful moment.

At least one person had gotten in without one. The young woman I'd let come in with me, Melissa. The talkative one who'd been eager to show off how much she knew about Alan. She'd chattered so freely to me, I could easily imagine her bragging about where she was going to all her friends.

"Some of those people might have leaked the information to others," I suggested.

"I guess, but not more than a couple of days in advance. Really, Quinn, it's so bizarre! Who would hear the band was shooting the video and arrange to break in here and sabotage the stage, right before the show?"

"They'd have had to get in at least twice," I pointed out. "The first time, to scope out the place and figure out exactly what part of the stage they were going to sabotage."

"You're right." Lalita laughed in bewilderment. "Almost easier to believe in the theater ghost!"

I said nothing to this. Would a shadowy supernatural entity also have to do advance reconnaissance? And if it did, would anyone notice? Could a servitor created from pure hatred "burn through" plaster as effectively as a blowtorch?

My conversation with Lalita opened up another possibility, almost as creepy. If the saboteur needed advance access to the theater, it could have been an inside job.

"Sounds like any of the people who were invited that night could've talked about it to others ahead of time," observed Tony.

The two of us sat in traffic leading up to the toll plaza for the Holland Tunnel. So we could get an early start, he'd spent the night at my place, which was not quite as romantic as it might have been. He'd had to work late on a story the evening before—par for the course—and got to my house around ten. After a shared nightcap and some enjoyable but rather hurried lovemaking, we'd both sacked out so we could be up at six for our trek into the city.

I had to admit to myself, our relationship these days left something to be desired. Instead of lovers eager to see each other whenever the opportunity arose, we were becoming more like a long-married couple. And that was on our good days, when we at least were getting along! I tended to blame Tony's demanding job, but at times, I wondered if that was the only issue between us.

On the other hand, given my inability to share much information, maybe it was just as well we hadn't had much time to discuss the Mad Love case until this morning. Anyway, for the time being, I'd have to put my personal problems aside and focus on my new role as psychic-sleuth-for-hire.

"The people who were invited to the Rialto probably knew enough not to broadcast the news of the concert far and wide," I continued, "but the same way I told you and Nancy and Rob, other guests could have told their close friends or relatives."

"Which raises the question, would any of those friends or relatives have a grudge against the band?" suggested Tony.

"Or *their* friends or relatives? Even in just a week, the news could have spread beyond the core group."

The tollbooth we'd been aiming for abruptly closed, forcing us to insinuate ourselves into the next lane. Amazing, how drivers who realize you have no choice but to merge will still refuse to let you in. It's not like the guy in the big silver SUV was going to get into Manhattan a whole lot faster, whether we were in front of him or behind him.

"Speaking of relatives," said Tony, after pulling off the daredevil lane change, "I've been digging deeper into Mayor Steve Randall's background. He could be a person of interest."

"Oh?"

"Very conservative guy, got a lot of right-wing support in the last election. Now he's eyeing a state senate seat. He's been stumping on issues like restoring prayer in public schools, right-to-life and—guess what?—'restoring the sanctity of marriage.'"

"Huh? Since when is that controversial?"

"It's code these days for opposing gay marriage, and the gay lifestyle in general as a threat to marriage."

I rolled my eyes. "Like, if there were no great stigma, all straight married people would instantly divorce their spouses and hook up with same-sex partners!"

Tony smiled thinly. "At any rate, Steve doesn't sound like the kind of guy who'd be crazy about the lead singer of his son's rock band coming halfway out of the closet."

And definitely not about his son being romantically involved with the lead singer! I bit my tongue to keep from saying that out loud.

Jeez, maybe Tony was onto something. I remembered Bardot telling me he "had his reasons" for making that announcement about his sexuality on the radio show. Was he testing the waters with his fans to see if they might eventually also accept the news about him and Jeff?

But rock fans were one thing. Mayor Steve Randall sounded like a much tougher customer to win over. Didn't he know his son was gay, or bi, or whatever? If he did, coming out against gay rights seemed like a rather heartless move.

"He ought to get along great with Reverend Willis," I wisecracked.

"Funny you should mention..." We'd finally reached the toll plaza, where Tony handed over a few dollars. He got a receipt in return, which he tucked neatly into the cupholder on his car's console, along with several others. "I came across a photo from about six months back of the two of them chatting like old pals at a political fundraiser."

"Randall and Willis?" I whistled. "Now, that's interesting. Willis has singled out Mad Love as the embodiment of what's wrong with pop culture today. He's asking his listeners to pray for their wretched, lost souls! If he's friends with Jeff's dad, why would he do that?"

"Why, indeed? Either he doesn't know Steve's son is in the band—which seems unlikely—or maybe that's why he's being so hard on them."

I got what Tony was implying, though it struck me as bizarre. "You think Jeff's dad might have put Willis up to it?"

"Who knows? Maybe he thinks if the Rev makes things hot enough for the band, they'll either repent of their decadent ways or break up. In the second case, Jeff would have to find himself another group, maybe one more in line with his father's values."

Sure, I thought, that'll happen. "Just how far do you think they'd go to...to break up the band?"

Tony considered. "Well, I sure hope neither one of them would risk Jeff's life just to get him to quit."

So did I. That would be a major sin by anybody's standards.

We picked up a little more speed now as we maneuvered through the crowded streets of lower Manhattan. I had to admire Tony's cool head as battle-scarred yellow cabs jostled within inches of his well-maintained Honda Accord. I would have had a nervous breakdown by now, maybe pulled over to the curb and just ditched my car in surrender. I had a horror of getting into an accident in Midtown, many miles from home, with some cabbie screaming at me in a foreign tongue and angry horns honking all around.

The press conference was being held at Sanktuary, a former church that had put in a few years as a trendy restaurant and now served as a Goth rock club. Unused during the day, it probably seemed to Mad Love the ideal spot to announce their new CD and tour dates for the summer.

"I hear they're still going to release the video, the one they shot at the Rialto," Tony said. "I'm surprised nobody put footage of the guy getting clobbered by the chunk of plaster up on You Tube. With what cell phone cameras can do these days..."

I winced. "If it had been a regular audience, that might've been the case. Probably, though, all of us were sensitive to the band's feelings about not exploiting the accident. I understand the final video uses only footage from the first take, before it happened."

I saw Tony check the car's digital clock and knew he must be concerned about making it to the press conference on time. The traffic continued to crawl as we headed north on Hudson Street. On the fringes of Chelsea, he tried to make a turn, then pulled up with a curse when he spotted sawhorses ahead.

"Damn road work—" he started to say.

But no, they were police barricades. Beyond them, I could see the steeple and the churchlike, brownstone facade of Sanktuary. The street in front churned with people, many shouting and carrying picket signs.

Just the first one I read was enough to turn my stomach: *God Hates Fags.*

CHAPTER 14

"Well, you did say Bardot wanted to lure all his enemies out of the woodwork," Tony reminded me. "Looks like he might've overshot the mark."

After we found a garage for the car and returned to Sanktuary on foot, I could see the picketers actually divided up into two factions. The ones who'd been detained across the street from the club—fortunately—carried placards with such sentiments as "Leading Fans to Hell!" There also were some offensive variations on Mad Love's name and a few truly vicious slurs and threats aimed personally at Alan.

The marchers right in front of the converted brownstone church offered rebuttals that seemed witty and almost innocent by comparison. My favorite: *If God hates fags, why did He make so many of us?*

Still, I wondered if Alan had seen any of the more scurrilous signs. How horrible it must be to find yourself suddenly the target of so much venom, coming from total strangers!

Several reporters and cameramen had stopped, probably on their way to the press conference, to cover the protest. Even Tony felt obliged to talk to a couple of anti-gay activists and take a few notes. I knew he was just doing his job, but even so, I edged toward the front steps of Sanktuary to distance myself.

Just then, the heavy "church" door opened, and a light-haired woman in a loose, frumpy, gray skirt suit backed out. She moved slowly, under duress, and still seemed to be trying to persuade the gatekeeper to honor her press credentials. He blocked her way, though, until she stalked off in a snit, facing away from me.

Something about her—maybe her appearance, her manner or maybe just her situation—gave me a sense of déjà vu. Before I could think about it any more, though, Tony showed up to catch me by the elbow and usher me inside.

We had no problem gaining entry, our *Sentinel* press cards passing muster.

At the foyer desk, we picked up press packets and hangtags already printed with our names and publication. Then we flowed with the crowd through an arched stone doorway.

Beyond lay a cavernous, stone-walled space with a vaulted ceiling, a row of heavy, wrought-iron chandeliers hanging from the central beam. I imagined that normally the terrazzo floor would have been left empty for dancing, but today it was strewn with small, round tables draped in black, four folding chairs pulled up to each.

At the front, three steps led up to the level of the former altar. In the evening, it probably served as a stage for performers. Right now, it held a long table draped with a banner that read, in agitated black letters, "Going Mad"—the title of the band's first headlining tour. A huge video screen hung from the ceiling just above.

Members of the press had begun staking out the small tables closest to the stage/dais. Tony grabbed a cup of coffee from the hospitality urn and started to head up front, too, but I hung back.

"I'll join you in a minute," I said. When he raised one eyebrow, I reminded him, "Remember, I'm here to mingle with the crowd."

"Okay, I'll save you a place." He forged ahead to the front of the room, where I saw him connect with one of the *Sentinel's* photographers.

Meanwhile, I spotted a young man who looked a bit out of place. Most of the reporters and photographers had dressed casually that morning, maybe due to the nature of the press conference. This guy, though, was decked out in a cheap-looking brown suit. His reddish hair was cut short, parted in an almost nineteen-fifties' style, and he wore a tiny gold cross on his lapel. I'd figured him for a right-wing Christian even before

I stepped near enough to read his hangtag: "William Canfield, *The Evangelist.*"

I held back a smile, hoping he didn't put himself in the same category as Matthew, Mark, Luke and John. No doubt that was just the name of his publication. For a second, I wondered why the official at the door had kept out the frumpy-looking woman but let in this guy. After all, the plan had been to bring all of Mad Love's possible foes out into the open.

At first glance, this tall, thin fellow, with eyebrows almost as pale as his complexion, didn't look dangerous. I did sense he might be a bit tightly wound, though, just from the twitchy way he kept scanning the crowd. Also his baggy suit could easily have concealed a weapon. I wondered if the guards had done any pat-downs in the vestibule.

I sidled next to Canfield at the refreshment table, poured some coffee into a Styrofoam cup and added artificial sweeter and some tepid creamer. Then I smiled and nodded toward the hangtag. "I'm surprised you'd have any interest in covering this event."

He squared his narrow shoulders. "On the contrary. Our readers need to know what's going on in the world today, and what they're up against. 'Know your enemy,' that's our philosophy!"

After a tentative sip of the coffee, I decided to let it cool a bit. "You consider Mad Love your enemy?"

"They're part of the conspiracy to erode family values, make a mockery of marriage and lead young people into lives of debauchery." He sounded as if he'd rehearsed that speech, or at least recited it many times.

"A conspiracy?" I probed this hint of paranoia. "By whom? Even if what you say is true, who on earth would benefit from doing those things?"

Canfield answered with a tight, unpleasant laugh. "On earth? Maybe no one. But Satan benefits! He wants to sow confusion, madness and disease among mankind. And he uses these 'entertainers' to help his cause—whether they're even aware of it or not."

"Interesting." I tried my coffee again; it had mellowed a bit, so I took a good swallow. I needed the caffeine to follow Canfield's twisty train of thought. "How do you propose to stop it, then? The Satanic plan?"

If he picked up on my sarcasm at all, it didn't throw him. "By exposing it. By combating this evil propaganda"—he waved a hand toward the stage and its banner—"with God's truth."

"And if that isn't enough?"

His shoulders stiffened again, as if he'd left the hanger in his jacket—I had to wonder what urges *he* was repressing. "Then, by any means necessary."

That last statement got my attention. I still didn't get any vibe that I could clearly connect with Alan's nasty messages and "gifts," but his language struck me as a bit...militant. I wanted to draw him out more, on how far he was willing to go to defeat the rock 'n' roll minions of Satan, but a tap on a live microphone interrupted our chat.

A blonde female MC who had enlivened her black pantsuit with a leopard-print blouse stepped onstage and urged everyone to take their seats. With a mixture of reluctance and relief, I bade farewell to Mr. Canfield and joined Tony at the table up front.

The MC, probably from Mad Love's PR firm, introduced Stern, Alan and Jeff. As they filed in and sat down behind microphones at the long table, I noticed each man adhered to his own style. Stern looked all business in a button-front plum shirt and a gray blazer. Longhaired Jeff dressed the most casually, in a black Lon Chaney/*Wolfman* T-shirt and an open denim jacket—still Goth, but with a humorous spin.

Bardot sported a black-and-purple striped T beneath a close-fitting motorcycle jacket. With his pale skin and dark, iridescent hair, he wore black like it was invented just for him. Not a bad trait for a rock star.

The crowd acknowledged the three of them with moderate applause. The press, as a rule, isn't a star-struck bunch—for the reporters, this was all in a day's work

Stern introduced a short promotional video for the tour with clips from past live performances, including about a minute of the one at the Rialto. A voice-over touted Mad Love's recent successes, hit singles and platinum album, and heaped praise on each of the five musicians.

Tony whispered to me, "Interesting, though, that only the two front men showed up today."

I'd been thinking the same thing. "Well, that's not so strange. Maybe they figured six guys fielding questions would be too many."

After making the band's upcoming tour sound like a reunion of all four Beatles, with Jim Morrison thrown in for good measure, the video ended. More applause, slightly more enthusiastic this time, though I could imagine Bill Canfield sitting on his hands. The MC then stepped aside and let the three men behind the table answer questions.

The first few were businesslike, involving the scope of the tour and the songs to be performed. Not surprisingly, Alan said most would be from the last album, *Night Tremors,* which had had hit so big, and the newest one, *Fear No Evil.*

Finally someone brought up the Rialto tragedy, and asked if that video ever would be released.

"Yes," said Stern, "we're putting it on the Web next week, along with a dedication to the memory of cameraman Ted McCloskey. The fine work he did on the shoot can at least be seen by our fans, as a tribute to him."

A female reporter raised her hand. "Do the police still think foul play might have been involved in that accident?"

"They're still investigating," Stern told her. Perhaps hoping to change the subject, he made the mistake of taking the next question from Tony.

"Your last tour, opening for Bigboy, also had more than its share of mishaps, and at least one of those also was considered suspicious. Does that give you any concerns about going back out on the road?"

I wanted to slide under the table. All three men on the dais now looked straight in our direction. Of course, they would see me sitting next to this hardnosed reporter who had just put them on the spot.

To Alan's credit, though, he answered calmly. "We'll certainly take all the necessary precautions, maybe more than usual. But we aren't going to let a few 'mishaps,' as you called them, keep us from touring."

Jeff chimed in here. "We need to bring the music in person to our fans, y'know? It's part of our job."

Alan nodded and asked Tony, "You have to take risks sometimes to do your job, don't you? We're performers—we can't spend our lives wrapped in cotton inside a box."

Stern then gave the nod to a thirtyish man with short, curly black hair and a physique that must have been honed by many hours at the gym. "Speaking of coming out of the box, Alan..."

A few people snickered, and I feared Stern would live to regret acknowledging this guy, too.

"Just a month ago, you came out as bisexual on a radio talk show, and the announcement caused quite a stir. How would you answer people who might say the timing was very convenient, and maybe you're exploiting your orientation to get more publicity for the new album and the tour? I mean, so you're bi—what's the big deal?"

With a frown, Stern leaned toward his table mic, as if ready to protect his client, but Alan already had begun to respond. "Y'know, I've been wondering the same thing. If you've actually *heard* the interview, the DJ and I were just joking around when that comment slipped out. And, honestly, I had a second where I could've said, 'Just kidding,' and taken it back. But I decided not to, because it would have been disrespectful"—I thought he threw a quick, sidelong glance at Jeff before he continued—"to the other people out there who are gay or bi or questioning, and afraid to be who they are. So I figured, let it stand. Maybe some of them will hear it and feel a little more okay about themselves. But, man"—he shook his head with a crooked smile—"I never thought it would be such a big issue! Like you, I figured most people were past all that."

I heard some murmurs of agreement, but more hands shot into the air—Bill Canfield's among them. This time, before Stern could even act, Alan spotted Canfield and pointed directly at him.

"*Mr.* Bardot, it amazes me that you have so little comprehension of the impact your announcement must have had on your fans," said Canfield, his voice quaking with emotion. "You admit you want those who might be 'questioning' to feel it's okay to live as you do. Have you even thought at all about the lives you could be ruining, of the children and teenagers who look up to you as a role model..."

A couple of the media people near Quinn exchanged muttered comments, and one woman just shook her head.

Alan leaned back in his chair, lips pursed in frustration, as if he'd expected something like this, but it was still hard to take. Finally, he pointed to the curly-haired man and joked, "This guy thinks it's no big deal; you think it's a huge deal... Maybe you two should just fight it out between yourselves!"

Jeff took the mic again. "Yeah, I thought we came here to talk about the tour and the music. How 'bout we get back to all that?"

A few people in the audience, possibly fans scattered among the reporters, applauded this suggestion.

Mercifully, the questions did return to more professional topics for the last few minutes of the press conference. Then the MC thanked everyone for coming, and Stern and his boys exited briskly through a side door. A few determined reporters— including Canfield and the curly-haired guy—tried to pursue them with more questions, but were thwarted by security guards.

When I also started for the stage exit, Tony looked at me like I was nuts. "Where are you going?"

"I'm supposed to check in with them before I leave. They'll probably want to debrief me." I saw him redden and thought maybe I should have put that another way.

"Security won't let you back there."

"They will," I assured him. "Really, Alan told me to stop by after the conference and let him know if I picked up on anything suspicious."

Tony's voice turned guarded. "And did you?"

Another one of *those* moments between us. "Maybe, maybe not. Anyhow, I promise I'll just be a second."

"You sure?" He shifted on his feet and looked at his watch. "'Cause, I've gotta go write this story."

I was about to suggest he make himself comfortable at one of the tables and work on his laptop, but his body language suggest he meant "go," as in back to the *Sentinel*. That ticked me off. This wasn't the Watergate scandal, with all the reporters scrambling to scoop each other, and Tony knew it. He was just giving me a hard time again, for what?

I heard myself matching his snarky tone. "If you can't even wait for me for fifteen minutes, maybe you should go ahead without me! I'll take the train home."

Someone near the stage called my name. A security guard with a slip of paper craned his neck to scan the crowd.

I swung back to Tony, saw steam coming out of his ears and tried to mollify him.

"Just hang here a minute. I might be able to get you backstage, too. Give me a chance to ask Alan—"

"Hey, don't do me any favors." He turned sharply, briefcase strap over his shoulder, and stalked away.

For a second I was too stunned to react, and by the time I shouted after him, he'd merged into the crush of people headed out the door. My own pride kept me from following him. I had a job to do, too, and I'd be damned if I'd let his childish tantrum keep me from seeing it through.

When the guard called my name again, I started back toward the stage.

This time, though, I found my way blocked by the curly-haired man who had accused Alan of coming out as a publicity stunt. His hangtag read, "Dan Fox, *Rogue Male*." Another intriguing juxtaposition.

He checked out my ID at the same time, and a smug smile spread across his tanned face. "Sounds like you have special access."

I just nodded and tried to get past him, but he grabbed my arm. The gesture startled me, especially since it sent a painful charge through my nerve endings, almost as if I'd whacked my funny bone.

Fox bent near enough for me to smell the coffee on his breath and spoke just loudly enough for me to hear him over the general buzz.

"If you talk to Alan back there, give him this message: Rocky still sees Elaine once in a while, and says someday soon the whole world's going to know about her."

CHAPTER 15

"**G**ot that?"

Dan Fox clutched my arm so tightly—and the electric-shock effect startled me so much—that I nodded almost in self-defense. With a nasty smile, he let go and vanished into the crowd.

I rubbed my tingling arm and tried to absorb what had just happened. Though Fox's "message" had sounded innocuous on the surface, I'd hardly needed the psychic jolt to sense the threat lurking beneath. But what on earth did he mean?

The security guard called my name again—for what would be the last time, judging from his exasperated tone. Rebounding from my shock, I waved in response and hurried over.

He showed me down a flight of stone steps to the club's basement. When the building had functioned as a church, I guess this would have been a community room. Now it had been tricked out with iron wall sconces shaped like arms holding torches, and high-backed, ornately carved furniture upholstered in purple velvet. A long, wooden refectory table held another coffee urn and a tray of sandwiches.

The MC in the leopard blouse was chattering nonstop to Stern, who sipped coffee and looked as if he'd gone somewhere else in his mind. Toward the back of the room, Alan and Jeff appeared to be taping a promotional TV spot with a reporter and a cameraman. Lark sat off to the side, in one of the medieval-looking chairs, looking perfectly appropriate in her usual hard-edged regalia. She pressed a cell phone to her ear, but wiggled her black-clawed fingers at me in greeting.

I sat down on a Gothic velvet bench, still feeling shaken.

For the first time since I'd taken on this job for Mad Love, I was truly afraid.

You'd think the last *tulpa* incident would have sent me over the edge, but I'd been able to tell myself that that was just a kind of telepathy. The business with Fox, though—even the way he'd grabbed my arm in the crowd—

If he'd had a weapon, he could just as easily have shot or stabbed me!

I rubbed my bicep again to ease the lingering sensation of his rough grip. He'd also left a psychic residue—the same slimy feeling I'd picked up from Alan's "old friend" email, the one he'd dismissed so casually. Still, I didn't think that message had come from Fox. My contact with him gave me a more watered-down impression, a sort of secondhand evil.

I heard a metallic tinkling, and black boots with witchy, pointed toes stepped into my downcast line of vision. Lark's voice asked, "Quinn, honey, you okay?"

I snapped my head up and forced a smile. "Just a little overwhelmed, I guess."

"Get you some coffee?"

"Thanks, but I've probably already had too much today."

She jingled off then to deal with some other issue. Meanwhile, Jeff and Alan finished their interview and wandered over to me.

"None of the other guys showed up today?" I asked.

"Well, right now the band's on a break," said Alan. "They're off spending time with their families."

Jeff cracked, "Bardot and me, we got nothing better to do."

I knew little about Alan's family situation, except that he'd grown up in California with his aunt and cousins. But Jeff had parents and a younger sister in New Jersey. I wondered if this said something about his strained relationship with them.

I commiserated with Bardot and Randall about the press conference. "Kind of put you through the ringer out there, didn't they?"

Alan shrugged it off. "Nothing we didn't expect. That guy at your table got straight to the point, though, huh? Asking if we were scared to go back on tour! You know him?"

I felt my face warm. "I *date* him. Sorry—I had no idea he was going to pull that."

Alan grinned widely at my admission. "No problem. Man was just doing his job."

"He wasn't exactly thrilled, either, that I got to come back here afterward and he didn't." I should shut up, I thought—why was I complaining?

"Aw, you should've told me. We could've given him a pass, too. Is he still outside?"

"Left without me." In a show of petulance, I added, "Alan, you're coming between me and my boyfriend. It's not fair! Do I try to come between you and your boyfriend?"

Yikes! For some reason, today I kept blurting out double-entendres.

They took the joke at G-rated face value, though, and Jeff clapped me lightly on the shoulder. "No, you don't, and I really appreciate it!"

Alan sat down next to me on the bench, hands braced on his knees, with an air of getting down to business. "How did it go with your crowd surveillance? Boy, that guy with the bad Eddie Haskell haircut has some issues, hasn't he?"

I knew he meant Bill Canfield, so I told him about my conversation with the *Evangelist* reporter. "He did sound kind of fanatical, and I didn't like his line about stopping you 'by any means necessary.' But even though I talked to him for about ten minutes, I can't say I sensed much beyond that."

"In other words, nothing like you got off the dead bird or the notes," Alan concluded.

"That's right. On the other hand..."

Just then, Stern called Jeff away. I actually was glad for the interruption and greater privacy, because I felt the rest of my input should be for Alan's ears alone.

"On my way back here, I got stopped by the guy who didn't think your coming out was such a big deal. His name is Dan Fox and he writes for *Rogue Male*. Ever heard of him?"

Alan shook his head. "Not my usual reading material. It's a gay skin magazine, and not one of the classier ones. Mostly online, I think."

That conjured up images I didn't really want to dwell on. "Anyhow, when Fox realized I'd be talking to you, he gave me a message." I tried to remember the exact words. "He said, 'Rocky still sees Elaine once in a while, and someday soon the whole world's going to know about her.'"

Alan, the relaxed and confident rock star, went through a startling transformation. He shrank back as if I'd struck him, and even his big, sea-green eyes seemed to blanch.

If Fox had wanted to deliver a hard blow, he'd apparently succeeded. "What's wrong?" I asked. "Does that mean something?"

Alan sprang up from the bench, then wavered for a second with a dazed look. "Sorry...gimme a minute."

He shot across the room to catch up with Stern, and the two of them actually disappeared into one of the limestone side alcoves to confer. From what I could glimpse, Alan did most of the talking, while Stern listened with a tightening frown. In this church-like setting, it reminded me of someone confessing his sins to a priest.

Jeff passed them with a curious glance and came over to ask me quietly, "What's going on? You got us some new evidence?"

"I have no idea." Since Bardot was being so secretive, I figured I'd see what his partner could tell me. "One of the reporters said to give Alan a message about 'Elaine,' and when I did he got very upset. Who's Elaine?"

Jeff raked one hand back through his long, wavy locks and thought for a second. "The only Elaine he ever mentioned to me was his mother."

That certainly wasn't what I'd expected, but I realized it might explain a few things. If someone was threatening his mother—

"She died," Jeff finished, "when Alan was about nine years old."

Bardot finally returned, but did nothing to relieve my confusion. He just thanked me, in a general way, for my help, and asked how I was getting home.

I started to explain about the train, but he waved a hand. "We'll call you a car. Least we can do, since we're responsible for your ride leaving without you."

I wanted to ask him more about the cryptic message, his mother and "Rocky," but sensed it was really not the time. In fact, he seemed so eager to get rid of me that I wondered if he'd ever contact me again. Had I stumbled too far into forbidden territory?

One of the guards ushered me out, while Jeff threw me a sympathetic look and shrugged, as if he didn't know what to make of it all, either.

I left by a back door, where at least I didn't run into any of the picketers. The cops seemed to be dispersing them now, anyway. The only hanger-on that I did see, lingering just outside a subway entrance, was the woman in the frumpy gray skirt suit who'd been shut out of the press conference earlier. She stood about twenty feet away and, as the driver of the Town Car opened the door for me, her gaze met mine. Her expression hardened to a glare, almost an accusation.

Once again, I had the feeling I knew her from somewhere, but this time I realized why. She bore a slight resemblance to Lark. Except this woman was shorter and plainer, her frizzy hair a redder shade of blonde, and of course, she lacked all the black leather and hardware.

In fact, compared to Lark, she looked utterly nondescript and harmless. Her fixed stare, though, gave me the creeps. I felt relieved to slip into the air-conditioned comfort of the car and let it whisk me away from all the chaos surrounding Mad Love.

I thought of giving Tony a call, then realized I didn't want him to know that, instead of taking the train home, I was traveling in comfort courtesy of the band. Even if I lied, with his sharp ears he might pick up on lack of any train-like rumbling in the background. But why the hell should I have to hide things from him when I was doing absolutely nothing wrong? After all, he'd left me stranded without a ride!

Well, this wasn't the first time his Sicilian half had clashed with my Irish half, and when that happened, things had gotten ugly. Neither half ever wanted to be the first to apologize, either.

Maybe only our more levelheaded WASP halves should ever be allowed to communicate.

To keep from fuming about that situation any further, I

pulled out my notebook and looked over the jottings I'd already made on Canfield's behavior and the rest of the press conference. I added my observations about Dan Fox, his strange message and Alan's equally bizarre reaction. Then I spent the rest of my ride home trying to make sense of it all.

First, I had to consider the source of the apparent threat—a writer for a gay porn e-zine that even Alan regarded with distaste.

Then there were two names new to me, "Rocky" and "Elaine." If Elaine was Alan's mother, deceased for many years, could "Rocky" be his father, possibly obsessed over her death? I pictured him still "seeing" Elaine often by poring over photographs or visiting her grave. Maybe he blamed Alan, in some way, for her dying so young?

But even if that were the case, why would Alan's father send him a message through a person like Dan Fox?

Our car emerged from the Holland Tunnel into a dishwater gray, diluted sunshine. I felt oddly relieved to be back in New Jersey, but still weighed down by the strange behavior of just about everyone I'd dealt with that morning—from Canfield, Fox and the weird girl outside the club to Bardot.

And, not least of all, Tony. Damn, last night I'd been lying naked in his arms, but today I was the Enemy again?

Tears suddenly welled in my eyes. Even if I finally scored a byline in *Celebrity Home* was it worth losing Tony? And what else might I stand to lose by getting so enmeshed with Mad Love and their secrets?

CHAPTER 16

O nce I got home and took off my businesslike blazer, I realized I had lost my temporary press badge. It had only been stuck to my lapel with adhesive backing, so that didn't surprise me. Certainly, it wasn't worth worrying about. It had only been good for the press conference, so no one else could gain access to the band, at some future date, by pretending to be me. Still, it might have been fun to keep as a souvenir.

Especially if Alan decided to cut me loose after today.

I should have been relieved at the prospect, but by now I'd come to really care about him and Jeff. I had to admire the classy way they'd both handled themselves under the stress of that morning's event, and I wanted more than ever to help them.

I also couldn't deny my curiosity about the latest wrinkle in the mystery.

Having missed lunch, I was starving, so I popped a couple of slim veggie burgers on my countertop grill. I set the timer, then opened my laptop at the kitchen table. While the burgers sizzled, I hunted online for connections between Alan Bardot and "Elaine."

I turned up only one reference to his mother. Apparently, she also had been a professional singer, though of the nightclub torch-song variety. It sounded as if she and his father had been separated for a few years before she'd died of unspecified causes.

A search for links between Alan and anyone named "Rocky" came up dry, so I took a break to concentrate on my lunch. The food smells attracted Bela, but when he realized there was no meat involved, he jumped up on another kitchen chair to watch the activity around the backyard birdbath.

Finished eating, I got up my nerve to check for any connection between Rocky and *Rogue Male*. That took me into some very X-rated Internet territory, and no doubt added some interesting cookies to my laptop's browsing history. The only tenuous link was an interview the magazine had run a couple of years back with an "indie filmmaker" named Rocky Montanna. Let's just say, his idea of art films were not mine, and much of the article's terminology would not have made it into the *Sentinel* or any other family newspaper. The head shot that accompanied the piece showed a rather puffy, fortyish guy with a hairline too even to be real and a self-satisfied smirk.

I was about to dismiss the filmmaker's name as coincidence until I noticed the byline at the end of the story.

Dan Fox.

Oooboy. I felt as if I'd just stepped in something I couldn't wait to scrape off my shoe.

But I still didn't get the association with Elaine Bardot.

So Fox did know someone named Rocky, though this was not necessarily even the same Rocky. Had Elaine been involved with him, maybe appeared in one of his dirty movies? Didn't seem likely, if she'd died about twenty years ago! Still, I sensed I might be getting closer to the real story.

I began to consider a new possible motive for the ominous messages sent to Alan, maybe even for the band's accidents.

Blackmail?

Then it hit me. "Rocky Montanna"…and my psychic warning that Bardot should stay away from the Rocky Mountains? When I remembered the singer's startled reaction when I'd told him about that vision, I knew it couldn't be just a coincidence.

My cell phone rang, spooking me, and I read Tony's number on the tiny screen. I was still so annoyed with him, I considered letting it go to voice mail. But I figured if he'd actually found time to pick up the phone, despite his pressing deadlines, I should be big enough to take the call.

"Guess you got home all right," he said.

"No thanks to you." I was tempted to tell him about my chauffeured ride, but it would only escalate the hostilities between us.

"Sorry to leave you in the lurch like that. But I knew Saperstein wanted me to get the toxic playground story out this afternoon..."

"Yeah, sure. I was talking to Mad Love for fifteen, twenty minutes, tops. It wouldn't have blown your deadline to wait that long." I told him Alan would have let him come downstairs with me. "But you didn't even ask about that. You actually gave up the chance at a scoop, and for what? The satisfaction of walking out in a huff? For the second time in a week?"

He heaved a sigh, and to my shock admitted, "You're right. I acted like a total jerk. Even I don't know what's going on with me these days. This 'assignment' of yours has got me totally bent out of shape."

"What more am I supposed to do? I already told you, I'm going to try to wrap up the case this week, one way or another."

"I know," Tony said, soberly. "But do you really believe you can?"

"Maybe not. But if it looks like it's going to take a lot longer, I can always back out of my arrangement with the band."

"I'd appreciate that. Meanwhile, until it's all resolved...you and I probably should take a break."

My stomach dropped. "C'mon, Tony. Don't you think that's a little—"

"It just makes sense. Every time you talk about this Mad Love stuff, I'm wondering what you know that I don't, and I'm getting steamed about it. It's not like we're even able to work together. Maybe I can help you a little, but you can't help me at all."

"I'm sorry," I told him. "I never imagined it would play out like this."

"Well, it has. All I'm saying is, if it *is* going to be over soon, maybe in the meantime we shouldn't spend too much time together. You're on vacation, so you won't even be coming into the office—"

His tone seemed to imply more than just a week-long hiatus, though, and that made me panic. "Look, this might not be necessary. I may be off the case even sooner."

"Oh? How come?"

"Something happened today... I may have uncovered something even Alan doesn't want me to know about." I laughed nervously. "People should realize, when you hire a psychic, you can't necessarily pick and choose what she finds out!"

Tony chuckled, too, and for a second we seemed to reconnect. Then my phone beeped and another familiar number popped up. *Damn.*

He heard the signal, too. "Got a call waiting?"

"Yeah, and I'd better take it."

The frost crept back into his voice. "Bardot?"

"Cheer up—maybe he's going to tell me I'm fired."

"That *would* be good news." Another sigh on the line. "Anyway, I've gotta get back to work. Give Mr. Rock Star my best." And he hung up.

With a growing sense of emotional vertigo, I listened to the silence for second, before picking up the call from my new "boss." If Alan was taking the time to phone me this afternoon—after the morning he'd been through—I doubted it was just to say he'd found my lost hangtag.

"Everything okay?" I asked him.

"Not sure. First, I want to apologize for all the craziness this morning."

"You mean the protestors? They didn't really cause *me* any problems. Pretty tough on you guys, though."

"We'll survive. But I mean the stuff that happened later, with that Fox guy. I'm sorry you ended up in the middle of that."

Men were apologizing to me right and left this afternoon. Glad that Alan was reopening the topic of Fox, I probed further. "His message really seemed to upset you."

"It caught me off guard, but we're handling it." Once again, he deftly changed the subject. "That's not why I'm calling."

His tone worried me, and I waited for him to elaborate.

"When I got back to my apartment, I found your press pass stuck under my door, with a note. It said, 'Tell that witch to back off, or she'll be the next one having an 'accident.'"

Fear rippled through me. "Shit."

"Yeah, exactly. Quinn, I never meant to put you at risk over this stuff!"

I recovered enough to shift back into my sleuth mode. "Any idea who could have left it?"

"Stern asked around, like he always does. The doorman, the security guard, a couple of my neighbors. Nobody saw anything suspicious."

Maybe, I thought, they just didn't know "suspicious" when they saw it. "Let's think about this, though. It had to be someone who was at, or near, Sanktuary this morning."

"That guy Fox?" Alan guessed. "No, you were wearing the nametag when I talked to you downstairs."

"I guess it could've fallen off later, and he could've picked it up...anybody could have. But it's got to be someone who knows where you live and has access to your building. That should narrow the field."

"It also sounds like somebody who knows about you—the kind of help you're providing for us. I mean, if they just wanted to call you a name, why not 'bitch'?"

I got his point—"witch" sounded like a reference to my being psychic. But I hadn't told anyone about the work I was doing for Mad Love except my closest friends.

"Who in your circle knows?" I asked him.

"Just me, Jeff, Stern and the rest of the band. I told the other guys just before the photo shoot at the jail, so they'd understand why you were there."

"And Lark," I reminded him. "She's known since the beginning."

"Well, sure, but she's got nothing against you, and she's sure got no motive to sabotage us. Believe me, she's well paid! The others, too—they've all got a vested interest in keeping the band together and successful. So it just doesn't make sense."

I recalled my discussion that morning with Tony, about who could have known about the Rialto show, and came back to the same conclusion. One of these trusted people must have talked to someone else—someone who *did* have a grudge against the band.

"Anyway," Alan said, "I can understand if you want to back out on our deal. There's no point in you becoming a target, too."

He was absolutely right, and it was kind of him to give me

an "out." But I was mad now. If there's anything I hate, it's being threatened.

I explained to Alan about my week off and my intention to solve his "case" in that time.

"I just might be able to do it," I added, "but I'll need two things from you."

"Anything!" he swore.

"First, I want to talk to the other band members. Any way to get them all together?"

"The cops have already questioned them, but... Yeah, sure. Monday we start rehearsing our act for the new tour. We'll all be together up at Pat's farm outside Warwick."

"Sounds perfect. What's the address?"

"I'll send you a text. It's way out in the country, so you'll need directions." The smile back in his voice, he asked me, "What's the second thing?"

I mustered my nerve. "You need to come clean with me, Alan. Remember, I signed the NDA, so you can trust me. I need to know about this business with Elaine, Rocky—everything."

When he finally answered, he sounded grim. "Stern won't like that, but...okay, you got it." He must have heard me waiting, in the silence. "Not over the phone, though. It's too long a story."

"On Monday, then?"

"Yeah," he promised, "on Monday."

CHAPTER 17

Nancy Sabatino tilted her delicate profile upward and shook her ponytailed head. "Dunno, Quinn…I'd say you're living on borrowed time."

She might have been referring to any of several aspects of my life, but it so happened she was talking about the tree in my back yard, beneath which both of us currently stood. The big old maple loomed about twenty feet from my back door, halfway between the house and the detached garage.

I had been asking her advice on my rhododendrons, which weren't flowering so well that spring, and she'd noted the radius of gloom cast by the overgrown tree. She'd also pointed out that about a third of the branches had no leaves, which could mean the maple was on its way out, anyhow.

"Get an arborist to look at it," Nancy said. "At least he can prune it back, but you may want him to just take it down."

My gut clenched the way it always seemed to, these days, whenever I faced a problem that required me to lay out a large amount of cash—cash I didn't have. "And how much is *that* going to cost?"

"Tree that big? Maybe a thou."

The amount rolled off her tongue too lightly. Like me, Nancy also had been downsized from full-time to part-time at the *Sentinel* last year, but she still had her lawyer husband's salary to compensate. "A thou" would be a much smaller chunk of her income than of mine.

"Another job that'll have to wait a while," I muttered.

Nancy peered up at the dead branches, which stretched like skeletal arms across the blue, late-morning sky. "Don't put it off too long. You don't want this thing to come down on your house."

"Haven't you heard? I'm going to write an exclusive story on Alan Bardot's apartment for *Celebrity Homes*, probably for several 'thou.' That ought to cover the tree removal and a few other home improvements." As we ambled back toward the front of the house, I added sourly, "Just as soon as I figure out who dropped that chunk of plaster on the cameraman at the Rialto!"

"Un-huh. You got a plan for that?"

I shrugged. "I must be getting closer. Now someone's leaving Alan notes threatening *me*. I always wondered what it would be like to be famous, but I can't say I ever daydreamed about having a stalker."

"Yeah, that's one part of the celebrity lifestyle you don't want to rub off on you. Has Bardot told the cops?"

"He said he gave them the ID tag and insisted they check it for prints, but they didn't find any. They never do, on any of these nasty 'gifts.' Beyond that, I don't expect much from them. I'm not a celebrity—nobody's going to follow me around twenty-four-seven just to make sure I don't have an 'accident.'"

Nancy and I mounted the steps of my wrap-around porch and sat on the wicker divan. My hornet's nest, now sealed with polyurethane, still occupied a place of honor on a corner plant stand, and she twitched her shoulders at the sight of it.

"I don't know how you can keep that thing around," she said. "What if the hornets decide to come back?"

"Nah, they won't, now that it's sealed," I assured her. "It's beautiful, in a way." Even allegorical, I thought privately. It reminded me these days of the weird twists and turns of the Mad Love case. Maybe I thought if I meditated on it long enough, I'd stumble on a revelation.

It was Saturday. Tony really had cut off all contact with me, so I was grateful Nancy had been free to meet me for lunch, just us gals. I had nothing against Rob, but I didn't dare talk about Mad Love's business in front him because of the ongoing litigation against the theater. As long as she promised not to repeat anything I told her to her husband, Nancy remained one of the few people with whom I could talk a bit more openly. At least about issues not covered by my NDA—such as this latest threat against me.

"Like you said," she continued, "it's interesting that this person used the word 'witch,' when not many people know about the work you're doing for the band."

"I guess it might also be one of the right-wing religious types. Some of them think any type of psychic powers come from the Devil. On the other hand, it's not very spiritual to threaten people with bodily harm."

"No, it's not. That's pretty scary, Quinn. If this is the same person who tampered with the band's truck and plane...I'd be afraid to even start my car in the morning."

Thanks for planting that idea in my head, Nance. "Well, so far I don't imagine this person knows where I live. And, even though it seems naïve to say it, I haven't *felt* any sense of danger here at home. He does know where I work, but luckily I'm not even going to the office this week."

"You will be going to Mad Love's rehearsal," she pointed out. "That's not 'backing off' the case. If this person thinks you're still poking around, in spite of his threat—"

"Mad Love will have their own security around, so I'll ask somebody to watch my car when I visit them. Frankly, though, I think the note was a bluff."

Nancy shot me a sideways look. "Is that another hunch?"

"Maybe...maybe more." I slapped my blue-jeaned thighs and stood up. "I'm hungry, so I'll tell you over lunch. Where are we eating?"

We took her SUV out on the highway to Mayberry's, a chain restaurant decorated with vintage memorabilia from local businesses, schools and sports teams. At just past noon, the restaurant was already fairly crowded and noisy. They gave us a booth near the bar area, and my side faced the wall-hung, big-screen TV. I guess I have a touch of ADD, because those flickering, changing images tend to distract me when I'm trying to have a conversation with someone.

Today, though, the TV was turned to a boring, local news channel, and the restaurant's busy atmosphere worked fine for my purposes. I could air some of my theories to Nancy without worrying about eavesdroppers.

We both ordered omelets, her choice the salsa special and mine mushroom-and-cheese. Then I brought her up to speed on what I'd been deduced so far.

"I'm not sure the person leaving Alan these notes is the same one responsible for sabotaging the truck and the plane," I said. "First of all, I don't think the 'crow' person wants to hurt Alan. If he did, he's had every opportunity. He's left things in front of Alan's door several times, with no one stopping him. Why not leave a bomb? Or something with poison in it?"

Nancy shuddered. "So what's the motive?"

"Jealousy. From the time I stepped on the dead bird, I got that. I think this person wants to eliminate anyone else who seems close to Alan. And he...or she...might even think I'm a new girlfriend."

"What about the shadow-thing you saw in the theater?"

"I'm still not sure where that fits in, but..." I confided in her about the similar incident during the photo shoot at the jail.

"Oh crap, Quinn, that's scary. What do you think it is?"

I shrugged. "Gale has suggested a couple of explanations, but it still could just be my own sixth sense taking some kind of visible form. At least it didn't show up at the press conference. I was almost waiting for it to drop one of those Gothic iron chandeliers on the dais, like something out of *Phantom of the Opera!*"

The waiter took our plates, and we both agreed to more coffee—probably frustrating the Saturday shoppers who now filled benches near the door.

"You told me some more stuff happened at the press conference," Nancy said, "but you didn't tell me much."

"And I'm afraid I still can't—at least, no details. But I think there's something embarrassing that Alan has been keeping secret, even from me. He promised to finally explain before the rehearsal."

Nancy giggled. "Wow, this should be juicy! What could embarrass a bisexual rock star?"

I felt obliged to defend Alan. "He's not so crazy—in some

ways, he's actually pretty conservative. He did fire a band member for using hard drugs, and he seems to be into serial relationships, not orgies. After all, despite my irresistible older-woman charms, he's never yet hit on *me*."

With an evil grin, Nancy reached across to pat my hand. "And that just tears you up, doesn't it, Quinn?"

"You have no idea!"

The waiter had just refilled our coffees when I finally found my gaze drawn to the bar's oversized TV screen. It showed footage of a rally, and I spotted the offensive picket sign, "God Hates Fags." When the camera pulled back, I also recognized the brownstone-church facade of Sanktuary.

"What the—" I scooted out of the booth and dashed to the bar, which, at this early hour, was less crowded than the main dining area. Why was the New Jersey station just now reporting on something that happened in Manhattan the previous morning?

The screen shifted to video of a more sedate gathering in a sunny park; a banner proclaimed it was North Burwick's centennial celebration. A tall, broad-shouldered man in a navy blazer and red-white-and-blue tie mingled with more casually dressed citizens, shaking hands and chatting. His dark blond coloring and broad, all-American face gave me clues even before a caption identified him as Mayor Steve Randall.

I caught the eye of the bartender and asked him to turn up the sound, then perched on a stool to listen. A voice-over by the news commentator suggested Mayor Randall had been blindsided at this low-key event by an unexpected question from a reporter.

The video then captured a male voice—one I knew well—yelling to Randall from somewhere outside camera range.

"In light of your stand on gay issues, are you aware of the anti-gay protest that took place yesterday in New York during a press conference by the band Mad Love?"

Randall glanced sharply in the speaker's direction, then faced away again with a slight shake of his head. It could have meant he didn't know about the event or just that he didn't consider the question worth answering. He tried to go back to chatting with his constituents.

The reporter, though, would not be dismissed so easily. "Isn't it true, Mayor, that you own son Jeff is the lead guitarist with that band? Does it bother you that he and the other band members were subjected to this kind of harassment?"

This time Randall's narrowed eyes shot poison darts in the reporter's direction, and he answered crisply. "My son is an adult, and he and I disagree on many things."

"But Mayor—"

He blocked any more controversy with a square, raised hand. Aided by security, he made a quick escape into the crowd.

I didn't realize I was trembling until I heard Nancy's voice from behind me. "Whoa, talk about being 'outed'! And wasn't that Tony?"

Not wanting to spoil my lunch with Nancy, I waited until she dropped me off at home before I pulled out my cell phone. Before I could make any calls, though, I saw that I had a text message from Alan.

It asked, *Yr BF again?*

I groaned. Even he must have recognized Tony's voice…or maybe just his pit-bull interviewing style.

'Fraid so," I answered. *So-o-o sorry. I M gonna kick his a**!*

After a minute, Alan wrote back, *Don't sweat it. We'll talk Mon.*

That calmed me down a little. At least he—and Jeff—must not be too angry to meet with me, as planned, during the next day's rehearsal.

But did Tony even care that he could have undermined all their trust in me? Or what that was he'd had in mind?

Furiously, I punched his number on the keypad. I was still going to kick his a**!

CHAPTER 18

Tony took my call right away, apparently not expecting the earful I would give him. I accused him of having ulterior motives when he'd suggested we "take a break."

"What is this, some kind of petty revenge?" I demanded. "You won't be satisfied until you've turned these guys completely against me and gotten me kicked off the case?"

His lightning-fast, witty rebuttal was, "Huh?"

"Or maybe you plotted this all out ahead of time. You were planning to ambush Mayor Randall, and you didn't want me trying to talk you out of it!"

Tony sounded genuinely surprised. "Hey, Quinn, everything's not about you. Steve Randall's relationship with his son is a legitimate part of my story. Doesn't it bother you that this guy is anti-gay rights and palling around with Reverend Willis, while Jeff is the target of protests and abuse?"

"He was against gay marriage, and he shook Willis' hand at a fundraiser. Neither of those things makes him a total villain. Maybe, like he said, he and Jeff have their differences, and that's why they've tried to keep their connection out of the press."

Tony snorted. "Not like they could expect to hide it forever. They have the same last name, and Jeff's bio online says he grew up North Burwick. Heck, he even looks like his Dad…just add a couple of decades, take away the long hair and give him a spare tire."

His caustic tone sounded as if he'd like nothing better. What, so now he was jealous of Jeff, too? I had to remind myself he didn't know Jeff and Alan were together and that he had nothing to fear from either of them. Unfortunately, I still couldn't enlighten Tony on that score.

"Even if you felt you had to make the connection," I went on, "you could've done it in one of your articles. To blurt it out at an event where there were TV cameras..." I'd worked myself up to such a pitch that, for a second, I ran dry of words. "You were just afraid I was going to crack the case first, so you had to shake things up. You didn't even care who might get hurt."

"C'mon. The only person who might've gotten hurt was the mayor, and if he's trying to distance himself from his son to preserve his public image, he deserves it."

"You also may have hurt *me*. Alan and Jeff know by now that you and I are...friends," I emphasized the word a bit too much. "I'm meeting with them Monday to ask more questions, about things they may want to keep confidential. Who knows if they'll still trust me?"

"Look, Quinn, we all want the same thing—to find out who's trying to sabotage Mad Love. A guy is dead, and there's a good chance somebody killed him while trying to nail one of the band members. Until we get to the bottom of this, I don't think there's any room for lies or secrets, no matter whose they are."

Easy for Tony to say, I thought. His only loyalty is to the *Sentinel*. But I'd signed an agreement promising that any of Mad Love's secrets they didn't want exposed would also be my secrets.

Reflecting on all this left me more sad than angry. I told him, "Y'know, I take back what I said before. You were absolutely right."

"Oh? About what?"

"Until this whole business is over, you and I *shouldn't* be speaking to each other."

This time, I hung up first.

I was still brooding over my argument with Tony on Monday morning, as I began my hour-and-a-half drive to Pat Jacy's farm outside Warwick, New York. Finally, I made myself calm down, remembering I shouldn't arrive at my destination all keyed up. I needed a cool head—a clear channel, psychics called it—when

I talked with the members of Mad Love. I wanted to hear what each of them had to say about the threatening notes and suspicious accidents, and also to get a sense of what, if anything, they might *not* be saying.

I crossed the border from northeastern New Jersey into New York State, as Route 287 became Route 87. Passing through Harriman State Park, I rolled down my window to better drink in the sights and scents of the lush spring greenery.

Again, I wondered how—and why—I'd let myself get so deeply enmeshed in the band's troubles. After swearing to Gail just a year ago that I had no interest in developing or profiting from my psychic abilities, why had I become so intent on solving this "case"?

Was I just curious to see if I could? And if so, was it worth risking my relationship with Tony?

I turned off onto 17A and wound my way through a rustic lake community. Soon after, the town of Warwick totally charmed me with its Victorian-era main street and proliferation of antique shops. Maybe I'd have some time to browse a little on my way back?

Depending on how long it took me to grill all five members of the band.

I re-checked my Mapquest directions—so far I've resisted getting a GPS, afraid it will dull my natural navigating instincts—then turned off onto a two-lane country road. Driving up here wasn't like the suburbs. The farms and other large properties were so spread out, I couldn't exactly follow a neat progression of house numbers to determine if I was getting near Jacy's place.

Finally, though, I spotted the life-sized rearing horse—the kind carved with a chainsaw from a solid tree trunk—that Alan had said marked the driveway. I also saw an older, battle-scarred magenta Volvo stopped there, as if waiting for me to pass before pulling out.

I put on my blinker and slowed down, so the driver would realize she could exit. As my driver's-side window aligned for a moment with hers, I saw it was a young woman with a long, thin nose and frizzy, strawberry-blond hair. The same one I'd seen shut out of the press conference in New York.

She also shot me the same kind of glare as on that afternoon. Then floored her accelerator and sped off with a spray of gravel.

Jeez! I thought. Had she come all the way up here for another try at an interview and maybe been rebuffed again? And Tony thought he was persistent!

I continued on my way—slowly, because I spotted three real horses turned out in a small paddock near the road. Since they were pintos, "spotted" was the right term. Not only did I not want to spook them by speeding past, but I enjoyed the chance to admire them and hark back to the horseback riding days of my teens and early twenties. Supporting myself in journalism had put an end to that expensive hobby.

Jacy, lucky man, could afford to keep horses. Since pintos had been favorites among certain Native American tribes, I wondered if this was a nod to his heritage.

On a rise up ahead, I spotted a classic, white Norman Rockwell-era farmhouse with a screened front porch. I drove straight toward the barn, though, because I'd been told that's where Jacy had his rehearsal studio. In the dirt yard outside, I found my way blocked by two more large, muscular creatures, but the human kind. The one with the thin black ponytail, I had seen before—he'd checked me in for the photo shoot at the jail.

If he recognized me, though, he gave no sign of it. When I leaned out of my car window and gave him my name, he gruffly demanded ID.

I flashed my press card and even took off my sunglasses so he'd be able to match my face to the photograph. Once he confirmed who I was, he acted almost apologetic.

"Lotta fans come around. They know it's Jacy's place and that the band sometimes rehearses here," the bodyguard said.

"Yeah," his friend chimed in, with a gap-toothed smile. "Just got rid of one of 'em."

"The woman in the pink car?" I asked. Neither of these guys seemed likely to know "magenta" when they saw it.

The man with the ponytail nodded. "She cruised right on in here, but stopped short when she got to us. Batted her eyes, tried to pretend she was lost, then asked directions to some place I never heard of. But the kicker was, she asked if she could use a phone in the *barn.*" He grinned. "I pulled out my cell and said I'd dial for her, and all of a sudden she didn't want to 'bother' us and drove off."

"Oh, well. It's fans that keep the band in business, right?"

"True. But some of 'em are nuts!"

Convinced of my sanity, at least, the bodyguard told me how to get to the rehearsal space.

An outdoor staircase had been built onto the barn, wide and sturdy enough to accommodate even the band's equipment. As I climbed, I could hear the rehearsal already in progress—I recognized the pounding rhythm of "Belly of the Beast" from the last album. With my hand on the doorknob, I almost hesitated to intrude. At the same time, how could I pass up the opportunity to watch and listen to Mad Love polishing its act for the tour?

Inside, the music was louder, but still not the same volume as if they'd been performing for an audience. The guys all occupied a low platform at one end of the loft space, set up with microphones, small amps and padding on the walls to muffle the sound. Donny sat behind his drums, Pat at the electric keyboard and Alan on a high stool, while Jack and Jeff stood with their guitars. A sofa and a few old armchairs had been angled to face the stage area.

During an instrumental break, Alan bopped along with the music. He saw me slip in, gestured toward the empty seats, then picked up his vocals again without missing a beat.

I smoothed out the sofa's Navaho-patterned throw blanket and settled there.

The number wound up with a sizzling crescendo from Jeff's guitar and an explosion from the bass, drums and keyboards, Alan's last notes soaring above it all. If they were trying to tighten up their act, it already sounded dead-on to me.

In the ringing silence that followed, I couldn't resist applauding.

Alan laughed. "Thanks."

Jacy spoke into his microphone. "Not a big audience, but an enthusiastic one."

"I wanna go through that number again," Alan told the

others, "but first, let's break for lunch."

"Ah, yes." Jack slipped the strap of the electric bass from his shoulder. "Time to help the lady psychic figure out who's trying to kill us!"

Deadpan, Jeff began to play the highly recognizable opening riff of a Bon Jovi hit. Alan joined in the joke by warbling, slightly off-key, "We're wa-a-anted, dead or a-live…"

Donny Morelli sniffed. "Oughta add that to our repertoire!" No taller than me, but with a torso pumped up from drumming, he stepped out from behind his kit and opened his cell phone. "I'll tell the ladies we're ready."

"Ladies?" I asked Alan.

"His wife and Pat's girlfriend are up at the house making sandwiches."

I joined Alan and Jeff in the rehearsal area. "Speaking of ladies…" I told them about the one who had driven onto the property and been turned back by the bodyguards. "I saw her before, too, during the protest at Sanktuary."

Tall Jack, looming in back of us, overheard me and shook his shaggy blond head. "Sounds like Barkin' Larkin. I thought we got rid of her."

Alan sent him a dark look. "Easy, man. She *is* Lark's sister."

I almost smacked my forehead, sitcom-style. "I *thought* they kind of looked alike."

"Yeah," said Jack, "in dim light, if you really squint."

I got his point—even with all her piercings, Lark was by far the better-looking sister. I also figured out what he'd meant by "Barkin' Larkin," and disliked him for it.

The same way the band had nicknamed Sternberg "Stern," they must have turned Larkin into "Lark." That flash of insight also lit up something else my memory.

I asked them, "*Melissa* Larkin?"

Alan, Jeff and Jack all turned to me. "You know her?"

"I sat next to her at the Rialto show. In fact, I was responsible for her getting in." I explained I had let her use my spare ticket. "It's weird that when I saw her again I didn't recognize her. But the night of the video shoot she had on a ton of makeup, and her clothes and hair were a lot different."

Donny closed his phone and picked up the thread of our conversation. Dryly, he said, "Next time, do a background check before you give away your extra ticket."

I guessed I'd stumbled onto another secret. "You guys were trying to keep her out? How come?"

The drummer tilted his close-cropped head and made sad-puppy eyes. "She's in *lo-o-ove* with Alan. Aren't they all!"

Bardot just frowned. "She got to be a real pain in the...neck. Finally, even Lark agreed we should keep her away from the band."

A perky knock on the door interrupted us. Pat ushered in two pretty young women in jeans and T-shirts and introduced them to me. Carla Morelli had the same working-class-Italian style as Donny, while Pat's girlfriend, May, was delicately Asian. They carried platters of wrap sandwiches, which they set on a bar toward the back of the loft space. The band members dove for the food.

Alan made an after-you gesture to me, but I hung back. In a whisper, I accused him, "You're really making my job difficult. How could you leave out the minor detail that you have an obsessed stalker?"

He rolled his eyes toward the ceiling, as if I was wildly exaggerating. "I don't think Melissa's *obsessed*. She's just a little... immature."

"You've warned her off, and she's still following you around. If she's frustrated, she might do something extreme to get your attention. Maybe even try to get rid of anybody she thinks might be keeping her away from you. Does she know about you and Jeff?"

Without answering my question, he protested, "Melissa can't be behind the sabotage. She doesn't know anything about machinery or construction!"

"She knew you were going to be at the Rialto that night," I reminded him.

He shook his head with a skeptical chuckle. "You really think little Melissa climbed up on scaffolding and sawed through that plaster? Anyway, she wasn't on tour with us when the other stuff—"

He was cut off by a racket from outside—shouted curses from the bodyguards.

Then one of them bellowed, "Fire!"

CHAPTER 19

With visions of the barn in flames beneath us, we all dashed for loft's exit. Well, some dashed faster than others. The other two women and I got out first, but not necessarily through chivalry on the part of the band members.

Swearing in desperation, Jack and Jeff fumbled to unplug their guitars, while Donny and Pat panicked over how to save the drums and electronic keyboard.

"Come on, come *on!*" Alan shouted to them—using all of his considerable lung power—from the doorway. Carla and May finally persuaded their guys to leave the bulkier pieces of equipment behind, but the guitarists stubbornly rescued their instruments.

By the time we'd all scrambled down the outside steps, we could see flames licking skyward from a manure pile a few feet from the main barn door. The ponytailed bodyguard struggled to unroll a hose from a reel on the barn's outer wall—he looked like he'd never handled such a foreign thing before. Pat finally snatched it from him and told him to go turn on the water.

From a safe distance, the rest of us watched them douse the fire. Our fears eased, and we cracked wise about our close call and the pungent aroma of the steaming horse manure. To be on the safe side, Pat had the bodyguard turn the pile with a pitchfork a few times, while he drenched the whole thing. Then he cross-examined the two guys on what had happened.

"Either of you smoking out here?" he asked. *"Anything?"*

They both shook their heads, and the ponytailed guy raised a hand to heaven. "Swear-ta-God, man!"

I saw Alan frown and sensed his suspicions brewing. "See

anybody else hanging around?" he asked them.

"Not a soul."

"I heard the horses actin' up," the gap-toothed guy volunteered, "so I went to the field to check on 'em. But Zack stayed here the whole time."

Warily, Pat asked, "What was wrong with the horses?"

"Nothin' I could see. They was running around, but they calmed down after I came out."

Hands on his narrow hips, Jacy turned back to the charred and smoldering mound. "Guess the thing *might* have just combusted. I've heard of that happening, but never saw it before... We'll have to move it farther away from the barn." When both bodyguards made faces of disgust, he laughed. "No, you don't have to do that. Just keep an eye on it, for now, and make sure it's out."

We all started back toward the loft stairs. As Jeff passed the smoldering pile, he paused to kick at a scorched ball of manure. "Talk about a hot mess!"

I smiled, but the incident left me uneasy.

The horses had been stirred up at the same time the manure caught fire? Unless the bodyguards were lying, it sounded like someone might have been creating a diversion. But why?

While I hung back, pondering, Alan put a hand on my arm. "I dunno, Quinn," he joked. "These things always seem to happen when you're around!"

I reminded him, "A lot of them also seem to happen when Melissa Larkin is around."

"Well, even if she was here earlier, she isn't now." He shook his head. "I'll talk to Lark, but I really don't see her sister being involved in any of this."

I gave up trying to convince him. "Then let's talk about the other secret you've been keeping from me—about this guy Rocky and your mother."

"My moth—" Alan looked confused. "Oh, because he said 'Elaine.'"

"Wasn't Elaine you mother's name?"

"Yeah. But it's also my tattoo." He watched the other band members climb the stairs back to the barn's loft and their interrupted lunch. "Let's walk for a minute, and I'll tell you the whole story."

We strolled down the driveway, the sun baking our shoulders, birds chirping in the trees and wildflowers brightening the roadside. The perfect setting for a romantic conversation, but I felt sure this would be something quite different.

"I grew up in Fresno, California," Alan began. "My mother... She used to sing me to sleep at night. Not just lullabies, but all the old torch songs. She had a beautiful voice. *She* was beautiful, too."

Imagining a more feminine version of Alan's dramatic coloring, sculpted cheekbones and long-lashed eyes, I could easily picture Elaine.

"My Pop was jealous and possessive, and they fought a lot. After she left him, she got jobs singing in clubs. In the beginning, she used to take me along, letting me sleep nights in the dressing room. Then she got a chance to tour with a band, and she left me with her sister Rose."

"The psychic aunt?" I asked.

"You remembered that! Anyhow, Mom would come back to see us once in a while, and toward the end she didn't look so good. I think it was drugs...and the wrong men. Finally, when I was nine, my aunt told me Mom had died. I found out later it was an overdose."

I could imagine how abandoned he'd felt, still just a young boy. "I'm sorry."

He nodded his thanks. "After high school, when I set out on my own, I got her name tattooed on the back of my left shoulder, just to keep some part of her with me."

We had come to a stop by the horses' pasture, and I glanced reflexively toward Alan's back. He noticed and, with a boyish grin, peeled up his dark-blue T-shirt to show me the tat. It was tasteful, almost old-fashioned, the name on a kind of ribbon unfurling over the wing of his shoulder blade.

He covered up his lean torso again, then rested his forearms on the fence and began to explain about Rocky. He prefaced that part by emphasizing, "None of this goes back to your boyfriend the reporter!"

"Absolutely not," I promised.

Shortly after getting the tattoo, Alan had left his aunt and cousins and set off on his own. He had done a little singing in high school and hoped to hook up with a band in Los Angeles, but that didn't pan out. He took minimum-wage day jobs, answered want ads and went to the clubs at night hoping to make connections.

At one of the clubs, he'd met Rocky Montanna.

"He was a filmmaker—had a company called Rocky Mountain Productions—and asked if I'd ever done any acting. I hadn't, but I was game to give it a try. So he started inviting me to parties at his place to 'meet some people.'" Alan shook his head at the memory. "They were a colorful bunch! I'd already experimented enough to know I was bi, but I'd never been around folks like this—transvestites, transsexuals, S&M types. They were into drugs and kinky sex stuff I'd never even heard of. At first, I mostly hung on the fringes, taking it all in, but not getting too involved."

I just nodded. Though I had an idea where this story might be leading, I maintained a nonchalant air—neither too prudish nor too curious—so Alan could tell it in his own way and at his own pace.

"One night, after most of the party crowd had split, Rocky talked me into a three-way with a guy and a girl. We were all kind of high, he said it would be 'safe,' so I figured what the heck. We did it right in Rocky's bedroom. What I didn't know was, he had a camera hidden and recorded the whole thing."

I was getting a clearer picture now. A little too clear—I started to feel like a voyeur, myself.

"Rocky told me the next day about the video and even tried to get me to watch it. He said I had 'real talent,' all that kind of BS, and he wanted to put me in his skin flicks!" Alan scowled. "God, was I mad. I couldn't believe he did that without even telling me! I might've been only about eighteen and a little full of myself, but I knew I didn't want to be in *that* end of show business. I made him give me the DVD and told him to screw off. I avoided him from then on.

"But he kept after me about it, calling and leaving messages.

I was starting to get gigs with bands, but Rocky would tell me I was wasting my time, that I could make more money with him. This went on for maybe a year."

"Ever think he might have made a copy of the DVD?" I asked.

"It occurred to me." He laughed dryly at his own naiveté. "That's one reason I came east. I figured if I put a whole continent between us, he'd finally leave me alone. And for a long time, he did."

"Until Mad Love got successful," I guessed. "So now he's blackmailing you?"

"Unfortunately, it's not that straightforward. If he came right out and said, 'Pay me a chunk of the band's earnings or I'll put your sleazy video on the Web,' the cops might be able to nail him. But so far, it's been just these mysterious emails and other hints that we can't even trace back to him."

"Like the bit about 'still seeing Elaine,'" I remembered.

"Yeah—that shook me. I'd been thinking, hell, I looked different eleven, twelve years ago, so how could he prove it was even me? But I guess, in the footage, you can see the tattoo."

I tried to think of a way out of Alan's sticky situation. "You could have it removed."

His face hardened. "Y'know, I'd hate to get rid of it just because of that bastard... Anyway, there are enough people in my life who've seen it by now. It's not like I've kept it a big secret all these years. Of course, not many know who 'Elaine' is. I doubt Montanna even knows—I never told him."

"You could always claim the video was faked, with some guy who looked like you."

"Probably...but it could still get messy." For the first time in his confession, Alan met my eyes. "Wow, it was hard telling you all this! Harder even than when I told Stern." He faced away again, a muscle tightening in his cheek. "Almost as hard as when I told Jeff."

"The others don't know?"

He shook his head. "I've made some jokes about people from my past coming out of the woodwork, now that we've made it, but...I'm worried about how the other guys would react. Man, I hate the idea that a stupid mistake I made back when I was still a kid could wreck things for all of us now."

As the two of us started back toward the barn, I tried to reassure him. "Even if the worst happened and he did release the footage, you've already gone public about your orientation. Besides, other celebrities have shown up in raunchy videos, and their careers survived."

"I know," Alan said, "and if it were just me...but you've seen what Mayor Randall is like! He still hasn't gotten over the idea that Jeff and I are together, and I think he's scared we'll somehow torpedo his political career. A scandal like this would just give his opponents more ammo."

The pain in those big, blue-green eyes told me something beyond Alan's words. He was afraid those family conflicts might destroy his relationship with Jeff.

We heard a shout from up ahead and saw Pat Jacy in the road. "If you want lunch, better hurry! The wraps are going fast."

Alan seemed relieved to be off the hot seat. "Enough about me, Quinn! Now you can go grill everybody else."

After this, I hardly dared to imagine what the others might tell me. Could things get any crazier?

CHAPTER 20

Before beginning my interrogations, I fortified myself by grabbing a turkey wrap. Pat may have been a declared vegetarian, but he'd compromised his principles far enough to offer a variety of sandwiches. I sat on a stool at the loft's bar and ate with one hand; with the other, I scribbled notes from my conversation with Alan.

Today I'd brought along the "spy" pen I'd gotten from cousin Michael, embedded with a digital recorder and a USB flash. Supposedly I could take notes and simultaneously record an interview, so I could play it back on my computer and make sure I hadn't missed anything. I'd tested it at home and it had seemed to work. I figured it might be just the thing to help me capture not only what each band member said, but how he said it, without making any of them too self-conscious.

I decided to start with Pat and invited him to join me by the bar. It seemed a good, private spot, at a distance from the rest of the guys, Carla and May.

I asked him about the farm, and he told me it had belonged to his parents.

"My Pop made pretty good money for a while at one of the upstate casinos—working there, not gambling," Pat told me. "He decided to follow his dream and breed Paint horses. When he and Mom retired to Arizona, they left me this place and a few of the horses, to boot."

"Most people might wonder why a rock musician would pick someplace so quiet and out-of-the-way," I noted.

Jacy grinned, white teeth contrasting with his dusky skin and lank, black hair. "I love being out here in nature. It's got its own rhythms, its own music... The success is great because I get to do what I love for a living, but I don't buy into it. You start craving that attention, wanting to keep the party going all the time, it'll burn you up. I think that's what happened to Barry."

That brought up one of the questions I'd wanted to ask. "How did he react when you guys fired him?"

"Oh, he was mad as hell, of course. Couldn't believe we'd make such a big deal out of one drug bust, said we were just using it as an excuse. Accused Alan of wanting to run the whole show and the rest of us of stabbing him in the back. The guy was totally in denial. He'd been screwing up for at least a year and wouldn't even admit he had a problem." Pat's dark eyes turned distant at the memory. "When Stern and Alan said we should let him go...it was a tough call, but I had to agree with them."

I said I'd talked to Barry, and he claimed to be totally sober now and happy working for his father's construction firm.

Pat brightened. "That's great! So maybe it was all for the best, huh? And nobody can deny, Jeff's been a terrific addition to the group."

When I asked how he felt about the relationship between Alan and Jeff, he answered readily.

"Hey, I have a cousin who's gay and kept it quiet all through his teen years," Pat said. "I used to sense that same frustration in Alan, trying to stay on the down-low for the band's sake. Since he's hooked up with Randall, he's mellowed out a lot. I think the two of them are really good for each other."

From that point, it seemed logical to move on to questioning Jeff. A week earlier, I wouldn't have planned to include him in my interviews, since he seemed a likely target of the attacks, but a lot had happened in the meantime.

I started off by apologizing to him for Tony's aggressive tactics with Mayor Randall.

Jeff smiled crookedly. "Your boyfriend's kind of a pit bull, isn't he? Was he getting back at us for not giving him an exclusive at the press conference?"

"No, I really don't think it was anything like that," I assured him. "Tony's an investigative reporter, and...well, the good ones *are* sort of like pit bulls. They don't let go easy! I just hope that incident didn't cause any problems between…you and your father."

"No more than usual." Jeff flipped a bar coaster between his fingers, his tone bitter. "Maybe it's just as well. At least he can't go on anymore pretending we're not related."

"That must be rough," I said. "I guess he knows about you and Alan?"

"Yeah, I finally told my folks a couple of months ago. My mom's getting used to the idea, and my sister Katy is totally fine with it, but Dad…" Jeff saw me scribbling in my notebook and stopped short. "This isn't going in the paper, is it?"

I crossed my heart. "No way, I swear. I'm just gathering background today so I can try to figure out who's making trouble for you guys."

He relaxed a bit then and went back to talking about his father. "Dad's still got this image of me in his head as the husky kid who played high school football and always had a cute girlfriend hanging around."

Sounding a bit like a bland therapist even to myself, I said, "Must be confusing for him."

"Hell, I was pretty confused myself, growing up. I liked women, too, so it was easier just to stick with them. But when I met Alan…" His warm brown eyes took on a faraway look for a minute, then the cutting tone returned. "My dad wants to believe this terrible guy seduced his squeaky clean, hetero son. It's so damn unfair! At first, Alan assumed I was dead straight, so he was afraid to do or say anything that might spook me and make me quit the band. I actually had to make the first move." When Jeff's gaze met mine again, he reddened a bit and laughed. "Too much information, right?"

"Not necessarily. I'm trying to get a sense of the group dynamics, so I don't know what might be important." I moved on to another topic. "Alan explained to me why he got so upset over the message from that Fox guy. He said he'd told you about it, too."

Jeff's lips tightened. "I knew there was something going on, that he thought someone was trying to shake him down for money, but not all the details."

"That probably was…awkward," I said.

"It was our first real fight!" He shrugged his wide shoulders. "At the end of the day, though… who hasn't done something stupid, or even dangerous, when they were younger? The one I'd really like to punch out is that Montanna guy, but who even knows where he is now?"

I wondered about that, myself. "Speaking of hard feelings… did you sense any resentment among the other guys when you replaced Barry?"

"A little—mostly from Jack and Donny. I just made an extra effort with them. Asked their advice on stuff, let them know I wanted to fit in."

Jeff seemed such a likeable guy, I imagined it would be hard for the others to freeze him out for long. Still, based on recent incidents, he might be the very band member someone was trying to kill. "And when you got involved with Alan? Did that change the group dynamics?"

"It did, at first. I mean, in a rock band there's always the tendency for the lead singer, and maybe also the lead guitarist, to get most of the attention. We don't want the other guys to feel it's totally become the Alan-and-Jeff show, so we try to include everybody in the major decisions. There's still some tension, but so far we've managed to keep things on an even keel." He leaned back on his elbows against the bar with a deep sigh. "Just hope that lasts. We've had some pretty choppy seas lately."

The other guys all had finished their lunches and were sitting around talking with each other and the two women. I sensed I might be holding up the rehearsal, and my request for Jack to join me next at the bar drew a frown from Donny. I overheard him ask Alan, "Really, man, how much more time we gonna waste on this BS? We got work to do!"

Oddly, it was Jack who came to my defense. "C'mon," he told his buddy, "you wouldn't deny me the chance to have my brain picked by our hot lady psychic!"

This made Donny relent, but the flattery didn't move me. I sensed Jack would have flirted with any passably attractive woman who wasn't already attached to one of his band mates.

He settled on the barstool next to me with a big, toothy

smile—one I'm sure had dazzled countless groupies. "How's it going? Anybody here giving off bad vibes?"

"So far, just the woman in the car who passed me on my way in," I told him, honestly. "You seemed pretty sure that was Melissa Larkin."

"Well...maybe not the way you described her. Last time I saw her, she had straight brown hair and kind of a dumpy figure. But that definitely is her car."

This news set me wondering. Someone else could have borrowed Melissa's car, of course. But a person also could lose weight and dye her hair. "Why did Mad Love start banning her from their events?"

Jack made a face, as if already bored by this topic. "Lessee... Alan hired Lark a few months before our tour to keep track of appointments and run errands. Once or twice, her kid sister pitched in to help. After a while, the sister kept showing up, even when Lark didn't need her or wasn't around."

"She'd go to Alan's apartment?" I remembered Melissa describing the decor before I'd seen it myself.

"Maybe. I just know Alan complained Melissa kept turning up unexpectedly and doing things he hadn't asked her to. When we went on tour, that solved the problem. Lark came along, but not Melissa."

"And after you got back?"

Jack shrugged. "She must've done something else to piss Alan off. Don't know what it was, but Lark's kept her away from us ever since."

I made a couple of notes, thinking the person I really needed to talk to about this was Lark.

Meanwhile, Jack tried to turn on the charm again. "Why all these question about Barkin'—about Melissa? I thought you wanted to know about us."

"I'm mostly interested in anybody who has a grudge against one, or all, of you." I smiled in a way meant to discourage rather than encourage him. "Barry, for instance. How did you feel about his getting fired?"

"I dug Barry. Like me, he thought the whole point of being a rocker was to have a good time. 'Course, he needed a little more

help having a good time than I do. I'm happy with a bottle of
Dewar's and a pretty lady...or two." He winked at me. "Even
when Barry got into the hard stuff, I would've cut him some
slack. Alan couldn't deal with it, though, probably 'cause of how
his mother died."

"Mmm-hmm, he told me about that," I admitted. "Was the
vote to fire Barry unanimous?"

"Except for Donny. He was just loyal—he and Barry go way
back."

I felt a firm hand on my shoulder and looked around into
Alan's startling eyes. I hoped at some point I would get over the
effect they had on me close-up.

"Hate to cut you short, Quinn," he said, "but we do need to
get back to rehearsing. I thought you'd have more time, but that
business with the fire put us behind schedule."

I looked at my watch—it was already three. "That's okay.
Donny's the only one I haven't talked to, but maybe I can get
him on the phone sometime."

"Sure thing. I'll ask him to call you."

The guys went back to their places on the low stage and
started working on a number from the new album. Carla and
May hung out on the couch for a while to listen, so I pulled up
an armchair and did the same. I enjoyed the glimpse behind
the scenes and the changes the band made in the way they'd
perform the songs onstage.

I commented that Mad Love couldn't possibly develop their
whole show in this space, and Carla laughed. "Oh, no way! To
work with the full stage, lights and special effects, they rent an
airplane hangar back in Jersey."

The band ran through a couple more rocking numbers from
the new album, everybody getting into it this time and moving
around more. They also did a slowed-down, eerily quiet cover
version of the Stones' hit "Gimme Shelter" that curled my
naturally straight hair.

When Alan moaned, "Rape, murder/It's just a shot away, it's
just a shot away!" the words sounded a bit too prophetic.

All the guys are so talented, I thought, and work together
so well. At least from what they'd told me, they all got along

pretty well, too. Yet the sabotage of the vehicles, the sinister messages and gifts left at Alan's apartment and the "accidents" at events that were closed to the general public...all of those things suggested an inside job.

One of the band members, or someone else close to them, was allowing these things to happen. Or worse, making them happen.

Watching the rehearsal, I remained conscious of the long drive home that lay ahead of me. When things started to get detail-oriented and repetitive, I waved discreetly at everyone and made a quiet exit.

Outside, the two bodyguards sat on hay bales near the barn playing cards. The manure pile—a miniature, spent Vesuvius—lay smelly but dormant as I passed. Something about that spontaneous fire still bothered me, too. Maybe my nerves were just overwrought from the strain of acting as a detective all day.

I started to unlock my car and found I had left it open. Probably, I'd been distracted by having to prove my identity to the guards when I'd arrived. Oh well, this was a farm, not downtown Elizabeth! Not that I'd left anything valuable inside, anyway.

I turned the ignition key and nothing exploded. I drove back out past the field, where the three spotted horses now grazed peacefully, and soon reached the highway.

The sun had sunk low, and when I made a southwest turn, the molten glare struck my windshield full-force. I folded down my visor and groped on the passenger seat for the cheap, tubular case that normally held my sunglasses.

It was gone.

Strange. I distinctly remembered tucking my glasses into the case and leaving it on the seat. I rummaged in my purse anyway, by Braille. Not there, either. Well, maybe it had slid to the floor of the car when I'd turned out of the driveway. I'd squint until I made the next turn and check more thoroughly when I got home.

I switched on the radio, searching for music, then decided instead to do just a little more sleuthing during my drive. It was time again for Reverend Willis' radio show.

Would he have anything to say about the protest at Sanktuary or about his pal Mayor Randall having a son in a "decadent" Goth rock band?

I was almost disappointed that this afternoon the Rev touched on neither of these topics. Instead, he was talking about angels.

CHAPTER 21

Reverend Willis expounded, in his actor's voice, about the many references to angels throughout the Old and New Testaments. He noted that they most often served as messengers from God—sometimes directly protecting people and sometimes warning them of things to come, so they could better protect themselves.

Even though I'd had some religious education in my younger days, it had been a long time since I'd given any thought at all to angels. I realized I didn't believe in them, which some people might find surprising, since I'd had first-hand experience with ghosts. Was an angel that much stranger a concept?

A woman named Sheila phoned in to testify that her guardian angel had helped her to kick her serious cheesecake habit and lose forty pounds. That weight-loss tip was new to me. I figured if Sheila could expand it into a diet book, her angel might make her not just thin but also rich.

Another caller drew Willis into some rather tedious analysis about the exact nature of angels, based on evidence from the Bible. Reminded of the medieval scholars who debated how many angels could dance on the head of a pin, I started to lose interest.

Just as I was about to change the station, I heard a voice that sounded familiar. "Hi, Reverend Willis, it's Bill Canfield."

My ears perked up. Hadn't that been the name of the Christian reporter who'd seemed so hostile at Mad Love's press conference?

"Hello, Bill, always good to hear from you," said Willis. "What's your question?"

"You said angels still walk among us today, offering us protection and guidance, if we're open to them. What about avenging angels?"

Willis hesitated. "Avenging angels? Not sure what you mean."

"In the Bible, God also sent angels to punish sinners. In Job, especially, it says 'If their souls should perish in their youth, yet their life shall be wounded by the angels' and 'Riches unjustly accumulated shall be vomited up, an angel shall drag him out of his house.' Do you think God still uses angels to frighten or harm the wicked?"

From the moment of dead air before Willis responded, I guessed the idea made him a bit uncomfortable. "That's an interesting question, Bill," he stalled. "You don't hear too many sinners today admit that they've been wounded by an angel! But you do hear reformed sinners say a particular person or situation influenced them to mend their ways. So maybe that was the work of an angel."

I sensed such a gentle interpretation left Bill unsatisfied. "So, if you know about somebody who's an unrepentant sinner, should you pray for an avenging angel to...set him on the right path?"

"Well, certainly, Bill, I would pray for that person to see the error of his ways," said Willis, still choosing his words carefully. "But I wouldn't think of that as an 'avenging' act. Remember Romans 12:19—'Beloved, never avenge yourselves, but leave it to the wrath of God, for it is written, Vengeance is mine, I will repay, says the Lord.'"

Oddly enough, that biblical quotation seemed to please Canfield. "That's exactly what I thought! Thank you, Reverend Willis."

"Uh...thank *you*, Bill. Brothers and Sisters, that's all the time we have today..." Willis sounded rather anxious to wrap up the discussion with Canfield, as well as his program.

Shaking my head over their exchange, I switched to a music station and some nice, loud rock 'n' roll. I wondered who Canfield had in mind as the target of his "avenging angel." Was he still on a vendetta against Mad Love, or had he moved on to another scapegoat?

For the rest of my drive, I pondered other things. I now knew the secret Alan had been hiding from me, and it was a doozy. I could certainly understand why he'd rather not have video of his bisexual three-way from more than a decade ago go viral just when the band was making it big. Whether they would actually lose fans over the scandal was anybody's guess. But one thing was sure—it would only add to Mayor Randall's disapproval over his son's choice of a partner.

The things Jack and the others had said about Melissa Larkin also piqued my interest, and I resolved to find out more about her obsession with Alan. That meant an in-depth chat with Lark.

And I still needed to talk with Donny, if only on the phone. As a longtime friend of Barry's, he might have some special insights.

Fatigued from my long drive, I finally pulled into my driveway at about six P.M. The turkey wrap was just a memory by now, and I mentally sorted through what I had in the refrigerator for dinner. About to step out of the car, I remembered the sunglasses. Leaned over to look and to grope around under the seat.

Still nothing.

I got out, opened the passenger-side door and made a thorough examination of the beige carpeted flooring. The cheap purple eyeglass case was nowhere to be seen.

Now *that* was weird.

I straightened up and considered possible explanations. The car door had been unlocked, so someone might easily have stolen them. But why? It's not as if they were some designer brand—I'd picked them up in the drugstore.

Leaving the mystery unsolved, I took my notepad, shut the car and headed up the walk to my house.

As soon as I unlocked the front door, I felt a change in the air.

Your nerves are just shot, I told myself. *The weird girl in the car, the fire at the farm, the vanishing sunglasses, all that spooky stuff about angels...*

But once I stepped inside, I knew it was more.

For the first time since I'd gotten rid of my ghosts six months ago, my house felt…wrong.

I might just be in a low mood, but by now I was starting to be able to sense the difference. This crawly feeling through my nerve endings was almost always a psychic warning of trouble. Unfortunately, it wasn't specific enough to tell me what kind of trouble.

I left the door unlocked behind me and started down the front hall with caution. The house was quiet, and I saw nothing out of place. Not that I owned much to tempt a burglar, but the living room's antique Oriental rug—which had come with the house—and some small, semi-valuable artworks on the walls remained untouched.

In the dining room, I could see all the dishes in place behind the glass doors of the old mahogany china cabinet. A glance into the little TV room told me the set had not gone anywhere.

In the kitchen, the vinyl placemat on the floor that anchored Bela's food dish had been knocked askew. Did that mean anything?

I called him and made those high-pitched whispering noises cats seem to find irresistible. (I once read that it sounds to them like a baby bird in distress, which made the idea seem a lot less cuddly.)

No response. Could that be what I'd picked up on—something wrong with Bela?

For the next fifteen minutes, I searched the house for him, pss-pssing all the while. I checked all the closets because, being mostly black and very quick, Bela can slip through a door while I'm holding it ajar and I may not even notice. It wouldn't be the first time he'd been trapped that way for hours, though never with any serious consequences.

I finally found him in my second-floor office. He sat hunched beneath the desk, as he sometimes does during a storm to escape the thunder. But this afternoon the weather was clear.

I cooed and tried to lure him out, but he wouldn't budge. That set me worrying again. Was he sick? I knew cats often hid away when they weren't feeling well.

With some effort, I pulled him out for a quick exam and saw

nothing wrong. He felt tense, though, and the hair along his spine bristled. As soon as I let him go, he scooted back under the desk and settled into his former position.

Back to the wall, watchful.

That made me look over my shoulder, too. I hadn't seen any sign of a human intruder, but...

Bela hadn't acted this way since the departure of the ghosts. He'd been very aware of them, though, sometimes even yowling and hissing at the empty air. Was he picking up on the same presence I felt? Had one of those spirits come back?

Like somebody who thinks she's beaten the flu, only to feel the chills and fever returning, I groaned inwardly. *Please, not again!*

On the other hand, the ghosts never had done me any real harm. Remembering that eased my fears somewhat.

I crept back downstairs, still checking around every corner, and finally locked the front door. As I passed through the living room, a shadow flitted across the bay window, just visible through the lace curtain.

I froze, heart hammering. Stole to the window and pulled the curtain aside. Saw no one in the yard.

Just a cloud or a blowing branch. The wind does seem to be kicking up.

Stepping back into the hall, I glanced at the cordless phone on the table there. Should I call someone for help? My first thought was Tony—but no. Even if we had been speaking to each other this week, he'd be in the middle of his workday, and he couldn't leave just because I was feeling spooked by shadows.

The cops? I'd seen no evidence of any suspicious *person* lurking around.

Nancy was a better bet. She lived in the next town, she had some experience with my paranormal adventures, and being a part-timer like me, she might be home.

I called her cell, but she didn't answer, so I left a message. Trying not to alarm her too much, I just asked her to call me as soon as possible.

After I hung up, I listened to the house around me and sent

out feelers. No suspicious noises, but still that vibration in the air. I picked up my notepad from the hall table and went back up to my home office to check on Bela.

He hadn't moved, but chirruped a plaintive greeting when he saw me.

"Don't worry, pal," I reassured him. "I won't let anybody hurt you."

He seemed a bit calmer now. Maybe our unseen threat had backed off, for the moment.

By now I was really hungry, but for some reason I still didn't feel comfortable going back downstairs. If Bela had decided to hide up here, maybe he had his reasons? I'd wait a little longer; see if the uneasiness passed.

Meanwhile, I could transcribe my notes from the day's interviews while everything was still fresh in my mind. I opened my laptop on the desk and went into the file I already had created for my Mad Love investigations. I'd finished copying Alan's awkward confession and had just begun the part about the manure-pile fire, when something dark flickered, again, at the corner of my vision.

Another shadow at the window. So quick it barely registered.

Definitely not a human prowler. On the second floor, with no roof below?

Another cloud or bird?

A snakelike hiss near my feet. Bela had backed farther against the wall, eyes fixed on the window, pupils huge. I trusted his sixth sense even more than mine, and my hair stood up, too.

Okay, this sucks. Something really is going on here.

And it didn't feel like the old haunting. Those ghosts only tried to browbeat me into helping them. This felt more like I was being...stalked.

But what the hell could I do? Grab a crucifix? Holy water? Foolishly, some might say, I didn't keep such things around the house.

I could flee to Nancy's place, but what if she wasn't home? And after seeing that shadow flit past the front of the house, I wasn't keen to go outside.

Call Gale? But she's in New York—what can she do?

She'd probably just tell me to use one of her psychic protection spells.

Would that work? I tried to remember one of the rituals her book had recommended for such emergencies.

Still in my desk chair, I planted both feet squarely on the floor and clasped—actually, wrung—my hands in my lap. I squeezed my eyes shut and tried hard to envision a ball of white light around me. Pictured it enclosing me, keeping me safe from any outside harm…

A sack of bricks wrapped in fur landed on my lap. At least Bela had grown brave enough to come out of hiding.

Good idea, pal. Room enough in the ball of light for both of us.

I wrapped my arms around his sleek form and tried again to concentrate, in spite of the pulse pounding in my ears. Too nerve-wracking to keep my eyes closed, though, when I had no idea what—

CRASH!

An explosion at the back sent a tremor through the whole house. Poor Bela dug his hind claws into my lap as he launched himself back under the desk. This time, I yowled.

My bubble of light burst and left me shaking.

What the hell? Someone blew off my back door?

I needed to know, but I couldn't move. Petrified, I just listened to the echoing silence.

No footsteps. Was the stalker just waiting for me to come investigate, so he could—

The ring of my desk phone almost gave me a coronary. Nancy!

But it was my neighbor, Dr. Zimmer. "Quinn, you okay over there?"

"Y-yeah, I think so."

"'Cause I just heard a bang"—he sounded like he was walking with his phone—"and I thought—Oh, Jeez!"

I started walking with my phone, too, down the stairs. I was jogging by the time I reached the kitchen.

A few ceiling tiles lay broken on the floor, and my favorite coffee mug also lay shattered. An orange sunset still glowed through the curtains over the sink, but strangely the back door window was black. When I tried to open the door, it scraped. The mudroom beyond was littered with rubble.

Dr. Zimmer—still on the line, and now standing in his own back yard—confirmed what I feared. "It was your tree, Quinn. A great big limb just fell on your roof!"

CHAPTER 22

In the deepening twilight, Nancy and I assessed the damage—first from inside the house, then from outside.

"Looks like the roof of your mudroom got the worst of it," she said. "The ceiling in there fell, too, but only one window broke. Homeowner's insurance should cover most of your repairs. What's your deductible?"

Still trying to deal with the spectacle of the enormous branch lying across a protruding first-floor section of my roof—and the lingering sense that something had deliberately dropped it there—I took a second to reply to Nancy's question. "I don't remember."

Whatever my deductible was, it still would probably be more than I could easily afford.

"Well, insurance also should cover your costs in having the branch—or should I say, *limb*"—she eyed the full length of the thing, probably about fifteen feet—"cut up and carted away."

"Yeah, but now I'm going to have to get the whole tree taken down, and I doubt it'll cover that." Dr. Zimmer already had given me a number for a tree service he used.

Nancy wrapped one arm around me in a reassuring hug. "You could leave the rest of the tree for a little while. This was the only part really hanging over the house. Maybe it's done its worst for the time being."

"No way," I said, firmly. "That sucker is coming down!"

She picked up on my forceful tone—probably along with the tension in my body—and eyed me curiously. "Come to think of it... You left me that phone message before the branch fell, but you already sounded nervous. Why?"

I couldn't discuss my reasons in the moonlit back yard, where the half-dead maple still loomed over us, as if listening. "Getting cold out here," I said. "Let's go inside."

When Nancy had returned my frantic phone call, I'd mentioned the mess in my kitchen, and she'd thoughtfully picked up some Chinese takeout on her way over. Rob was tied up with business, so she had the evening free, anyhow.

I got out some plates and we ate in the dining room. Meanwhile, I gave her the short version of my eventful day. I skipped the details of my interviews with the band members, since all that was confidential. I did mention the young woman turned away from the farm by the bodyguards, the unexplained fire and Reverend Willis's radio show. I also told her about my sense of foreboding when I'd arrived home, and Bela's agitated behavior just before the accident occurred.

At first, Nancy tucked into her General Tsao's chicken with enthusiasm, but soon my story distracted her enough to slow her progress. "Oh, wow. You actually felt something was going to happen? And the cat picked up on it, too?" She remembered the broccoli floret between her chopsticks and popped it into her mouth. "Well, you must feel better, anyway, now that you know what the premonition was all about."

I did feel more relaxed, by that time, chiefly because of Nancy's levelheaded company. At first, I didn't think I'd be able to eat, but the fragrant chicken lo mein got the better of me. Bela had calmed down also, and brushed against our ankles hinting for some chicken.

I didn't think the threat was over just because the branch had fallen, though. Whatever had *caused* it to fall seemed to be gone. At least, for now.

Though I hated to burden Nancy with my suspicions, I needed to confide in somebody. "The thing is, it felt a lot like the 'premonitions' I've been having about Mad Love's accidents. I'm worried it might be…related somehow."

"Related? You mean, whoever put a whammy on them could have done the same thing to you?"

"Sounds ridiculous, I know, but…remember, after the press conference, my name badge went missing, and later Alan found it under his door with a note saying 'that witch' should back off. So somebody out there knows my name and where I work."

Nancy pondered this. "But not where you live," she added, optimistically.

"Might not be hard to figure out. I'm in the phone listings."

Again, my friend had paused over her dinner to fix me with a steady gaze. "So...you think this person made the tree branch fall."

"I'm not saying someone climbed up there and sawed through it. But there was no *person* obviously responsible for the Rialto accident, either." A pattern occurred to me. "Jeez, it likes dropping heavy things on people, doesn't it?"

"It?" Nancy echoed.

No, I wasn't going to ask her to believe in a servitor, thought-form or whatever. So far, she wasn't treating me like a totally insane person...why push things? I just answered with a shrug.

"Just in case there is something to your theory, can you call Tony to stay with you tonight?"

That *would* be comforting, I thought. I'd probably sleep better with his arms around me. Then I remembered our last romantic night together and how quickly his attitude had changed the following day.

"We're taking a break this week," I told Nancy. "Just until I've solved the case."

"Oh, c'mon, Quinn—"

"His idea, but I agreed to it. At least I won't have to weigh everything I say to him and bite my tongue every five minutes." Especially after the dicey things I'd found out that day during my interviews with the band, I definitely should avoid any temptation right now to leak information to Tony.

"Then d'you want to stay at our place tonight?" Nancy glanced down at the furry black beggar with the white bib who hugged the foot of her chair. "The two of you?"

I'd taken refuge with the Sabatinos once before, during the worst night of my haunting, but I hated to make a habit of it. No reason they should suffer because I'd decided to play paranormal detective. "Thanks, but right now I feel like the danger's passed, so I'll see how things go. Bela makes a great early warning system. If I feel that sense of menace starting up again, though, I might show up on your doorstep."

"Any time. After what you went through last year, I don't like to leave you at the mercy of"—she gestured with her empty chopsticks—"whatever might be at work here. These things really seem to target you!"

No kidding. Gail had warned me that could happen. Which reminded me…

"I do have other resources," I pointed out to Nancy. "After you leave, I'm going to call for backup."

"The cops?"

I could only imagine what they would make of my story about a phantom stalker. "No, somebody who'll actually believe me and may have some useful advice. Someone who's been there and done that."

"Ah," Nancy smiled, "your Obi-Wan Kenobi! Good idea. Tell her there's a disturbance in the Force."

It was after nine when Nancy left and I settled on my living room sofa to call Gail. I worried it might be too late for her—I didn't know when she went to bed—but this wasn't the kind of question that could be handled by email.

Luckily for me, Gail answered the phone promptly and assured me I wasn't disturbing her. I gave her the same rundown as I had Nancy, but included a few more details, such as the shadow I believed I had seen through my windows just before the branch fell.

Alone in the house, I found myself almost whispering. "I'm really worried this *thing*, whatever it is, could be after me now," I finished. "Is that possible?"

Bless Gail, she was the one person I could always count on to take such questions seriously. "I don't know. You think it has something to do with the name tag you lost at the press conference? But you got that back, right?"

"In a way—it was left at Alan's door. He may still have it."

"Did you lose anything else recently? Maybe something more personal?"

I started to say no, then remembered the sunglasses. I told

her how they had disappeared during my visit to the farm. "You don't think—"

"Someone may have taken them for a ritual. They'd be more effective than the name tag. If you've owned them and worn them for a while, they have your skin cells, your DNA."

I gave in to a hollow laugh. "Honestly, Gail! What are we talking about, a bloodhound? It can use those things to track me?"

"Many traditions teach that to harm someone from a distance, you must possess an item that has been in close contact with the person."

I scanned the shadows of the dim room around me, once again alert for spooks. The sight of Bela settled in the armchair and peacefully grooming one hind leg reassured me we probably were safe for the moment.

"Terrific," I groused to Gail. "Nancy invited me to stay at her place to get away from this thing, but if you're right, even that won't help. I might just bring this...servitor... along with me."

"You *might* be safer in the company of other people, but yes, it could follow you."

"So what do I do?" I wailed.

"Have you used the protection ritual I gave you?"

"I tried to this afternoon, but I couldn't really concentrate. I was too rattled."

"Try again, at a time when you're not being threatened," Gail advised me, calmly. "Repeat it two or three times a day. You want to build up a positive field around you this entity won't be able to penetrate."

The concept reminded me of an old toothpaste ad that promised to create "an invisible shield" against decay. Still, I figured I was in no position to scoff. "Okay. Anything else I can do? More active, maybe?"

I heard a sniff. "You could quit this case and let everyone involved know you're giving it up."

"Are you serious?" I couldn't believe I was hearing this from Gail Kleinholtz, the Germanic medium with nerves of steel who'd helped the NYPD solve a few grisly murders. "Is that what you would do?"

"Probably not, but you're not as experienced as I am. This is such an unusual case, even I can't tell you exactly how to handle it. When I think of the amount of will and concentration it would take to raise such an entity... The person behind this could be seriously unbalanced, Quinn. I don't want to see you hurt."

I reflected, miserably, that it might already be too late for me to back out. "Even if I say I'm quitting, how do I know this nut case will call the thing off? Anyway, I'd be leaving the Mad Love guys to deal with it on their own. No, Gail, I think I just need to step up my game and find out who's behind this."

"All right," she said. "Then figure out who wants to hurt the band, who might have seen you at the press conference and resented your interference...and who could have stolen your sunglasses."

I was about to start brainstorming on these questions with her when call waiting announced that Tony was trying to reach me. Since it was past ten o'clock, I figured it wasn't just to chat. Maybe Nancy had told him about the accident at my house. Crap, I should have asked her not to.

I thanked Gail for her help, letting her go to bed, and returned Tony's call. When he asked, "How are you?" I assured him I was fine and started to explain about the tree branch. From his confusion, though, I soon realized he wasn't calling about that.

"Damn, I guess you haven't heard," he said. "Some wacko shot Jeff Randall."

CHAPTER 23

Tony swung by the house to pick me up and, as if Randall were our blood kin, we sped over to Hoboken Medical Center. As we followed the curving northbound ramp to the Garden State Parkway, I got on my cell phone and tried to reach Alan.

No answer, so I left a quick message. "I'm sure you've got more important things to deal with, but if you can spare a second, please give me a quick call and just let me know about Jeff."

At this time of night, the parkway traffic was pretty light. Tony and I passed the first half-mile in awkward silence, until he remembered my initial response to his call. "What was it you said about something falling on your house?"

He hadn't stayed long enough to see the damage from the tree limb, so I explained about that, though not about my premonition.

"Must've been quite a shock," he said, gravely. "Sure you're okay?"

"Physically, yeah—I was upstairs at the other end of the house. It did shake me up at first. Nancy came over, with some Chinese food, and talked me down."

"Why didn't you call—" He stopped himself with a frown. "Sorry. I guess this turned out to be a hell of a time for me to suggest we take a break."

"Well, you couldn't have known a tree would crash into my house...or somebody would take a shot at Jeff. God, I wonder what that's about?"

"Might be connected to all the other things happening to

the band. I've talked to the cops in North Carolina and Florida about the equipment problems Mad Love had during their tour. They questioned the locals and the band's road crew, but never came up with any suspects. Maybe now they'll be able to connect the dots."

"That would be a relief," I said.

Eyes on the road, Tony frowned. "Interesting thing, though... neither of those so-called accidents really endangered any band members. The business with the plane was sure to be discovered the minute they took off, when there was plenty of time to land again—it just kept them from getting to their concert. And the truck that crashed was just carrying equipment."

"You're saying, shooting one of the band guys would be a much bolder move."

He nodded. "As a cop might say, not the same MO."

I bit my tongue to keep from blurting out anything else. To me, the sabotage sounded more in line with Rocky Montanna's blackmail scheme. It would frighten the band members without actually injuring any of them. After all, it would do no good to put them out of commission if the blackmailer was looking for a cut of their profits.

But that was an insight I still couldn't share with Tony.

A light drizzle blurred the highway arc lights, and Tony switched on his wipers, but cruised well above the speed limit. We had never worked as partners at the paper—our beats were very different—and I had to admit it was kind of a rush to be racing through the night with him in pursuit of the same story. Tony's intensity about his work could be kind of sexy. In fact, it was one of the things that had attracted me to him when we first met, four years ago. And no denying he was terrific at his job—a couple of his investigative series had taken major awards.

If he and I *could* work together, we really might have shot at cracking this case. Could we manage to stop arguing for that long?

Soon we left behind the relative emptiness of I-78 East for 1 & 9 North, which thundered with eighteen-wheelers even at this late hour. Tony floored the accelerator, and I figured we'd reach the hospital in about ten more minutes.

My cell phone rang—Alan getting back to me.

"I'm so sorry," I told him as soon as I answered. "What happened?"

"Oh, God." He shuddered a breath. "Jeff and I were coming out of my building. We were about twenty feet from the front door, on that plaza with the big pillars. I hear somebody shout my name, I swing around and there's a guy pointing a gun. Next thing I know, Jeff knocks me behind a pillar, and I hear two shots. Some woman on the street screams. The building security guard runs out and yells for the shooter to drop his weapon. He actually did, and the guard grabbed him."

I tried to picture all of this taking place on the modern, manicured plaza in front of Maxwell Towers. Then again, John Lennon had been killed in front of the Dakota, one of the most elegant old apartment buildings in Manhattan. "And Jeff?"

"He's slumped against the pillar with b-blood soaking through his T-shirt." Alan broke off for a second, then went on in a more heated tone. "While I'm trying to stop the bleeding, the cops drive up at the curb. They're handcuffing this maniac and he actually starts *laughing.* 'You can't arrest me,' he says. 'I'm doing God's work! I'm an angel of the Lord!'"

I felt sick. It sounded like to me somebody stirred up by Reverend Willis's diatribes against the band. My groan made Tony glance over in concern. Partly for his benefit, I confirmed with Alan, "But Jeff's alive? He's in the hospital—"

A sigh of relief on the line. "Yeah, I think he's okay, or he will be. They said the bullet went right through his shoulder... didn't even hit bone. He had surgery, but it went fast. He should be waking up soon."

"Alan, what did the shooter look like?"

He snorted. "Like nobody you'd ever pick out of a crowd. Tall and skinny, pale, slicked-down hair, cheap suit."

"Could it have been that guy from the press conference? The one who gave you such a hard time about being a bad influence on young people?"

A beat of silence. "Shit, you're right! I think it *was* the same guy. I was so rattled, it didn't register with me. How did you know?"

I told him about the call Bill Canfield had made to Willis's radio show. "I got a bad feeling from all his 'avenging angel' talk. I should have called you right then and warned you, but...I had some craziness at my house tonight, too. Nothing compared to what you guys went through."

"Don't feel bad," Alan said. "In a way, you did warn us. You said when you talked to Canfield he sounded like a fanatic. Too bad we didn't check him out right away—damn!"

"Well, all that really matters is, he's off the streets now and Jeff will recover."

"Yeah." Alan's voice thickened with emotion. "Can you imagine—the guy literally took a bullet for me! Not that I wouldn't have done the same for him..."

I reminded him, "Back at the Newark jail, you saved Jeff from the falling light stand. So you guys are about even."

That made him chuckle. "Y'think?"

Once again, I vowed silently to do everything in my power to end the threat against Mad Love. Of course, if the only threat had been Canfield, maybe the case was already solved. I could only hope so.

Tony kept throwing me sidelong glances, and I guessed why. In addition to being concerned about Randall's condition, he probably was hoping for a bedside interview. But now did not seem the right time to ask for that kind of favor.

I just told Alan, "I'm on my way to the hospital now, with my friend Tony. They've called a press conference."

"I know," he said vaguely. "Stern's making some kind of statement."

"If Jeff is awake, I'd like to talk to him about the shooting. I'll certainly understand, though, if he's not up to it."

"Gotta be his decision. I guess the police will want to question him, too, even though I gave 'em the whole story."

"Maybe I'll see you later, then." A bit choked up, myself, I tried to think of something else to say. "Alan, I'm *so* sorry this happened."

"Not your fault, Quinn. From the sound of it, though, our pal Reverend Willis has a lot to answer for. Some 'man of God,' eh?"

"Yeah, right."

After I hung up, I gave Tony a quick summary of what had happened at Maxwell Towers and Jeff's optimistic prognosis. "As for you getting access to him, I couldn't ask Alan just yet. He's a wreck."

Tony reached over and squeezed my hand. "That's okay. Once we get to the hospital, we'll see how things play out. At least it sounds like Randall's going to be okay."

His touch and his words raised my hopes that maybe we could go back to being a team instead of wary competitors. There were still a few secrets I had sworn to keep from him, but I had a feeling some of those would soon be dragged into the open, anyway.

We crowded into a paneled conference room at the rear of the hospital with at least a dozen other reporters, half of them accompanied by TV cameras. Mad Love wasn't quite big enough to inspire a full media frenzy, but any sort of celebrity being shot in front of a luxury apartment building by an obviously deranged man was hot news.

First, a grizzled Dr. Lucas, still wearing his surgical greens, made a statement concerning Jeff's injury and prognosis. In more clinical language, he said pretty much the same thing as Alan had told me.

"Mr. Randall lost a fair amount of blood, but the bullet passed through his shoulder without doing too much damage. He's a strong, healthy young man, and we expect him to make a complete recovery."

Someone asked if the injury would affect Jeff's ability to perform with the band.

"He'll need a period of rehabilitation," Lucas said, "but barring any unexpected problems, he should be back to performing before too long. For any further details, you'll need to ask Mr. Sternberg." He glanced in Stern's direction and offered him the podium.

Stern looked as ragged as I'd ever seen him, unshaven and wearing a rumpled blue windbreaker. I could imagine the level of stress he'd been going through with all of the recent developments.

"I spoke to Jeff a few minutes ago," he announced. "He's awake and resting comfortably, and very grateful for the emergency room staff here at HMC who took care of him so quickly. We also want to thank the security guard and others at Maxwell Towers who helped subdue the gunman before he could do any more harm.

"As for the future, I know fans may be wondering how this... unfortunate event...will affect Mad Love's upcoming tour. Even if we have to adjust some dates, at the moment we intend to go ahead with the tour as planned. We'll keep the fans fully posted as the details are worked out."

Though Stern had not invited questions, a reporter shouted, "Is it true the gunman said he was 'an angel of the Lord' on 'a mission from God'? What did he mean?"

Stern answered with a tight smile. "I'm sure the only one who knows what he meant is the shooter, himself—and maybe his psychiatrist. Thanks, everyone."

Ignoring any further questions, Stern left the podium.

Tony had been tapping away on his laptop throughout the press briefing and now looked up with a frown. "We came all the way out here in the middle of the night for that? It's nothing more than Bardot told you over the phone."

"Stay here," I said. "I'll see what I can do."

Fortunately, most of the other reporters seemed satisfied with the information they'd been given and were starting to disperse, using their phones and laptops to transmit their stories. I was able to intercept Stern on his way out.

"I spoke to Alan earlier," I said. "He told me once Jeff was awake, we might be able to talk to him. If he agrees, of course."

Stern appraised me for a minute with cool, gray eyes. Suddenly, I felt like the worst cliché of a parasitic journalist and fully expected him to tell me to go to hell.

"Alan said you were able to tell him the shooter's name even before we heard it from the police."

I smiled a little. "That wasn't any psychic flash. I heard Canfield call in to Willis's radio show just yesterday afternoon, ranting about angels."

The manager stared a bit longer, and I realized I actually had gained some credibility in his view. "You with that reporter boyfriend?"

"Yes, but he—"

"C'mon with me. Both of you."

CHAPTER 24

Using a special key card, Stern brought us to a VIP wing of the hospital that I would not have known existed. The walls here were tinted a pale gray to match the polished, marbleized tile of the floors. The area had its own visitors' lounge, where Alan and Donny sat in square-cut, designer tweed chairs and drank coffee from real ceramic mugs. They looked almost too disreputable for such an elegant setting in their faded jeans, sweatshirts and jaw stubble.

Stern introduced Tony to Donny, since Alan no doubt remembered my "reporter boyfriend" all too well from the Sanktuary press conference.

"Jeff's awake and not feeling too bad," Alan told us. "Donny and I popped in to see him as soon as they moved him up here, and Jack and Pat are on their way. Right now, his folks and kid sister are in there. After they leave"—Alan glanced at Tony—"I'll ask him if he wants to talk to you."

"I'd appreciate it," Tony told him, respectfully.

He and I sat down opposite the two band members on a sofa that matched their chairs, with a glass-topped coffee table between us. Stern flipped open his cell phone and stepped back out into the hall.

I felt sorry for him—his job as manager seemed to stretch out twenty-four/seven. I asked Donny, "Does Stern have a family?"

"Ex-wife and a daughter in high school. Probably sees more of us than he does of either of them."

Meanwhile, I heard Tony ask Alan, "So, this shooter was the same guy from the press conference? He did sound pretty intense that day, but I wouldn't have figured he'd do anything like this!"

"Me, neither. Guess you never know." Bardot sounded calmer now than he had on the phone, but his hand still shook a little as he took another gulp of his coffee. "But from what Quinn tells me, Canfield is a big fan of Reverend Willis, and that guy's been riling people up against us for months, ever since we got back from our tour. In the back of my mind, I always was afraid something like this might happen."

For a minute, he and Tony speculated further about the connection between Willis and the shooting. Meanwhile, I studied both of them.

I had kidded Tony that Alan reminded me of him, but to some degree it was true. They were similar in height, build and coloring—maybe I had a "type"? Each also seemed ambitious, in the best sense of being passionate about his work and desiring to do it as well as possible.

One thing I liked about Alan, though, was that he didn't take himself too seriously, an attitude symbolized by that purple streak in the front of his hair. Even though he was famous now, with people to run his errands and fans constantly telling him how great he was, he didn't appear to buy into his own hype. He also seemed more in touch with his feelings than the typical guy.

Bardot's androgyny intrigued me, I guess, even though it was the very quality that put him out of my reach.

Maybe, by making comparisons, I'd been selling Tony short. Yeah, he could get a little full of himself now and then, but, he *had* done a lot of good on his investigative beat—uncovered some corrupt situations and spurred some positive changes. He usually came through for me, too, in a pinch. Like when I needed a hornet's nest removed from the ceiling of my porch.

And though Alan would always be prettier—another mixed blessing—Tony did have one advantage at the moment. He was the only man in the room who'd shaved within the last twelve hours.

An audible yawn from across the coffee table brought my attention back to Donny. His short, spiky hair looked positively electrified this morning, and his eyelids drooped with fatigue. Clearly, early hours didn't agree with him.

"Well," he said to me, "I'm just glad they finally caught the guy who's being doing all this stuff! Now maybe we can stop always looking over our shoulders. Besides, it'll take the heat off Barry."

I remembered that was a subject I'd wanted to discuss with him. "You and Barry have been friends for a long time, haven't you?"

"Since high school. We started a band senior year; called ourselves Vertigo. Other members came and went, and after a few years, Jack joined us. Our lead singer quit and Alan came on—that's when we became Mad Love."

"If you and Barry started the group, no wonder he was angry about being let go," I said.

Donny straightened in his seat, a defensive gleam in his eye. "Sure, he was angry, but it doesn't mean he tried to hurt anybody. The problems on our tour...Barry couldn't have done it! He was back in Nyack working construction."

I nodded. "That's what his father told the cops."

He picked up on my implication. "I *know* he was, 'cause I talked to him from the road. I'd call him during the daytime, and I could hear the machinery an' stuff in the background. He'd got over the hard feelings by then, at least with me. He'd just ask what kind of crowds we were getting and where we were headed next."

That caught my attention. "So he had the band's whole tour schedule?"

Donny chuckled. "It's no secret—it's all up on our website. Doesn't even take too much more digging to find out what hotels we're at or when we're flying out. Hell, even groupies manage to hunt us down—"

Shouts echoed from the hospital corridor. I recognized one of the agitated male voices as Jeff's.

"Aw, shit!" Alan sprang to his feet and bolted toward the noise, the rest of us trailing after.

A middle-aged, brunette nurse was ahead of us all, striding purposefully toward the open door of Jeff's private room.

"Your reputation! God, that really is all you think about, isn't it?"

"Of course not! I care that you put your life in danger, all for—"

The nurse disappeared into the doorway, and her firm voice rose above the others. "Sir, your son is recovering from surgery. He can't have this kind of agitation. I'm sorry, but I'll have to ask you to leave."

We all halted a few feet back from the doorway, not wanting to add fuel to the domestic fire.

We heard a few lower-decibel grumbles and curses, then a second woman's milder plea. "Come on, dear; let's go downstairs and get some coffee. We'll come back later."

Finally a red-faced Steve Randall stalked out, his slim, fiftyish, blonde wife clinging to his arm and his coltish teenaged daughter close behind. He pulled up short when he saw Alan at the front of our group.

"You're responsible for this!" Mayor Randall bellowed, stabbing the air with a finger. "If it wasn't for *you*—"

Then his gaze jumped to another spot, just over my shoulder, and he shut his mouth. He must have recognized Tony and still had the presence of mind not to blow up in front of a reporter. He shook his head in disgust and let his wife tug him away.

Jeff's teenaged sister hung back just long enough to send Bardot a look of apology before she followed her parents.

I also felt moved to console Alan and put a hand on his shoulder. "He didn't mean it. He's just upset about Jeff."

The lean shoulder slumped beneath my touch. "Nah, the man hates me."

Tony's voice, behind us. "Uh...maybe this isn't the best time..."

I cringed, but Alan faced around with a hint of a smile. "The interview? Wait here a sec."

He stepped into Jeff's room, and they conferred quietly for a minute. Then Alan put his head out again with a devilish grin. "No problem, guys, c'mon in!"

Donny's phone rang. "Hi, honey!" He took it back to the visitors' lounge.

Tony and I found Jeff propped up by the adjustable bed, his shoulder-length, Tarzan hair fanned out over the pillow and his right arm in a sling. An IV tube drained into the back of his other hand. Some of the usual healthy color had gone from his face and the sky-blue hospital gown barely stretched to accommodate his athletic torso, but he greeted us cheerfully.

"Sorry you had to hear that." Jeff's voice sounded hoarse, probably from the breathing tube during surgery. "Even when I'm flat-out in a hospital bed, my Dad can't resist telling me how to run my life." He motioned with his free hand for us to pull up seats. "What d'you want to know?"

Tony, bless him, did not attempt to pry into Jeff's personal conflicts with his father, and I doubt the guitarist would have talked about those, anyway. He simply asked Randall about his own recollections of the shooting and whether it left him with any concerns about the tour.

The last question brought some of the warmth back into Jeff's cheeks. "Hell, I'm more determined than ever! I don't know if Canfield was working alone or if somebody else put him up to this, and I can't speak for the rest of the band, but nobody's gonna intimidate *me*. I can't wait to get a guitar in my hands again, and I can't wait to get out on tour and see all our fans." Fire in his eyes, he told Tony, "You can put that in your paper!"

Tony smiled, transcribing the quote onto his laptop. "I will. I'm glad to hear you're not changing your plans, and I hope Canfield's arrest means the end of all the band's problems."

"Amen." Then Jeff croaked a laugh and added, "As Reverend Willis might say!"

Privately, I reflected that even his father the politician couldn't have delivered a more rousing sound bite.

The nurse knocked at the doorjamb. "Excuse me...Mr. Randall needs to rest now."

Obediently, Tony and I stood and wished Jeff a speedy recovery. Alan stooped over the bed, wrapped his arms around his partner—carefully avoiding the sling—and gave him a quick kiss on the lips. "I'll be back later."

"I'm not going anywhere," quipped Jeff.

As we stepped back into the hall, Tony raised an eyebrow at me, which I ignored.

"I hope you can find your way out of this top secret wing,"

Alan told us. "It's like the Pentagon. I couldn't even tell you how I got here."

"I'm sure we'll manage," I said.

He shook his head. "God, d'you believe Randall? Just out of surgery a couple of hours, and he's ready to go back to work! Every time I close my eyes, I still see that lunatic pointing the gun at us, but Jeff—" He broke off, looking down the hospital hallway, his eyes glistening. "I don't know if I'd be as brave. He's still got his fighting spirit."

Tony lightened the mood with a sly smile. "It probably helps that he's really pissed at his father."

Alan laughed. "Also, that he's on some serious painkillers!"

We found Stern, who was able to direct us back down to the hospital parking garage. On the way, Tony finally commented to me, "I'm starting to understand why they made you sign a non-disclosure agreement." When I gave him a warning look, he raised his hands in surrender. "Hey, it's off the record. Their relationship has nothing to do with my story—though it does help explain why the mayor's so bent out of shape."

"His dad never wanted Jeff to be a professional musician, anyhow," I explained. "I guess finding out he was involved with Alan was the last straw."

As we walked to Tony's car, he slipped an arm around my waist. "Now I also understand why you kept telling me I had nothing to be jealous about."

By this time, I had to acknowledge the same thing to myself. "I guess even when a person's bisexual, sooner or later he's going to fall in love and choose a partner. Looks like Alan's made his choice."

"Guess so." We strolled together in silence for a bit. "But even though I may not be the psychic one, Quinn, I'm sensing you still like him."

"I do *like* him," I admitted, carefully. "Strange as it might sound, he's become a friend, and—"

"Hey, I saw you puttin' your hands all over him!" Tony pawed my shoulders like a manic golden retriever until I had to giggle.

"I was not—not like that, anyway!" I realized the scene we'd witnessed in the hospital room had finally freed Tony up to make a joke of his jealousy.

We reached his car, and he drew me around to face him. "I'll take some of the blame. Maybe I just haven't been trying hard enough to get Bardot out of your head."

I didn't agree out loud, but leaned happily into the embrace. "Well, my not being able to share information with you did make things tough."

"True. But now that the culprit is in custody, and even Alan and Jeff don't seem concerned who knows they're a couple, why don't we forget about this 'taking a break' business?" He massaged my back through my sweater and it felt delicious. "How about after I file my story—and both of us get a little rest—we go out someplace nice for dinner?"

I couldn't resist teasing him. "You mean, like a real date? Been a while since we've done that!"

"Exactly. We'll get a bottle of wine and toast to the end of Mad Love's problems and to no more secrets between us. And after that…maybe your place?" Tony waggled his dark eyebrows like Groucho Marx to suggest how the rest of the evening might go.

"Hmm…I don't have to be at work tomorrow, but you do," I reminded him.

"I'll bring a change of clothes."

We kissed—for a rather long time, considering it was a public parking lot. If that was a taste of how he intended to get my mind off Alan, I was very much looking forward to the rest.

For the moment, I did not mention to Tony that I was not so sure all the threats to Mad Love were in the past. Heck, why spoil a good thing?

CHAPTER 25

That evening, Tony and I had a lovely, relaxed dinner at The Coach House in downtown Crane's Crossing. Even though I drank more wine than I should have, and did confide a bit more about Mad Love's situation, I managed not to say anything about the looming threat of blackmail against Alan.

Back at my place, Tony gave a long whistle of sympathy over the damage the fallen tree branch had done to my mudroom. Even then, I said nothing to suggest it might have been the work of some supernatural force.

Over the past year, Tony had come to accept the reality of the ghosts in my house and of my special affinity for such things. Still he probably would find the servitor explanation for the band's accidents much harder to swallow. No doubt, he'd blame Gail for filling my head with bizarre, frightening theories. We'd have another fight, and I'd be left alone in the house for the night, which was *not* what I wanted.

So, by keeping a few more secrets, I earned the pleasure of Tony's company. We really steamed up the sheets that night, for the first time in a while. Afterward, I felt safe and protected, lying next to my man. I'm not normally into games, but I started to think if making Tony jealous had this effect, maybe I should have tried it sooner.

At one point, during our pillow talk, he confessed it wasn't just the competition between us over the Mad Love case that had made him so surly. "When you started getting phone calls and texts from Bardot, and spending all this time around him and the band, I could see you were enjoying it. And...I didn't know how I could compete with that."

"Well, it *was* a bit heady," I admitted, "but mostly because this is the first time I've ever tried to use my abilities to help someone else. The funny thing is, I never thought I wanted to. Now that I've been sort of recruited, though, it's exciting to think I might be able to make a difference." I brushed the dark forelock back out of his eyes. "But it's a professional excitement. You, of all people, should know how that is."

He responded with a skewed smile. "Yeah. Besides, after hearing the way Bardot talked about Randall today, and seeing their big good-bye smooch, I'm feeling not-so-threatened anymore."

"Good." I massaged his naked shoulder. "Whatever it took, I'm glad you've got your...er...confidence back."

Of course, a leopard can't change his spots entirely—or a journalist his fonts? The next morning, while I poured us some cereal for breakfast, Tony fetched the *Sentinel* from my front walk, eager to check out his story in print. While sipping coffee, he also flipped open his laptop to see how the other news outlets had played it online.

One of his emails, though, brought him up short. "Whadya know? I seem to have a message from Reverend Willis."

"No kidding?" No mystery how Willis would have known how to reach him—our *Sentinel* email addresses appear at the ends of all our stories. "Maybe he found out what you were up to last night! We'll be the next ones he denounces on his radio show."

Tony didn't even chuckle—he was too busy reading the email. Because of his frown, I asked what it said.

"Mostly what you'd expect. He deeply regrets what Canfield did, it came as a complete shock to him, he would never condone violence...yadda yadda. But he does say something odd at the end."

"Oh?"

"'Your article all but accused me of inciting this attack on Mad Love, and I want to state that was never my intention. For the real source of the problem, I suggest you look closer to home.'" Over the raised lid of the laptop, Tony met my eyes. "Wonder what the hell he means."

"Closer to home?" I echoed. "Does he mean *you* stirred up the violence? Or maybe the media?"

"Or somebody within Mad Love is responsible?" Tony guessed. "But that's ridiculous. Canfield was from Willis's camp. He didn't even know anybody in the band, not personally."

"Maybe you need to ask the Rev himself what he means," I said.

Tony blotted his mouth with a napkin, then powered off and shut the laptop. "I will...in person. The radio station's not too far from here. I can pop over there this morning."

He called his editor about his plans, then quickly showered and changed into his fresh clothes. Oh, well, it wasn't as if I'd expected a lazy morning-after with him, not on a workday.

About twenty minutes later, Tony emerged looking sharp in dark slacks, a button-down shirt and a classic blue blazer. I gave him an admiring once-over. "You should pass muster, even at a Christian radio station."

"Thanks. I figure if I get in Willis's face, he'll be less likely to play guessing games with me."

"Go get 'em, tiger!" Before he headed out the door, I grabbed him for a big good-bye smooch of my own.

After he left, I continued to wonder if Willis could have inside knowledge that someone in the Mad Love's own camp was sabotaging them. But how, unless he really had a hot line to the Almighty?

I'd considered the theory before, though, and it still worried me. In fact, left alone without any other distractions, I felt a growing sense of unease. Nothing to do with my own safety this time, though, which suggested more trouble for the band.

I glanced at the clock—just past nine. Almost twenty-four hours since Tony and I had left the Mad Love guys at the hospital, and I'd heard nothing more about Jeff's condition. With all the personal stuff he and Alan were going through, I hated to phone either of them.

I still had Stern's cell number, though, and after yesterday I seemed to have his respect, too. No harm in giving him a call, just to make sure everything was okay.

He answered in a measured, almost cautious tone. "Hel-lo?"

When I started talking, I heard him relax. "Quinn! Sorry, I didn't recognize your number."

"That's okay. I hate to be a bother, but I just wanted to find out how Jeff is doing."

"Pretty well, considering. They discharged him last night, and he's over at Alan's now."

"They let him out already? That's good."

"Yeah, I guess the hospital was tired of fielding questions from the press, and Jeff was getting antsy, too. He can heal just as well at Bardot's place. We even have a bodyguard staying at the apartment, to be on the safe side."

I wouldn't have minded recuperating in Bardot's ultra-hip apartment, even without any romantic benefits. "How does Jeff's family feel about that?"

"Oh, his dad's spitting nails, of course. Guy's a piece of work!" After a beat, Stern broached a new subject. "I see your boyfriend broke the news this morning about the shooter's connection with Reverend Willis."

"Yeah. That's another situation that should have interesting repercussions."

"It already has." Stern adopted the careful tone again. "I heard from Willis myself this morning."

"Oh?"

"He left a message on my office phone. I never met or even spoke to the guy before, but he was ranting at me! Said he didn't send Canfield to shoot anybody and he won't be threatened."

"You threatened him?"

"No, but apparently somebody called him and said he'd better get 'his people' under control. Said if anything like this ever happened again, he'd meet his Maker a lot sooner than he'd planned."

"Huh!" I sat down in the nearest kitchen chair to assimilate this new idea. An unknown person actually protecting Mad Love?

"Willis assumed it was me, but he had to admit my voice didn't sound the same. Of course, I told him I don't go around bullying people like some kind of thug."

"It wouldn't have been anyone in the band? Maybe one of

the other guys had too much to drink?"

"I guess that's possible, but I'm betting it has to do with... our other situation."

Despite my lack of sleep, I caught on quickly. "Your would-be blackmailer? Of course! As long as he thinks his scheme still might work, can't squeeze money out of a dead man."

"You got it. Montanna wouldn't want anything to happen to Alan, and even an injury to Jeff hurts the band's earning capacity."

I wondered if the phone call to Stern could have caused my own sense of foreboding. "Sounds like you've still got troubles. But at least these bad guys would rather have your clients alive than dead."

"Yeah, guess that's one bright spot," Stern admitted dryly. "By the way, Quinn, did you send Jeff a gift basket this morning?"

"Sorry, not me."

"That's funny. When I came by Alan's apartment, there was a basket of oranges outside the door, with a florist's tag that said 'Get Well Soon'! But no signature. Maybe it came from Jeff's family."

Like a sore tooth that flares when you probe it with your tongue, my sixth sense started to throb again. "Did they open it? Did Jeff eat any?"

Stern chuckled. "No, I think everybody's kind of afraid to touch it. Because of all the dead bird stuff, y'know? Probably silly, but—"

"No, *not* silly," I said. "Leave it alone. Do you have security people who can check it out?"

"Yeah. You really think—"

"Call them. And I'll be right over."

CHAPTER 26

I parked in the lot behind Alan's building and hurriedly logged in my name and license plate at a desk in the rear lobby. Meanwhile, I noticed the uniformed guard simply nodded to three other people who came in after me. Only one had a key, but she held the door for the other two.

A question occurred to me, and I wondered if I had time to ask it. Maybe… After all, Stern would have relayed my warning not to open the gift basket. That should buy me at least a few more minutes.

In a teasing way, I asked the middle-aged guard (Jerry, according to his brass name tag), "How come those folks didn't have to sign in? I guess they live here?"

"Oh, yeah," he said genially.

"Isn't it hard for you to keep track? I hear the building has about four hundred residents."

"Well, I've been here ten years, and we haven't had that much turnover. After a while, I know most of the faces, even if I might not remember all the names."

That made me wonder. If somebody came in and out often enough, would a guard just assume he or she lived there?

Stretching the truth a bit, I said I was writing an article about Mad Love and their recent problems. "Alan's had a few anonymous packages left outside his door. They're probably just from fans, but after this recent shooting, he's gotten more nervous."

Jerry stroked his comb-over. "Cops questioned all of us about that. I told them the only folks I see going up to Bardot's place are his usual crowd."

"His crowd?"

"His entourage, I guess you call it." Jerry flashed a row of ivory teeth with a gold crown toward the back. "The other band guys…I know all of them. His manager. The lady designer who worked on his apartment. And there's a coupla gals who do stuff for him. Run errands."

"A couple?" I asked. "I know about Lark. She's the tall blonde with all the hardware."

The guard made a face. "Never understood why kids wanna do that to themselves, 'specially a pretty girl like her. What's her name—Lark? She signs in as Jessica Larkin."

"It's a nickname." Conscious of the minutes passing, I prodded him. "But you said there was another girl."

"Yeah, a littler one. None o' those piercings—even dresses kinda dumpy."

My pulse quickened. The guys said Lark had been ordered months ago to keep Melissa away from the band. Was Alan's assistant still secretly allowing her sister to help her with some chores? Or was Melissa slipping in and out of the condo building without Lark's knowledge?

I told the guard, "Alan got another delivery today he wasn't expecting—a basket of oranges. You didn't see who delivered it, did you?"

Jerry shook his head. "Something like that usually goes to the front desk, and they wouldn't send it up unless they buzzed the apartment first."

It would go to the front desk if it came from a regular florist or gift basket service, I thought. But Alan's strange "presents" had been delivered right to his door.

I knew I had to get moving, but asked Jerry, "Will you be here for a while?"

"'Til four," he said, with another friendly smile.

Starting to put the pieces together in my mind, I hurried on up to Bardot's apartment.

Stern let me in with a vexed expression. "Glad to see you. Maybe you can talk some sense into Alan—he's already started unwrapping the damn basket!"

In the living room, Bardot and the mustached bodyguard

I'd met at the farm bent over something on the art deco cocktail table. Yellow cellophane and gilded, wire-stiffened ribbon already lay to one side, and the two of them were setting aside oranges as if they were live grenades. The guard wore thick work gloves, Alan black leather motorcycle gloves with cutouts at the knuckles, which might have been part of a kinky stage costume.

Jeff, his arm still in a sling to support his wounded shoulder, looked on from the safe distance of the hall doorway. With a tremor, he asked, "Bardot, haven't you ever heard that old expression, 'Curiosity killed the lead singer'?"

"Hey, it's either me or you," Alan shot back. "And you already had one brush with death this week."

"Ya forgot me," cracked the bodyguard. "Guess I'm dispensable..."

"It shouldn't be any of you—it should be the cops!" I scolded. Watching them set my teeth on edge. There was nothing obviously gruesome about either the basket or its contents, but at some deeper level, the sight repelled me. It was the same kind of reaction I'd had to the cardboard file box of hate mail.

"That's what I told them," Stern fumed, also keeping his distance from the mess on the coffee table. "But when Bardot gets something in his head—"

Unfazed, Alan lifted out the fourth of eight oranges. "Oh, hell, we could see the basket wasn't wired to blow up or anything. We've got gloves, so we're not really *touching* anything or leaving any prints of our own. Probably a false alarm, anyway. So far, it's just fruit, a little plastic grass, and—*Hel*-lo!"

From the bottom of the basket, he plucked a long, coal-black feather.

"Damn," breathed Stern.

"Looks like there's a note, too." Alan unfolded a piece of lavender paper and read dramatically. "'And my soul from out that shadow that lies floating on the floor shall be lifted—nevermore!'"

"From 'The Raven' by Poe," I muttered.

"I knew that!" He threw me a crooked smile.

Stern also glanced at me, far less amused. "You were right,

Quinn. It's our bird-brained stalker again."

"Looks like he's after me this time," Jeff noted. "I've got a well-known thing for oranges."

"Who knows about that?" I asked him.

"The band guys and probably lots of people from our last tour."

Alan nodded. "I used to kid him about it because I'm not into fruit at all. When we had a catered spread, I'd save him a couple of oranges."

Whoever had sent the basket, I thought, must have known that Jeff, but not Alan, would eat the contents. Still, could it be just a macabre get-well gift from one of their Goth fans?

Based on the vibes it gave me, probably not.

"Alan, can I borrow your gloves?" I asked.

Wearing them, I stepped into the bright sunshine that poured through the window wall and held one of the oranges almost up to my nose. The thousands of tiny dimples in the peel acted as camouflage, but when I squinted I could detect a tiny, clean puncture. About an inch over, I found another…and another…

Probably one for each segment.

I dropped the orange back onto the table like it was a hot coal. Bile rising in my throat, I wiped my gloved hands on my jeans. "It's injected with something."

The taut silence among us was shattered by the chime of the doorbell, and we all jumped. The bodyguard answered it cautiously.

Lark stepped in, wearing an unusually practical outfit that day—black leggings with a gray tunic—and carrying a huge hobo purse. When she saw our relieved expressions, she stopped short.

"Oh, crap. What happened *now?*"

CHAPTER 27

Stern called a private lab—no doubt, the same one that had done the necropsy on the crow—to collect the basket and its worrisome contents. They promised to pick it up within the hour and to have the test results by the following afternoon.

"I don't get it," said Lark, perched like a macabre but graceful stork on the wide arm of one of the living room's deco leather chairs. "I thought the guy who caused all this trouble was in jail."

The rest of us all exchanged glances. Jeff was the one who finally said, "Guess there's more than one person out there who *really* doesn't like us."

Alan sank down on the sofa and rumpled his iridescent hair with one hand. "But it doesn't make sense. I mean, if it's blackmail, why would he want either one of us dead?"

This time, the rest of us all looked at him sharply, and Lark echoed, "Blackmail? Who said—"

Stern cleared his throat. "He's just guessing, Lark."

Plainly, the other three wanted us ladies out of the way so they could discuss certain sensitive issues.

"Hey, Lark," I said, "you're the only member of the band's inner circle I haven't interviewed so far. How about we take a walk and leave the guys to map out their strategy?"

Though still looking confused, she came along with me.

We left by the building's rear exit, where Jerry the guard gave us a nod of recognition. I was glad to see him still at his post...I might need him soon.

Alan's building was one of several that backed up to a waterfront park and walkway. As Lark and I stepped out into the dazzling June day, all the sharply-cut gems of the midtown Manhattan skyline—Empire State, Chrysler and RCA buildings—glittered almost within reach. On our side of the Hudson, we passed a playground and tennis courts, saw young moms and nannies pushing strollers and a couple of people walking dogs.

I asked Lark how long she'd been Alan's assistant—a little over two years, she told me—and what she'd done before.

"I worked for an event planner." She smiled. "I liked that, and I actually left it to try starting my own small company. I asked my kid sister Melissa to go in on it with me, but...that didn't work out too well. Then our Mom got sick, and Melissa started taking care of her."

That conveniently brought up the subject I really wanted to tackle. "Y'know, I met your sister once. In fact, I got her into Mad Love's performance at the Rialto."

Lark's pierced left eyebrow jumped at this news. "Seriously?"

We had reached a landscaped, park-like peninsula that jutted out into the Hudson, with a walkway and arc lights. We sat down on one of several Victorian-style, wrought-iron park benches. I explained the whole coincidence with Melissa, while Lark listened wide-eyed.

"That's so bizarre!" she said. "Sounds like she was trying to bluff her way into the video shoot. She does things like that."

"I wondered, at the time, how she knew so much about Alan, even the decor of his apartment," I went on. "But I understand when you first started working for him Melissa helped you with your errands."

"Yeah." Lark turned her gaze out over the water, the silver stud through her left nostril glinting in the sun. "She used to. It wasn't as if I really needed the help—or as if she got paid for it—but she *begged* me. Then, after a while, she got a little too intense about it."

"Mmm...I heard something to that effect. If you don't mind telling me, why did Alan finally ask you to keep her away from him and the band?"

She frowned at the memory. "It was a few months ago, right after the tour. All the band guys go to this hair stylist in the East Village—Donny knows the owner. Jeff was fairly new to the band, and the others were trying to talk him into get some kind of color streaking, like Alan's. He wasn't going for it, though."

We both chuckled at this, since Jeff wasn't the overly flamboyant type.

"Anyway," Lark resumed, "he and Alan were kidding around, like they always do, when I saw Melissa's face. She suddenly caught on, y'know, that they were together. She looked shocked, like she was going to be sick."

I could easily imagine, having seen variations of that expression on her a couple of times. Aimed, ironically, at me.

"A few minutes later, she whispered something to Alan. I have no idea what, but it seriously pissed him off. You know he's not that thin-skinned, he can take a joke, so she must've really overstepped. As soon she left the room, he took me aside. He said very calmly that he'd hired me but not Melissa, and he didn't want her hanging around anymore."

"That didn't upset you?" I asked.

"Yes and no. I felt sorry for her because I knew by then what a humongous crush she had on him. But in spite of that— or even because of it—I knew Alan was right. If she was going to harass my boss, she could get me fired, and I really like my job." Lark sighed. "Melissa's twenty-four, but in some ways, she still acts like a kid. Sometimes she just doesn't know where to draw the line."

"When you told her she had to stay away from Alan and the band, how did she take it?"

"Oh, she was mad. But not yelling or crying mad. She just gave me that same kind of look, shocked and betrayed. Like, how could I do this to her, my own sister, when I knew she was so in love with Alan? I tried to talk to her, explain it was hopeless with him and she should find some guy who could return her feelings, but she wouldn't accept that."

I tried to break my news gently. "Lark, she still hasn't accepted it." I told her about Melissa showing up outside Sanktuary before the press conference and trying to get into Pat's barn the day of the rehearsal. "I think she's the one who's been leaving Alan these sick notes and 'gifts'...and maybe she sent Jeff the basket of oranges."

The tall, blonde woman swung horrified eyes toward me. "No! I can't believe it."

"Why not? After everything you've told me, it certainly sounds possible. Being so close to you, she probably has ways of finding out Alan's schedule, of getting into this building—"

Lark's eyes, ringed in black liner, turned fierce. "If this is one of your psychic hunches, you're wrong this time! I can't believe she'd keep coming around here after I warned her to stay away."

"I'm not making this up," I told her, sadly. "Let's go back inside. There's somebody I think you should talk to."

Lark might not have believed me, but she couldn't ignore it when Jerry told her pleasantly that a shorter young woman who looked a little like her still popped in about every other week.

"I'll let her in when she's lugging something heavy or got her arms full o' dry cleaning," he said.

"So, you let her in, even though she hasn't got a key?" I tried to ask casually, not making it an accusation.

His rounded features bent in thought. "Actually, I think she's got a key. I'm pretty sure I seen her unlock the door a coupla times."

Probably borrowed Lark's, I thought, just long enough to make a copy. "When was the last time you saw her here?"

"Maybe two weeks ago. 'Course, I'm not on duty every day. Calvin has the desk Friday through Sunday."

By the time Lark accompanied me back to the marble-columned lobby, she looked queasy.

"I didn't think Melissa even had the time or the energy to keep doing stuff like that," she said. "Our mom has cancer— she's home—and even though we've got a part-time nurse, Melissa mainly takes care of her. The rest of the time, she's at her job at Celebration Crafts in Secaucus. She's actually a pretty good artist, and she seemed really into that..." Lark's voice thickened and choked off the rest.

Gee, I thought, a crafts store would be the perfect place to acquire the materials and the skills to put together a professional-looking gift basket. And maybe even to get the feathers, rubber stamps and other props used in those messages to Alan.

Though Lark and I never had been on a hugging basis, I put an arm around her shoulders. "I'm sure it's a shock. I didn't want to believe it either. When I met her, I liked her." Even Alan had dismissed the idea of "little Melissa" being a threat, I recalled.

Lark glanced toward the elevators, her eyes filling. Soon, all of her raccoon-like eye makeup was going to look even scarier. "I need to go back up there. I'm supposed to help out Jeff this afternoon, but now… If Melissa was responsible for all this, what can I say to them?"

"For the time being, I wouldn't say anything." When she stared at me in surprise, I explained, "Up to now, Melissa hasn't done anything dangerous. At least wait until the cops find out what, if anything, is in those oranges."

"Oh, God—" Lark groaned.

I knew what she was thinking. If they did contain anything toxic, her sister would be in very deep trouble.

Just as the elevator arrived, my phone rang. I saw Tony's work number.

"You go on ahead," I told Lark, and she did.

The sound of Tony's voice consoled me a bit after the morning's tensions. "How did you hit it off with the Rev?" I asked.

"My hunch was right," he announced proudly. "This business about him persecuting Mad Love on his radio show? Guess who put him up to it?"

"Mayor Randall."

"Can you believe it? He thought if he could ruin the band, Jeff would break it off with Alan and go back to a straight lifestyle, in every sense."

I sat down on a narrow, upholstered seat near the lobby's indoor waterfall. "Strange Willis would let himself be used that way."

"Except in principle, Willis was fine with it. He's one of these people who thinks gays can change if they just try hard enough, so he didn't mind helping Randall 'rescue' his son. But he swears he never incited anybody to violence, and he's genuinely upset that one of his listeners tried to shoot somebody."

I remembered that when Canfield had called in to the radio show Willis *had* tried to calm him down.

Tony sniffed. "Only problem is, he made me swear to keep all this off the record. The only part I can print is how he regrets that one of his listeners resorted to violence and how he'll never mention the band again on his program."

"I'm proud of you for agreeing to keep it quiet," I told him. "I know you're giving up a big scoop, but it would only have caused more problems between Jeff and his father."

"I wonder if he even suspects his father was involved. I thought I had issues with *my* dad—Say, where are you, anyway? I'm hearing echoes and other voices, and…running water?"

"It's a fountain. I'm in the lobby at Maxwell Towers." I told him there had been another minor crisis, but this time it was averted before anyone got hurt.

"You're kidding. There's *another* stalker?"

"Could be just a nutty fan this time," I lied. "I wish I could tell you more but—"

"I know, the NDA. Well, I'm glad everybody's all right. Be careful, babe!"

"I will." It had been a while since Tony had called me "babe." As endearments go, it struck a pleasantly retro, *His-Girl-Friday* note, which probably suited our relationship.

He added, "Bardot must have figured you solved the case for him, anyhow."

His leading tone made me ask, "Why do you say that?"

"You've got a present sitting on your desk. I figure it's a thank-you from him, for all your hard work." Tony paused, as if strolling by the desk for a better look. "Hey, how does *he* know you like chocolate truffles?"

I made it from Hoboken to Elizabeth in a little over half an hour, luckily without any speeding tickets. As I cruised toward the front of the *Sentinel* building, I caught a glimpse of gaudy color at the curb farther up the street.

Even from a distance, I knew it had to be Melissa's magenta Volvo.

I grabbed the first street parking space I could find, but then hesitated. Did I dare go up on foot to investigate? If Melissa were still in the car, she might just run over me!

While I stood on the sidewalk, undecided, I spotted Alan's strawberry-blond stalker across the street near the *Sentinel's* front entrance. Wearing jeans and a gray hoodie, she loitered by the dispenser that sells copies of the paper. She was reading the day's headlines—or pretending to—so she didn't notice me at all. Did she think I was upstairs in the office? Was she waiting for the ambulance to arrive, so she could gauge whether or not her attempt to poison me had succeeded?

At the next break in traffic, I trotted across the street, effectively cutting her off from her car parked a long block away. I was just a couple of yards behind her when I called out, on a hunch, "Hey, Raven!"

She jumped like a rabbit and spun to face me. At closer range, I was startled at how bony her face looked—more so than when I'd first met her at the Rialto. Her eyes darted to my left, so I dodged that way, still blocking her escape to her car. I reached for her, but she took off at a dead run in the opposite direction.

My adrenaline kicked in. Call me crazy, but I chased her.

One grown woman chasing another down a busy sidewalk may not be as odd a sight in urban Elizabeth as in some other places, but we did draw some stares. Melissa bumped a couple of folks, while one man jumped out of our way—I at least tried to cut around people. Even so, I was gaining on the kid, though I had no idea what I'd do when I caught her.

Instead of crossing the next street, she simply veered right and headed around the block. Maybe she thought she could get back to her Volvo that way. But for someone almost ten years younger and a lot skinnier than me, she seemed to be fading fast.

Before she made it to the end of the block, I caught her by the hood of her sweater and then by her upper arm. The arm shocked me—my fingers closed all the way around it.

Prepared for a struggle, I spun her to face me. "What do you think you're—"

Her eyes rolled back in her head. Like a straw-haired doll, she collapsed in my arms.

CHAPTER 28

Kneeling on the sidewalk and cradling Melissa's full weight—admittedly, not much—I panicked.

What had I done? By chasing her, or by grabbing her, had I harmed her somehow? Made her pass out?

Or—

She *was* still alive, wasn't she?

A few people had paused on the sidewalk to gawk, and I yelled out to them, "Call 9-1-1!"

A sharply dressed black businessman whipped out his cell phone to do so.

Meanwhile, I carefully lowered Melissa to the dirty sidewalk. I put my ear to her chest and listened for breathing or a heartbeat. But over the traffic noise I couldn't pick up anything.

I felt her neck for a pulse. Weak, but yes, there was one.

Had she just fainted, or was it something more serious?

Years back, I'd taken a couple of lessons in CPR, but my memories of it were vague. I was afraid to try anything when I didn't know what was wrong with her. What if I made things worse?

Some of my anxiety also came from another source. As soon as I'd touched Melissa, I'd gotten a jolt of that emotional cocktail of rage, hurt, betrayal—the same as I'd felt when I'd stepped on the dead crow, but this time at full amperage.

No doubt about it, Melissa was Raven. She'd left all those ominous messages and creepy gifts.

Still worried about possibly injuring the unconscious woman, I cupped one of my hands over the other and gave her a few quick chest compressions. Almost instantly, her eyelids fluttered, and I exhaled in relief.

She half-rose on her elbows. "W-what happened?"

"You were running from me, and you passed out." I put a firm hand against her bony shoulder. "Stay where you are. The EMTs are on their way."

"No!" Melissa shoved my hand aside. "I'm fine... Oww!" She tried to stand, but one leg gave out, and she sank to the pavement again.

I still clutched her arm, trying to ignore the psychic malaise that radiated from her like a noxious perfume. "Why are you here, hanging around my office?"

She hesitated a beat too long before playing dumb. "Your office? I don't even know... Who are you, anyway?"

My first instinct was to tell her to cut the act and to accuse her of sending Alan the threatening notes and sending both Jeff and me tainted treats. But so far I had no proof of any of this. If she was guilty of some or all of those things, better to let the cops do the questioning. They surely would, if Jeff's oranges and my chocolates turned out to have been doctored.

A big, square, orange-and-white vehicle with flashing lights pulled up to the curb. This inspired Melissa to make a new and more desperate bid for freedom. I worried that she would refuse treatment and escape before *anyone* could question her. But her ankle seemed to give way, and she looked like she might even black out again.

The EMTs who stepped from the ambulance—one male and one female, both in navy-blue shirts and pants—could clearly see the problem.

The strong-looking, shorthaired woman asked us what had happened. I said Melissa had fainted and fallen, and luckily she didn't mention I had been chasing her around the block. The woman examined her ankle, while the man unloaded a stretcher. Melissa still protested that she didn't want to go to the hospital, but when the EMT gently palpated her ankle, she couldn't help hissing in pain.

"You need to at least get this X-rayed," the woman told her, with quiet authority. "Had anything to eat today?"

Melissa admitted to tea and a slice of toast for breakfast. The EMT glanced at her watch. "It's almost four now...nothing since then?" She continued to question Melissa, while calmly taking her vitals, as if to make sure the girl wasn't starving, homeless and/or under the influence.

Now that Melissa was in more capable hands than mine, my panic eased, and I started to see the situation more clearly. She had not been able to outrun me, and had collapsed from the effort, because she was not well.

A hand on my shoulder startled me. Tony stood there, his dark brows knit with concern.

"I looked out the window and saw the ambulance, and I was afraid it was for you," he said. "What's going on? Who is that girl?"

I kept my voice down. "I think she's the one who sent me the chocolates. She's been stalking the band, and I guess she figured out I've been helping them."

"The crazy fan you told me about?"

I nodded, my attention going back to the EMTs. I could see they were ready to leave with Melissa, and I asked the guy, "Where are you taking her?"

"Elizabeth General."

I opened my cell phone again and told Tony, "I've got to call Lark."

"Who's Lark?"

"Alan's assistant—" I shook my head helplessly. "Sorry, it's a *long* story."

Lark went completely to pieces over this new shock. "Oh my God, I've got to get over there! Elizabeth General? I don't even know where that is."

I tried to give her an idea of the route from Hoboken. "Take your time and don't have an accident. I'm sure once she's at the hospital she'll be all right."

"I hope so. Oh, jeez, what about Mom? It's after four—the home health aide will be gone by now. If Melissa isn't coming home, I need to... But..."

Obviously, poor Lark couldn't be in two places at once. "You go to the hospital and deal with Melissa. Maybe I can go check on your mom. Where is she?"

"Lyndhurst."

I'd driven through it—a small, working-class town near the Meadowlands. It would take a little time, but I could get there. "Okay, give me the address."

"Thanks, Quinn. You're a lifesaver!"

I hardly felt I deserved the praise. After all, I *had* been chasing Lark's sister when she'd dropped from exhaustion. And, in fact, I wasn't offering to look in on their mother for purely humanitarian reasons.

Melissa lived in that house, too. If I could poke around a little, I just might find enough evidence to wrap up this case.

Tony offered to blow off the rest of his workday and come with me to Lyndhurst, in case I needed help with Melissa's mother. I told him it probably was more important for him to have the box of truffles checked out, ASAP, and explained about the gift basket sent to Jeff.

Giving him Stern's number, I said, "He's already got a private lab analyzing the oranges."

Reluctantly, Tony let me drive away solo.

I headed north through Newark via Route 21 toward the Meadowlands. En route, I wondered mostly what I would and would not be able to do for a bedridden cancer patient, at least until someone else with more experience arrived to spell me. Lark was trying to reach a cousin who lived nearby and had helped out in the past, so I figured I might not be left alone at the house too long.

Strange, but at no time during my drive did I consider that I could be walking into a psychic minefield. It didn't even occur to me until I parked across from the shabby little two-story house, the lower half brick and the upper a faded, watery blue, the lawn weedy and overgrown.

This place, I realized, just might have been the point of origin for some very bad stuff.

With few other people around, I paused on the curb, shut my eyes and conjured up Gail's cocoon of white light. Then, though not at all convinced of its protective powers, I finally crossed the street to the Larkin house.

As per Lark's instructions, I found the front door key under a stone frog that nestled among some straggly bushes. When I stepped inside, the atmosphere repelled me on a strictly physical level—a stench of stale cigarette smoke clung to the walls and carpeting of the living and dining rooms.

I ventured ahead cautiously, not wanting to alarm Lark's invalid mother. "Mrs. Larkin? Hello?"

No answer.

I stole down the hallway, where the smoky odor disappeared beneath an even more nauseating sickroom smell. Like Melissa, I hadn't eaten anything since breakfast—though at least I'd had more than a slice of toast—and that turned out to be a good thing.

The first bedroom door stood open and I glimpsed a rented hospital bed with all the hardware. In it rested Mrs. Larkin, her head and shoulders just visible above a pink thermal blanket. Her pale face had a deflated flabbiness, as if in her illness she had lost a lot of weight very quickly.

I said her name again, quietly. When she still didn't respond, I felt a flutter of panic...but no, her chest rose and fell gently. She was just sleeping, and I had no reason to wake her.

I leaned against the doorjamb then, and clenched my jaw to hold back a flood of raw emotion.

My father, the world's nicest guy, had lain in bed much the same way about four years ago. He had quit smoking a while back, but the damage already was done. My mother, who had some training as a nurse, was able to care for him so he could spend his last few weeks at home. More comforting and dignified for him, it still had been pretty hard on Mom and me.

As a result, I always had trouble remembering Dad as the witty, fun-loving and slightly chubby man—who'd been as much as friend to me as a father—without also picturing him lying ashen and gaunt against his pillow. I was visiting one afternoon, stopped by his room to find he had passed on and was the one to relay the news to my mom.

It comforted me to think that whatever afterlife might exist for really good people, Dad certainly was there now. So far, he'd never dropped by to tell me otherwise, and with my newly developed psychic talents, that might have been a real possibility.

The warble of my cell phone yanked me back to the present. To avoid disturbing Mrs. Larkin, I stepped into the hall to answer it.

Lark. I quickly reassured her that her mother seemed okay.

"I reached Cousin Janet," she told me. "She's getting out of work now, and she's just in Nutley. She knows what medicines Mom gets, and all that, so she can take over from you soon."

"Sounds good," I said. "How's Melissa?"

I heard Lark choke up again. "God, Quinn...I saw her in Emergency right after they brought her in. Under those baggy clothes, she was skin and bones. I had no idea! I knew the last year or so she was dieting, but I didn't realize she was starving herself!"

"Do they think that's why she fainted? She's not sick otherwise?"

"They're going to run tests, but from what she told them, she's just not eating enough. She must be anorexic."

And even that, I thought, might be the least of Melissa's problems.

"I feel so awful that I didn't notice any of this." Lark went on, with a hint of self-mockery. "I was *so* busy with my glamorous job and my new husband...I did stop by sometimes to help with Mom, but Melissa always seemed cheerful and able to cope. I never realized she was going off the deep end with her dieting!"

"Don't blame yourself too much," I said. "Even when I met her at the Rialto, she was thin, but not as bad as today. And from what I've heard about anorexics, they can be pretty good at hiding what they're up to. Anyway, now that she's in the hospital, let's hope they can get her well."

"Yeah, thanks. I'm going to try to talk to the doctor now."

After Lark hung up, I remembered I had another job to do at the house, and I might not have much time left.

The next door down the hall was closed. Emanating from beyond it, I felt the now-familiar brew of toxic emotions that seemed to radiate from everything Melissa touched.

Did I dare to explore what could be Ground Zero?

CHAPTER 29

The door was unlocked. I supposed, since her mother was bedridden, Raven didn't worry too much about anyone invading her privacy.

I stepped into her room cautiously, almost expecting some spectral watchdog to leap at me from a shadowy corner. Maybe to guard against such a surprise, I switched on the ceiling light.

The bedroom did not look as if it belonged to a twenty-four-year-old working woman. The walls, ceiling, carpet, drapes and bedspread all appeared to be the same shade of twilight purple. The cheap, outdated French provincial furniture, with only a twin-sized bed, might have been bought for Melissa as a young teen. The desk held an older desktop computer with a tower and a rudimentary printer. I wondered if an expert might be able to tell whether it had produced any of the creepy notes Alan had received.

The dark walls formed a backdrop for dozens of tacked-up paintings and drawings of romanticized Gothic characters with delicate bodies, big heads and wide, long-lashed eyes. The women wore gossamer robes and sometimes wings—a black bird perched on the shoulder of one damsel with long, rippling, golden locks.

They were all done in the same amateurish style, and I had no doubt they must have been painted by Melissa. I remembered Lark saying her sister had artistic leanings. In here, Melissa had created a darkly magical world into which she could escape whenever reality became too painful.

Another painting showed a pale man with tousled, black-and-purple hair, chiseled cheekbones and sad, emerald-green eyes. He was trying to claw his way out of a thicket of twisting branches.

Was that supposed to be Alan?

Oddly, I saw no posters of him or the band. When I half-closed the bedroom door behind me, though, I found a collage on the back. Magazine photos, all of the same ivory-skinned model with cascading waves of strawberry-blonde hair, posed in various high-fashion outfits. One runway ensemble that included a leopard-printed miniskirt and platform boots reminded me a bit of the getup Melissa had worn to the Rialto.

Valery, Alan's ex-girlfriend.

Of course. Melissa had bleached and frizzed her hair, and dieted herself down to a skeleton, to look more like Valery.

Now, though, the model had been replaced in Alan's affections by his lead guitarist. I shuddered to think what drastic physical changes Melissa might contemplate to try to compete with Jeff!

I grew conscious of all the sad, almost accusing eyes watching me from the artwork on the walls. Could those elfin presences somehow report my every move back to their creator? With a shiver, I told myself that I mustn't sink too far into Melissa's mindset—I might end up just as crazy.

The few areas not plastered with her artwork were occupied by her clothes. Behind a folding wicker screen, a pipe rack held flamboyant bits of Goth and groupie outfits. I almost tripped over a boot and found many pairs of footwear jumbled under her bed. Hangers against the opposite wall held what Harry Potter would have called her "muggle" clothes—boringly conventional separates she probably wore to work. They included the sober gray suit she'd used to try pass for a reporter at Sanktuary.

The wardrobes were so opposite that I wondered briefly if Melissa suffered from an actual split personality. But this seemed a more conscious decision to present two different faces to the outside world.

The room also gave me an oppressive, claustrophobic feeling, maybe because of all the insulating layers. Didn't Melissa have a closet?

The hangers against the wall. I'd seen that kind of gadget

before—it hooked over the back of a door.

I pushed the clothes aside and took hold of the closet doorknob. The contact gave me a sick sense of vertigo, and I hesitated. Did I really want to know what lay beyond?

The inside was painted the same purple as the rest of the room, and I had to pull the chain of an overhead bulb to see anything.

A single, straight chair. A small table covered with a pentagram cloth, the kind sold in any New Age store. At each corner, a stubby black candle had melted down into a small brass holder. A larger brass bowl in the center held a scorched, gluey mixture that I didn't want to investigate too closely. It included a few strands of silky brown hair, almost certainly human.

The short hairs on the back of my own neck prickled. Again, I tried to shake off the sensation of being watched.

Wall shelves to either side held a tidy assortment of books, baggies and jars. The reading matter included tomes on witchcraft, voodoo, Santeria and a few other magical traditions I didn't recognize.

I pulled out a small volume with an ornately patterned spine and saw the embossed title *Book of Shadows*—the term for a witch's personal collection of spells. A few folded sheets of white paper tucked between the pages turned out to be computer printouts of incantations with fetishes and rituals.

Let's just say, Raven wasn't wishing anybody a happy birthday and many more to come.

I lost my nerve to read any more of the book, because I'd already glimpsed the contents of some of the zip-top bags and jars—powders, herbs, small bones, more tufts of hair and something that looked like congealed blood.

One other image dominated the small shrine. Front and center, Raven had tacked up a poster of Mad Love with its new lineup. A thick, black X had been drawn across Jeff's face and the rest of his body also had been mutilated in various ways.

I felt a floating sense of unreality. Melissa couldn't hope to compete with Jeff, so she had set out to destroy him. Was it possible that in this depressing little house, through sheer, deranged passion, she had created a supernatural thought-form—a servitor—to carry out the deed for her?

At least I didn't get any sense of that presence lurking around her room. Maybe at the moment its creator was too preoccupied with other things to defend her *sanctum sanctorum* from my invasion. Or just too physically weak?

On one of the lower shelves, I came across what was, in some way, the most shocking discovery of all—the sunglasses I had "lost" during my visit to Pat's farm. I picked them up with a shaking hand, recalling what Gail had said about the servitor tracking me by my DNA.

Could that really have happened? The shadow outside my window, the branch crashing down on my house—

The doorbell chimed, nearly scaring me out of my shoes. In a panic, I tossed the *Book of Shadows* onto the small table, yanked the ceiling cord to kill the light and shut the closet door behind me. I almost felt like I should wipe my fingerprints off everything I'd touched in the room, but there was no time. As quietly as possibly, I turned off the bedroom light, stepped into the hall, closed that door also and hurried to let in Mrs. Larkin's cousin.

Janet had a round, pleasant face, divided by a sharp sundial blade of a nose, and short, wavy auburn hair. Her flowered tunic and green knit pants stretched to accommodate wide hips.

"So good of you to come and help out like this," she told me, with a smile. "Lark said her sister took ill?"

"It might be nothing. She could just be overdoing her diet."

"Um, I wondered… Girls today go crazy with that stuff, trying to look like those skinny actresses and models. How's Aggie doing?"

I took a second to realize she meant Mrs. Larkin. "Sleeping, last time I checked."

By the time we reached the woman's bedroom, though, her eyes were open. The doorbell must have roused her.

Janet smoothed her cousin's wispy gray hair. "How're you feelin' today, honey? Okay?"

Aggie winced and shook her head a little. "Where's Lissa?"

"She's gonna be a little late, that's why I'm here. You need something?"

"I want Lissa!" The woman's voice rose in irritation. "Why isn't she here? She has to give me my medicine!"

"Aw, are you hurtin'? Don't worry, I'll get it for you."

I stepped back out into the hall to give Janet room to maneuver, and also so Aggie wouldn't question what I, a stranger, was doing in her house. She seemed agitated enough as it was.

Janet crossed the hall to the small bathroom and took a brown prescription bottle from the medicine cabinet. At Aggie's bedside, she poured clear liquid into a special dosing spoon and helped her patient swallow it all.

"There." Gently, she readjusted the crushed pillows beneath Aggie's head. "Just take it easy and you'll feel better in a minute, okay?"

As Janet passed back through the hall with the bottle, I asked her, "What is that?"

She struggled to pronounce the name on the label. "Rox… Roxanol. Anyway, it's morphine. By now she's built up a tolerance for it, poor thing."

"Is that why you keep it in the medicine cabinet?"

The woman nodded sadly. "Better not to leave it in her room. She might overdo because she doesn't realize how strong it is. She once told me it tastes 'like apple cider.'"

As I drove away from the Larkin house, I realized I was hungry as hell. While there were real, biological reasons for this, I also might have been influenced by the mental image of Melissa/Raven wasting away from unrequited love.

I could satisfy my needs much more easily, by hitting the Burger King on Route 3 on my way home.

My cell phone rang just as I was turning into the parking lot, but I pulled into a space before I checked the message. Tony. He said someone from Mad Love's organization—it sounded like one of the bodyguards—had come by to pick up the chocolates. Afterward, he'd gotten tied up at work over the breaking news that a psychiatrist had declared Bill Canfield mentally competent to stand trial. Tony ended by asking how I'd made out on my trip to Lyndhurst.

I knew he'd be busy for a while longer, so I went inside the restaurant, picked up a grilled chicken sandwich and a diet Coke, and sat at a table to finish them off before I called him back.

"Any idea when Canfield might go to trial?" I asked him.

"Oh, who knows? The lawyers could go back and forth for months, and it could still end in some kind of plea. We'll probably have the lab results on your chocolates a lot sooner. How did things work out with the old lady?"

Once again, I mentally sorted out what I could tell him from what I couldn't. "Just fine, but it left me kind of wiped out. Brought back a lot of sad memories."

"Ohhh…because of your dad, right?" Tony had met me while I was still recovering from his death. "Damn, I didn't think of that. You really should've let me go with you."

"Then you'd have missed out on the Canfield story," I pointed out. "I'm fine, but I'll be a lot better if you can come over tonight."

"Count on it. I probably can get out of here in another hour and then I'm all yours."

Best news I'd heard all day. "All I've got for supper is a frozen pizza, but it's the kind you like, and I'll open a bottle of Chianti."

"As if I needed any more incentive," he said, with a low, sexy chuckle. "See you soon!"

While I had the cell phone out, I called Stern and left a message to have his lab check both the oranges and the truffles for morphine. So he would take my advice seriously, I also explained my suspicions. Luckily, the people at the tables nearest to me remained far too involved in their own conversations to listen in on mine.

I got back in my car and drove the rest of the way home in sluggish rush-hour traffic. The afternoon had heated up, and my old four-cylinder Cruiser struggled to maintain full-strength air conditioning and peppy forward motion at the same time.

Meanwhile, I wondered what would have happened if I'd assumed the truffles came from Alan and wolfed down two or three with my usual gusto. I've always gotten a buzz from good chocolate, but the morphine might have been more than I could handle. How much could I have eaten before I detected the funny taste? Maybe not enough to kill me, but at least enough to make me pretty sick.

The same could be said of Jeff and the oranges.

So Melissa lacked professional-caliber skills as a poisoner. As a practitioner of what they used to called the Black Arts, though, she still might have the potential to do serious damage. Assuming she *had* created the spook that dropped the chunk of proscenium on the guy at the Rialto.

I arrived home at twilight and found pale confetti scattered along the curb in front of my house. Wood chips. Yikes, I'd forgotten—the guys had come by to take down my dead tree. I walked around the house and, yes, the big maple had disappeared except for a four-inch-high stump. Studying its diameter and dense rings, I felt a bit guilty about having ordered such an arborcide. But after all, it was in self-defense.

With that threat removed, and Melissa hospitalized for exhaustion, I hoped I wouldn't have to worry about any more nasty *tulpa* tricks for a while.

Back on my front porch, I checked my mailbox and found the folded bill from the tree service. I'd look at it later—I was depressed enough already. At least my insurance should cover most of it.

A shiny black SUV glided to a stop in front of the house next door, the one that used to belong to the Dykstras. It had just gone up for sale. A Victorian of the same vintage as mine, it needed even more TLC. Could this be a prospective buyer? Well, with such a luxury ride, maybe he could afford to restore a hundred-and-seventeen-year-old money pit.

For some reason, the vehicle's presence bugged me, though I couldn't pinpoint why. Maybe it was just the connection with the Dykstra place. The house and its last owner still had some scary associations for me.

While I scanned the rest of my mail, I kept watch from the corner of my eye, but no one got out of the SUV. Finally, I shook off my unsettled mood and went inside.

No servitor vibes in the house tonight, but I still was

haunted by all the weirdness I'd found in Melissa's bedroom, and its possible significance. I needed to share my story with somebody who would believe me, but keep it confidential, and who could possibly offer some advice. Only one person met all of those qualifications.

I hated to phone Gail for any reason but an emergency, so I emailed her. I described Melissa's physical condition and everything I'd found on and around Raven's closet altar. I also asked what, if anything, I could do to help the troubled young woman get back in touch with reality. Then I hit Send.

Back down in my kitchen, I poured myself a little of the Chianti. A few sips started to calm my nerves. Not as effectively as a few truffles with morphine filling might have, but it would do.

Minutes later, Tony rang the bell. I opened the door with wineglass in hand, and he grinned. "Started without me, did you? Yeah, I saw your other boyfriend sneaking away!"

"Other boyfriend?" Pretty funny, when I barely had time for one.

"Some guy in a Lexus." He nodded toward the street. "He was parked next door with the window rolled down. When I got out of my car, he rolled up the window and beat it. Darned suspicious, if you ask me."

"The Dykstra house is for sale He was probably just checking it out." I led Tony into the kitchen and poured him some wine.

"Hmm...I don't know if I want him moving next door to you. Fancy ride, wavy black hair, wrap-around shades...looked like a pretty slick character."

I laughed. "Oh, well, that explains it. He must be the Realtor!"

CHAPTER 30

Over the next twenty-four hours, my life settled back to something close to normal. I received another freelance assignment from a regional shelter magazine, which renewed my hopes for future solvency. A contractor gave me a reasonable estimate to repair the mudroom roof.

Lark told me on the phone her sister was being transferred to a Behavioral Health Center at the hospital, where they cared for uncooperative anorexics and others whose physical ailments were complicated by mental issues. If Melissa stayed there until she was truly cured, I thought, maybe the worst of Mad Love's problems really were under control.

At any rate, Monday I would return to my regular part-time job at the *Sentinel*. I imagined that, after dealing with all of Mad Love's life-and-death drama, coping with the usual perfectionistic interior designers and publicity-shy homeowners would feel like the real vacation.

I also got a response from Gail to my latest email. She agreed Melissa must have been practicing her own blend of black magic and voodoo, trying to hex anyone she felt stood between her and Alan.

We may never be sure whether she actually conjured up some destructive entity, or whether your intuition simply showed you that shadow figure to warn you an accident was about to occur, Gail wrote. *Either way, the girl seems to have tapped into something, so be on your guard around her. If you do meet up with her again, protect yourself as well as possible.*

I'm sure Gail was thinking of the imaginary sphere of white

light. On the other hand, I envisioned a large crucifix, some garlic, a bottle of holy water and possibly a gun loaded with silver bullets.

Remember, though, my mentor added, *a destructive thought-form feeds on negativity. No matter how you might feel about Melissa right now, try not to direct any fearful or angry feelings toward her. If you harbor negative emotions, they will just give her more power over you. You must think of her with compassion and hope that she will change her ways and move toward the light.*

To me, that sounded like a mighty generous response to someone who'd tried to kill me, but what did I know? Gail was the expert in this area.

She regretted she couldn't come to Jersey to help me in person, but she was off to New England to assist some family with a really nasty haunting—one also being recorded for a TV reality show. She asked me to keep her posted, though, and promised that if my situation didn't improve she would put me in touch with another capable, experienced psychic in my area.

I signed off hoping that wouldn't be necessary. I supposed if I had no more close dealings with Melissa, I could try to keep a positive attitude toward her.

Tony had just started on another big story that kept him working late, so we spent the next night apart, and the following morning I got a call from Stern. True to my prediction, both the oranges and the truffles had tested positive for morphine—the same liquid formula found in Mrs. Larkin's pain medication.

"Does Lark know?" I asked him.

"I discussed it with her, and, of course, she was very upset and apologetic. She's been through a lot the last few days, too. Anyhow, we're all meeting this afternoon at Alan's place to decide how to handle this and other matters. We'd like you to join us, if you can."

A major damage-control session? How could I say no?

When I arrived at Alan's apartment, I found myself the only woman present. The band members had settled in the funhouse-themed game room. The first time I'd seen this space, I'd gotten a kick out of all the garish monster and demon faces grinning at me from the dark walls. Today, though—after my experiences of the past couple of weeks—I found them unnerving. They reminded me too much of the real phantom that might be stalking the band...and me.

Stern, who had let me in, nodded toward three open pizza boxes on the bar, each with a couple of wedges left.

"Help yourself," he said. "They're 'artisanal,' whatever that means. One's got barbecued chicken, another's got three kinds of mushrooms and the third one's a Margherita."

I peeled off a slice of the mushroom pizza, then took a paper plate and a bottle of water. I started to alight on one of the barstools, but Pat Jacy, always the gentleman, gave up one of the art deco side chairs for my comfort. He settled on the zebra-printed ottoman.

A beefy, almost albino-blond guy leaned against the doorjamb close to the big T-rex sculpture, the arms folded across his broad chest crawling with tattoos. I figured him for a new bodyguard—from what I'd seen, two or three seemed to rotate in their duties.

I also noticed Lark's absence.

The other guys, with plates and bottles of their own in front of them, offered me token greetings.

Then Stern got down to business. "First, Quinn, we all want to thank you for your help in sorting out this whole mess with the Canfield guy and Melissa Larkin. At different times, you warned us about both of them, and you've gone way beyond the call of duty to follow up. If you hadn't stopped Jeff from eating those oranges—"

Embarrassed by the praise, I reassured the lead guitarist. "You probably wouldn't have finished even one. I'll bet the taste, or the buzz, would have warned you off."

"Maybe," Jeff said. "But don't forget, the doc's got me on painkillers, and he also prescribed sleeping pills for me at night. I'm tapering off them now, but combined with the morphine...it could've been lights-out for good."

I cringed because I hadn't thought of that. I wondered if Melissa had.

Alan, next to Jeff on the sofa, frowned and rubbed his lover's back. Today, the guitarist had gotten rid of his sling, but still moved his arm stiffly. Alan, for his part, looked a little thinner in the face, more boyish and vulnerable than ever.

"Anyhow, Quinn," he said, "we're all very sorry Melissa also targeted you. Like I said before, when I asked you to help out on this, I never meant to put you in any kind of danger. It's great you made the connection right away with the candy and didn't eat any, but you could have."

Stern broke in again. "We just want you to understand that... we realize the seriousness of the situation."

I looked from him to Alan and back again, curiously. Were they afraid I'd sue them? Was Lark absent today because they'd fired her? Had her drawn and quartered?

"But we've all discussed this"—Alan glanced around at his band mates, as if for support—"and we've decided not to press any charges against Melissa."

I exhaled, understanding now the source of his tension.

"It wasn't totally unanimous." From the chair next to me, Jack spoke up, an edge to his voice. "This chick tried to *kill* Randall, and who knows whether the treatment she's getting is going to do any good? She could get out and take another crack at it."

Donny, who slouched with his beer against the old fortune-telling machine, grunted in agreement.

The tattooed blond guy interrupted, his mild tone and pleading gesture at odds with his hardcore appearance. "Guys, we're *really* grateful for this. Melissa's very sick, that's true, but she's getting the best care. I swear, she'll be closely supervised until we're sure she's no danger to anyone. You'll never, ever have to worry about this kind of crap from her again!"

Stern must have read the confusion in my face. "Sorry, Quinn, I should've introduced you. This is Tad Lindquist, our road crew manager...and Lark's husband."

"Ah," I said. "I wondered why she wasn't here."

"She's running around today, making arrangements for Melissa to be moved to the new center," Tad explained. "I came instead."

"So…she's still got her job?"

Alan hurried to defend his assistant. "Lark's been a tremendous help the last year or so, not just to me, but the whole band. She handled so many details while we were on the road… and even when I asked her to keep Melissa away from us, she did try. We just don't think she could've known—"

"I didn't mean it like that," I assured him. "I was *afraid* she'd been fired, but I agree with you completely. I don't think Lark's to blame for any of this, and I know how sorry she is that things got out of control."

Stern nodded gravely. "We know you've got every right to be angry and afraid, yourself. But we're just hoping—"

"Don't worry. I have no plans to press charges, either."

Jack shook his shaggy blond head, as if he thought I was a fool, but the others in the room visibly relaxed.

"I'm sure she has mental problems, even beyond the anorexia." I asked Tad, "Do you and Lark know about the altar she's got set up in her bedroom closet?"

When he looked blank, I told all of them about the drawings, the poster of the band and the collection of spells and other artifacts Melissa had assembled. "She had my sunglasses, and… Jeff, is there any way she could've gotten some of your hair?"

He nearly choked on a mouthful of pizza and stared at me. "You're kidding, right?"

Alan's eyes bugged, too. "Shit, she could have. She was hanging around the salon that day we were getting haircuts. If she picked up some from the floor, who'd have noticed?"

"C'mon." Donny made a skeptical face. "What does it matter? You're acting like she could actually *do* something with it. Throw a curse, or—"

Alan cut in. "But that's what she was trying to do! Those messages implying the band was 'cursed' must've come from her. And when we actually had a few serious accidents, maybe she *thought* she caused them, so she sent more notes taking credit for them."

"One seriously fucked-up chick." Jack stalked past me to the bar for another beer.

"Yes, I think we can all agree on that." Stern slapped the

arms of his leather chair decisively and glanced at me. "Quinn, another slice?"

When I told him I was good for the moment, he went on with his explanation, as I'd hoped he would.

"On the other hand, whatever *she* thought, Melissa could not have sabotaged the equipment on our tour or injured that cameraman during the video shoot. Someone else was behind those incidents. That's the other reason why Tad is here today."

All eyes veered toward the tattooed man. At the sudden attention, he straightened against the doorjamb and uncrossed his booted feet.

"Right after the plane engine got tampered with last year," he said, "the cops questioned me and all the guys on my crew. Did anybody hire on at the last minute? Could somebody without credentials have blended in and pulled off the sabotage? A couple of the roadies did remember seeing this pock-marked dude who never talked to anybody, but always seemed to be busy with some job. We couldn't account for him on our payroll, and after the plane incident, nobody ever saw him again."

"We're thinking the guy was planted by our friend the filmmaker," Stern said.

From this forthright statement, I assumed the other band members finally had been briefed on the looming blackmail threat. Pat wore a rueful expression, but Jack and Donny looked as if they'd bitten into something rancid. I was just as well pleased I hadn't been included in that discussion—they probably hadn't made it too easy on Alan.

"You mean, Montanna?" I asked. "I thought he was out in L.A."

"Guess he's gone bicoastal," Alan quipped.

"I always thought it seemed strange he harassed the band without ever asking for money," Stern said, "but he was playing it smart. This week, he finally tipped his hand."

"Canfield's attack on me must've shaken him up," Alan said, bitterly. "Can't get golden eggs from a dead goose, right?"

"He called—first time I ever heard his voice—and made me a proposition," said Stern. "He offered the band 'protection' for a hefty cut of the proceeds from the new album and the next tour. He suggested that, with his underworld connections, he can make sure no one bothers us again."

"What a crock." Donny smacked his empty beer bottle down of the top of the fortune-teller's glass enclosure, making me wince. Its campy appeal aside, the boardwalk artifact had to be worth thousands.

"Yeah," Jeff agreed. "With friends like that, we wouldn't need any other enemies."

"Why's he after our money?" Jack asked. "Porn is a legit business these days—he should be raking it in."

"You'd think so, wouldn't you?" Stern crossed to the bar to throw away his paper plate and napkin. On the way back, he paused before the wall of windows with the Manhattan skyline as his backdrop. "But I've had a private detective checking out Mr. Montanna's professional activities on the coast. By the way, his real name is Rocco Montagna, but I guess he felt that didn't have the right Hollywood vibe. Anyway, it turns out the adult-film business has fallen on hard times."

"Makes sense," Alan sniffed. "Too much competition these days from cable TV and free stuff on the Internet."

Stern nodded. "Montanna apparently has tried to make up the difference by running a side business in kiddie porn, which fortunately is still illegal. But lately the feds have started cracking down hard on that stuff, so he's desperate for a new source of income."

"Guess he heard about our success—especially Alan's success," Jeff noted, "and felt entitled to cash in."

I sank back into my vintage chair, overwhelmed. "Whew. You guys sure have got yourself..." I flashed back on the complex maze of the hornet's nest that I'd preserved on my porch table. "What are you going to do?"

"Pay the man, of course!" Alan saw my horrified expression and laughed out loud, for the first time that afternoon. "Don't worry...we've got a plan."

"We've been in touch with the authorities," said Stern, "and all they really need is evidence of extortion. We hope to get that soon. Obviously, Quinn, is this part is too dangerous for you to be involved in any way. It's better if you don't even know any more details. But we really did want to thank you for your help so far."

"Glad to do it." I wondered if this really was it—they would finally nail Montanna, and their problems would be over. At any rate, Stern's tone had the feeling of a polite dismissal.

Alan took it that way, too. He got up and saw me to the door.

"As far as the magazine article goes," he said, "a deal's a deal. As soon as we wrap up these loose ends and the bad publicity dies down, I'll set things up with *Celebrity Home* for you to do the story on my apartment."

I almost had forgotten about all of that. It reminded me of another unresolved issue. "What about the suit against the Rialto?"

He followed me into the hall. "Stern thinks if we can prove Montanna planted a man among the work crew to make trouble for us, and the theater owners couldn't reasonably have known about it, the cameraman's family might be satisfied. With any luck, we can settle that whole business out of court." He walked me toward the elevator. "Oh, and I'm sure I don't need to tell you, but none of the stuff we discussed today is for publication."

That made me hesitate. "Alan, you need to understand... Tony's investigative story involves finding out who's been sabotaging the band and whether the same person also killed the cameraman."

He jerked his head dismissively. "I mostly mean the stuff about Melissa. Believe me, if the FBI busts Montanna, Tony'll be the first to know." We reached the elevators, and he pushed the Down button for me. "I have to admit, when you first came across those emails from that scumbag, I played them down because wanted to keep that whole situation under wraps. But you didn't let me get away with it—you kept telling me you sensed he could be dangerous."

"I'm still sensing it." On an impulse, I gave Alan a quick good-bye hug, which seemed to catch him by surprise. "You guys be careful, okay?"

Riding down on the elevator, I also wondered about what

Jack had said. Just because Melissa was hospitalized might not guarantee the band had nothing more to fear from her.

Even though it might be contrary to Gail's advice, I thought I needed to have a heart-to-heart talk with Raven.

CHAPTER 31

I arrived on Melissa's floor of the hospital toward the end of visiting hours. A motherly black nurse had just delivered her supper tray.

"I guess it's okay," the nurse told me, in a hushed, conspirator's tone. "Try to get her to eat something."

Melissa did not enjoy the same kind of elite accommodations as had been provided for Jeff in Hoboken. Still, Stern might have pulled some strings for her, because she did have a private room.

She sat near the window in a vinyl-upholstered armchair, the top of the adjustable table effectively pinning her in place. Her tray held a standard-issue hospital meal of sliced turkey, mashed potatoes and mixed vegetables, with what looked like a chocolate-pudding cup on the side. For good measure, an IV bag on a wheeled stand fed more nutrition into her left arm.

In the limp blue hospital gown, Lark's sister cut an eerie, scarecrow figure. The gown's baggy dimensions only emphasized the scrawniness of her arms and legs; her hair formed a straw-like halo around her hollowed face. She ignored her food, but showed some idle interest in the TV mounted high on the wall. Judge Judy was scowling at a dowdy middle-aged couple, who stammered and interrupted as they accused each other of all kinds of misbehavior.

Despite this background noise, Melissa heard my step and glanced around. When her eyes widened in shock, I almost laughed.

"Hi, Melissa. Surprised to see me up and about?"

She continued to gape as I approached and sat on the foot

of her bed. I nodded toward her tray. "Nurse says you'd better eat some of that, unless you want to be hooked up to that IV for a long, long time. Darn, I should have brought you some truffles for dessert! By the way, how did you know those were my favorite?"

The birdlike young woman managed a tight smile. "Lucky guess."

Yes, I was definitely getting the vibe now. Melissa might look fragile, but there was an aura of menace pulsing from her. Whether it was just general craziness or real power, I couldn't say. But I remembered Gail's advice to keep my thoughts toward the girl supportive and positive, and struggled to follow it.

"You're also lucky I'm not the kind to hold a grudge," I told her, my tone sarcastically mild. "But I am curious as to why you tried to poison me. I mean, we hardly even know each other!"

She focused on the TV again. "You were always around him, keeping him away from me."

I wondered if it would do any good to talk sense to her. "Melissa, I'm not involved with Alan. Like I told you when we met a the video shoot, I'm a writer—"

"You're more than that. Lark told me you're some kind of... psychic."

Too bad I hadn't asked Lark to sign an NDA where *my* activities were concerned. Of course, in the beginning she'd probably had no idea there would be any harm in sharing this bit of gossip with her sister.

"In a way, I am. The band asked me to help them find out who's been making trouble for them. In particular, why the block of plaster fell on the cameraman at the Rialto." Melissa's keen brown eyes flickered back to me, and I pushed further. "You wouldn't know anything about that, would you?"

A dry laugh. "Me? How could I have had anything to do with it? I was watching the concert. I was sitting right next to you!"

"I know," I said. "And right after the accident, you left."

"I...got scared."

Scared just because someone got hurt, or because the *wrong* person got hurt? Gail had suggested if the "practitioner" throwing the curse was inexperienced or unstable, she might not have full control over the result.

I shifted my approach. "You've been sending Alan those messages, signed with the raven stamp. Why 'Raven'?"

The bony shoulders shrugged. "The guys gave Lark a cool nickname. Why shouldn't I have one?"

The anti-Lark? I wondered. I sensed a lot of jealousy, and not only because Lark had a glamorous job and access to the band. At the Lyndhurst house, I'd gotten a feel for the sisters' early home life. Lark had broken free from their needy, demanding mother and shabby, working-class neighborhood. Sure, she'd tried to help her sister do the same, but Melissa couldn't cope with that much real-world responsibility. So she'd been left behind.

"And Alan wrote that song for me." A glow suddenly warmed Melissa's sharp features. "About the raven flying home to the moon. It was a secret message from him, that he knew we belonged together! If the rest of you would just stop interfering—"

Ironic, I thought, that the romantic image Alan admitted borrowing from Barry Callahan would be the one Melissa interpreted so personally. Ordinarily, I would have felt the girl's twisted mental state was better left to a professional and none of my business. But she had tried to poison me, which made it my business.

I decided to try some tough love.

"I know you don't want to hear this," I told her, "but no one is keeping Alan away from you."

"They are...they all are!" Her color improved with her anger. "Even Lark. She told me—"

"She told you to stay away from Alan because he asked her to."

"That's a lie. She only said that because—"

"Alan liked you okay as a friend, but he could see you wanted more from him. You pushed too hard, and you were rude to him about Jeff. He's not in love with you, Melissa. He's in love with Jeff. But you must know that, since you sent Jeff those oranges."

On the TV, Judge Judy reamed out the feuding couple, who admittedly sounded as if they didn't have a working brain between them. I wished I could turn down the volume, but Melissa's hand—like a delicate bird's claw—rested lightly on the remote. I'd just have to talk over the din.

She shook her head now, as if I was the naïve, deluded one. "Jeff seduced him and confused him. Alan likes women! He slept with Valery and with other girls, and now there's you—"

She gave me way too much credit, and this time I did have to laugh. "I'm *not* Alan's girlfriend. The only reason I was even at the video shoot was because I was doing a story on the renovation of the Rialto."

The arrow of her stare pierced me. "Lark told me...that night at the theater, before the accident, you...saw something."

I remembered Alan had found my ID tag on his doorstep, with the note referring to me as "that witch." More of Melissa's handiwork, no doubt. The thought shook me for a second, until I decided to use it to my advantage.

"Okay, Raven," I said quietly, "let's have an honest conversation, witch-to-witch." When she flinched, I told her, "I've been to your house. I've seen your altar and your potions and your spells. I even know you grabbed my sunglasses up at Pat's farm and tried to throw a curse on me." I didn't acknowledge she might have succeeded, with some costly damage to my roof. "So let's say you have some actual skills along this line. But you're headed down a very dark path."

She half-faced away again, and in the flicker from the TV, I saw a tear roll down her pale cheek. "All I want is—"

"You want Alan, but you can't have him. And you know what? Even if you bumped off Jeff and me and everybody in his entourage, it wouldn't do you any good. Then Alan would totally hate you! You don't want that, do you?"

"God...no!"

"Then you have to stop what you're doing, right now. You're hurting other people and making yourself sick for nothing." As I said this, I suddenly felt the deeper implications of it. Could her superhuman psychic efforts in creating the thought-form have contributed to her exhaustion?

At the same time, I could sympathize with the poor girl. Being crazy about someone who did not and never would return your feelings—I'd been there. Who hadn't? It sucked, for sure. Part of me wanted to reach out and comfort her with a touch, but I had no idea how she would react. In her agitated state, she might recoil and hiss at me, like a feral cat.

"There are good people here at the hospital who want to help you get better," I went on gently. "If you're smart, you'll let them."

Melissa glanced down at her untouched dinner, a very literal reaction that suggested I might be getting through to her. I figured I'd better use the moment as best I could.

"Yeah, Alan is a great guy. But if you really care about him, you'll wish him happiness with Jeff or whoever else he chooses, and success for the band. You know your wishes have power, so use them to make yourself healthy and happy. Not as Valery or even Raven, but as Melissa."

She continued to stare down at her tray, wiping away more tears with the back of her hand. I started to feel proud of my armchair psychology, thinking maybe I had helped her make a breakthrough. Still, I figured I'd used up all my best stuff and should probably leave her to her dinner. I shouldered my purse and stood.

"It's not over," she murmured.

I halted by her chair. "What?"

"Alan's in danger, and you can't help him. He still needs me." She looked up at me fiercely. "He needs *me*."

I tried to figure out how, or even whether, to respond to this. Meanwhile, the nurse bustled back in, chattering merrily, as if to a parakeet. "How'd you do, Ms. Larkin, with your supper? Did you eat any—"

Melissa's head snapped up and showed her tear-streaked face. The nurse swung toward me in accusation.

"You say something t' upset her?"

This called for a quick and cool response. "Just that all her friends feel badly for her and hope she gets better real soon." Before I had to do any more explaining, my cell phone rang. I didn't immediately recognize the number, but the call gave me the perfect excuse to split.

Cell phone use is prohibited in many areas of hospitals, so I waited until I'd reached the lobby before I checked the message. Probably the last voice I expected to hear was Barry Callahan's, and his first words chilled me.

"I know you're not just a magazine writer—Donny told me how you've been helping the band." I started to panic, until Barry reassured me he was fine with my sleuthing. "But I need to meet with you, tonight. It's about the sabotage and the accidents." I heard him draw a deep breath. "When we talked a couple of weeks ago...I didn't exactly tell you the whole story."

CHAPTER 32

What the hell was I doing?

When Barry had asked me to meet him at a job site in Harrison at six o'clock, I'd agreed without much hesitation. I'd been there before, after all; it was his workplace, and it would still be sort of light out. Besides, I—and everybody else—had pretty much ruled him out as having anything personally to do with the dirty tricks against Mad Love.

So I'd hopped back in my Cruiser and headed north on the Parkway, then east on 280. Now I'd crossed the Passaic River and headed once again into the bleak landscape of abandoned warehouses and empty lots.

Funny, but when I'd driven out there on a bright afternoon, the area had not looked quite so menacing. As my poor car jostled over rutted gravel, I prayed I wouldn't break an axle out here.

The red brick factory stood apart from other, more decayed properties in the area, cordoned off by orange plastic fencing that didn't even work as a psychological barrier. Oversized graffiti with flashy dimensional effects still covered a couple of the outer walls, a comforting reminder of local gang activity.

I seriously considered turning my car around and fleeing for the safety of home, sweet home.

But Barry had information for me, and he'd practically begged for my help. He'd said he didn't trust Tony because he didn't want his name in the paper. I'd tried to reassure him that Tony would respect his wishes, but the guy insisted on talking to me instead and letting me pass the information to the authorities. He didn't even want to do it over the phone, but insisted we meet in person.

Now, all of a sudden, that seemed like a bad idea. If Barry was that afraid of someone, did I really want to be his go-between? Was it safe for me to meet with him out here in the middle of nowhere?

Pulling closer, I saw a Kelly-green van with "Callahan & Son" in white letters parked near a rear loading bay, alongside a couple of tractor trailers and, farther back, a generic black SUV. I would have expected a few more vehicles at such a large job site, but the crew must have quit at five. That's why Barry had wanted to meet afterward—he knew we'd have total privacy.

I stopped near the front entrance, pulled out my cell phone and punched in Tony's number. I might be worrying over nothing, but better to be safe than sorry.

When I got a recording, I left a message telling him where I was, who I was meeting and the time. "If you don't hear back from me in an hour," I finished, trying to sound humorous, "feel free to call the cops!"

Before I left the car, I took one more precaution. I opened my glove compartment and fished out a slim canister of pepper spray I'd stashed there while working full-time in Elizabeth. I'd never had to use it and hoped I wouldn't tonight, but it was going in my purse, just in case.

A stiff, sour-smelling breeze gusted off the dark river as I crossed the pavement to the factory entrance. A billboard there, new since my last visit, announced the site would soon become Rio Vista Condominiums. A full-color rendering showed the building dolled up with new windows, fancier trim and various roof and doorway peaks intended to make it look more residential. The devastated terrain that surrounded it tonight apparently would sprout a lawn, shrubbery and curving walkways.

Wow. Would the kind of people able to afford such luxury ever find their way out to this desolate location?

I searched the windows for any sign of life and spotted a dim yellow glow on the third—the top floor—where Barry had told me to meet him. I tried the old glass-and-iron double doors, found them open, and climbed the two flights of filthy industrial stairs.

On my way up, I began to hear music. Barry was listening to rock, either on a radio or a CD. I hoped I wouldn't walk in and find him playing air guitar, reminiscing about his glory days.

He wasn't. He stood near a drafting table spread with plans for the renovation, but didn't seem to be looking at them at the moment. Instead, he just stared out the nearest window, hands in his jeans pockets, his posture tense and vigilant.

My steps echoed on the sawdust-powdered floorboards, and he spun around. His grin seemed forced, but he sprang forward to welcome me.

"Quinn! Thanks for coming. You don't know how much it means to me."

He grabbed my outstretched hand in both of his, and right away I knew this guy was terrified. No sixth sense needed—his palms were clammy, and I doubted it was from swinging a hammer.

"I'm happy to do anything to help end all this harassment of the band," I said. He offered me a bottle of water from a big, Styrofoam cooler, but I passed, eager to get down to business and get out of there. "What can you tell me?"

Barry shut off his CD player, settled on a stool by his drafting table and gestured toward a three-foot-high stack of boxed sheetrock. I brushed off some sawdust and sat there. Aside from the metal lamp screwed to Barry's drafting table, the only light came from a few caged, temporary fixtures strung across the rafters. The vast ceiling stretched above us in a maze of old pipes and ductwork, not yet upgraded. A wheeled, red pipe scaffold towered nearby.

"Sorry I didn't say anything about this the first time we talked," he began, "but I was scared. The only reason I'm telling you now is because I heard somebody took a shot at Alan and wounded Jeff, and then sent them a poisoned fruit basket."

My antenna went up. "How did you know about the fruit? The cops never released that information to the press."

A skewed smile. "Donny and I still talk now and then. When I heard about the shooting, I gave him a call, and he told me about the other stuff. Anyway, it sounds like somebody's starting to play rough, and I've got an idea who it might be."

I said nothing. Though pretty sure the culprits in those two crimes were already in custody—of one kind or another—I didn't want to discourage Barry if he had something more to share.

He sighed, with a lift and drop of his wide shoulders. "A couple of months after the band released their first album with Jeff, and right before they left on tour, a guy came by one of our job sites to talk to me. Said he was some kind of reporter. He asked me about my connection to Mad Love and was I upset they'd kicked me to the curb that way…kinda like you did when you came here the first time."

With a nod, I took out my spy pen and a small notebook. Barry didn't object, so I made some jottings, meanwhile subtly activating the digital recorder.

"This guy, though, kept harping on how the band had really disrespected me, and wouldn't I like to get even with them? Frankly, he got my attention, and I asked for details. He said his boss was looking for somebody to screw things up for Mad Love on the next tour." Barry slipped from his stool and paced a few yards across the cavernous room beneath a web of shadows cast by the huge scaffold. "I asked him why anybody would want to do that, and he just said I wasn't the only one who had a beef against Alan Bardot—" He stopped abruptly, head snapping toward the open door that led to the stairs. "Did you hear something?"

I hadn't and shook my head. He stole to the door and peered down over the railing. Apparently satisfied, he ambled back to his drafting table and sat down again.

Great, I thought. Either Barry was seriously paranoid, or we really did have something to worry about. Whether from his behavior or some other source, I was getting an uneasy vibe again.

Speaking a bit more quietly, he went on with his story. "Anyway, this dude said they needed somebody with good mechanical skills for the job. Offered me a nice chunk of change, plus my airfare to follow the tour. But mad as I was over being fired, I just couldn't do that to the other guys—especially Donny and Jack. The things he wanted done…it sounded like people could get hurt. So I told him I'd just started on the job with my pop and couldn't get away for that long."

"What did he say?" I asked.

Barry brushed a strong hand over his short-cropped blond hair. "He wasn't happy. I guess he figured he couldn't force me, but he dropped the pal-sy act real fast. He told me, 'You and I never had this conversation,' and I knew it was a warning."

"They must've found somebody to do the sabotage, anyway," I noted.

"Yeah, and that's where I might have information for you. The next week, one of my guys quit. Gave some excuse about moving out of state to take care of a sick mother. I didn't think much of it at the time, but looking back, I figure this dude got to him, instead."

"Do you know where he is now? The guy who left your crew?"

"Not for sure, but I still have his name and the address he gave me when I hired him." Barry picked up a sheet of paper from his drafting table. "That's why I asked you here tonight, to give you this and to talk to you in person. I got no idea if somebody's listening in on my calls. They can intercept cell phones, y'know."

I just nodded, wondering who he thought "they" were.

"An' I'm pretty sure I been followed a couple of times. Big black SUV, new-looking. Common type of vehicle, I know, but—"

A prickle ran down my back as I remembered the one sitting outside my house a couple of nights earlier. And also...

"Barry, there was a black SUV parked way at the back of this building when I came in. I figured it was yours."

He stiffened on his stool. "I drove here in the van."

A dark chuckle echoed from the stairwell. "A good actor waits for his cue, and that sure as hell sounds like mine!"

Two men stepped through the doorway. Both aimed shiny automatic pistols at me and Barry.

CHAPTER 33

For a second or two, I almost thought it was a joke. The pair threatening us looked like bad guys from Central Casting—maybe cut-rate James Bond villains.

Then I recognized the barrel-chested guy in the Fu Manchu biker moustache from his photos on the Internet. Rocky Montanna, in the flesh. Accompanied by a towering, long-haired henchman who looked vaguely Polynesian.

Once I comprehended the guns were real, I couldn't focus on much of anything else. My first thought was that I could die, right now, in this isolated construction site. My second was that my intuition had tried to warn me, but like an idiot, I'd ignored it.

Rocky strolled forward now, chiding Callahan. "Barry, Barry, you kept your mouth shut for almost a whole year. You couldn't do it a little longer?"

Barry said nothing, but his gaze darted sideways. Rocky also noticed this and ordered him to step away from the drafting table.

"You, too," he snapped at me.

On wobbly legs, I obeyed, leaving behind my purse with the pepper spray—not that it would do me much good against firearms. I also left behind my notepad and my pen with the recorder, still running.

Terror sharpened my senses now, and I took in every detail about this bizarre pair. Closer up, Montanna looked to be in his mid-forties, medium-height and with a tan he probably hadn't acquired on the East Coast in April. The shirt that strained across his chest was embroidered with palm trees and his black pants had a silky sheen. His dark hairline looked as artificial as in the Internet headshot. The young henchman was costumed in a black muscle shirt and camo pants tucked into combat boots.

It was all so surreal, I still had the sense of being in a bad *noir* movie. Any minute now, the director would rescue me and Barry by yelling, "Cut!"

"The funny part is," Rocky went on smoothly to Callahan, "you blamed me for trying to have Bardot shot and Randall poisoned, and I had nothing to do with those things! Believe me, I wish those boys only good health and a shitload of success. I just want my share of it."

Barry finally found his voice. "W-who are you? I don't even know what—"

"I'm Mad Love's new head of security. Well, I haven't been officially hired yet, but we're going to fix that right now." While his muscleman still covered us, Montanna pulled out a cell phone, dialed and waited for an answer. "Alan, sweetheart, good to hear your voice again after all this time." He chuckled. "Where the hell am I? Wouldn't you like to know!"

With a gun still pointed at me, I didn't dare sneak a look at my watch. But I wondered how much time had passed since I'd left the message for Tony suggesting he send the cops out here. Had he heard it yet, and if so, had he taken it seriously?

"Yeah, I blew off that little rendezvous with Sternberg tonight in the city," Montanna went on. "Thing is, I don't trust that guy. I figured he'd just have the feds lurking in the shadows. Besides, it's *your* autograph I want on our contract, *capice?*"

He paused again, then grinned. "Such language! You kiss your boyfriend with that mouth?"

Barry glanced again toward the drafting table. I wondered if he had a gun stashed there. Made sense, if he often worked at this desolate site alone at night.

"Calm down 'til you hear my proposition," Montanna continued on the phone. "Maybe you don't think you need my protection, babe, but I've got a couple of your pals here who can tell you otherwise. We're all hanging out right now in this atmospheric old factory, somewhere out in East Jesus, and I think they'd *really* like you to sign that contract."

I felt a weird vibration through my head and realized my teeth were chattering. With some effort, I willed them to stop.

From the corner of my eye, I saw Barry also trembling. He shifted his weight, as if he might make a lunge for the drafting table. I prayed he wouldn't, because the big Polynesian guy surely would drop him before he got there.

Leaving me totally alone with these two whack jobs.

"No, they're not band members. I did plan to grab one of your guys, which might've been tougher, but then these two practically fell in my lap." Montanna listened again, then stalked toward us holding out his cell phone. "Bardot wants to hear your voices."

I hated to cooperate in this lousy scheme and help lure Alan into a trap, but Barry had no such compunctions. "Alan, man, who *is* this dude? He's a freakin' psycho—"

(I'm censoring a bit here.)

Montanna took back the phone briefly. "Your former lead guitarist, remember him? Maybe you don't especially care what happens to Barry, but you just might have warmer feelings for our other hostage." He stuck the phone almost in my face, and I froze. "At a loss for words, honey? Just say your name."

My face grew hot from a mixture of fear and fury. "Quinn. Matthews."

Montanna gave me a sarcastic wink. "Sultry! That'll really bring him running." As he withdrew the phone again, I caught a whiff of his musky aftershave and fought down the urge to vomit.

"Anyhow," he told Alan smoothly, "nobody has to get hurt, as long as you cooperate. Right now, Mr. Fox is waiting in a car in front of your building. You'll come here with him—no one else—and bring the first payment, in cash." A pause. "Well, I *am* sure you *can* get that much, even on short notice. Go to a freakin' ATM!"

(Censoring again.)

"Sell one of your art deco knickknacks at an all-night pawn shop! I want you and the money here in an hour, tops. Oh, and don't worry about leaving your boyfriend alone. Zack'll make sure he doesn't try anything stupid. Yeah, the bodyguard...he's working for me, too."

As Montanna hung up, I wondered if there was even a remote chance all of us would get out of this situation alive. Yes, Alan might show up with the money and sign the contract, but was this guy stupid enough to think that would be the end of it? Stern already had told the FBI about Montanna's threatening calls and emails. This would just sew up the case for extortion...

Especially if my innocent-looking pen on the drafting table was still recording all of this. I didn't dare to even glance in that direction.

Rocky tucked the phone back into the pocket of his tight pants and smiled at us. The guy actually had a dimple in his chin and probably was good-looking at one time, before decadent living had left him puffy around the eyes. I could hardly believe Alan ever had trusted him, but I certainly could understand why the singer had come to hate him.

"Might as well make ourselves comfortable," he said. "Us, not you two. Malo, tie them up. Use those electric cords."

His henchman grabbed some spare cables from a corner pile and started toward me and Barry. Meanwhile, my purse, still on the table, began to play the old theme from *The X-Files*— the ringtone I used for Tony. All three men stared at it, while my heart bounded with fresh hope.

"Who's callin' you?" Rocky asked me.

"M-my boyfriend," I said. "I should've been home by now."

As the tinkling tune played again, the thickset man nodded sharply toward my purse. "Get rid of him."

I figured I'd be dead anyway if I didn't take this gamble, and grabbed the phone.

"Sorry, I was tied up with a long interview," Tony said. "Got your message. I guess you're okay?"

I kept my tone casual. "No, actually. I got kind of tied up, myself." Well, not yet, but I was about to be. Montanna frowned at me, but I pretended not to notice.

"Huh? You're *not* okay?"

"Yep, that's right. So why don't you just go ahead and do that other stuff, like we planned?"

"What other—" His voice dropped to a hush. "You really want me to call the cops?"

I turned positively perky, not like me at all. "Sure, sweetie, that'd be great! Gotta go now, but hope to see you soon. Luv ya!"

I'd barely hung up when Montanna snatched the phone from my hand. He made kissing noises at it before he tossed it back onto the table.

I hardly cared. Tony was going to call the cops and send them right to our address.

Then, a chilling thought. I just prayed he *would* call the cops and not follow me down here himself.

Malo already had lashed Barry's arms behind him with the cables and now did the same to me. The effect probably was less painful than it would have been with ordinary rope because the cables were insulated, with a rubberized covering. Then he shoved the two of us down to sit on the pile of sheetrock and wait for Alan to show up.

As if that wasn't bad enough, Montanna insisted on making conversation with us. The guy sure loved to hear himself talk. I haven't spent a lot of time around people who used hard drugs, but he had to be on something.

Great. Barry and I are being held hostage by a guy who's not only desperate for money and bent on revenge, but probably also high. Even for a blackmailer, he wouldn't be thinking too straight. And he might have an itchy trigger finger.

Gun still in hand, Montanna studied me now with an intensity that made me squirm. With my modest endowments, I doubted he was sizing me up for one of his porn flicks.

"Zach tells me that, besides being a reporter, you're also some kind of a psychic," he said at last. "Guess you should've seen this coming."

I figured a little banter might stall him until the cops showed up. "Unfortunately, precognition isn't one of my talents."

"No?" He leered. "What is?"

"I see dead people. Now and then."

Montanna still looked amused. "Well, you might be seeing yourself and Barry dead, if our friend Bardot doesn't get a move on."

Callahan sounded close to tears. "She wouldn'a even been here tonight if I hadn't called her. Damn, Quinn, I'm really sorry!"

"Actually, Callahan, it's the other way around. I wouldn't have bothered grabbing you if you hadn't arranged to blab everything to her. Besides, I figured Bardot would care more about her, and from the way he sounded on the phone, I was right."

Had Alan really sounded worried about me? I didn't read too much into it. He probably just couldn't stand the idea of another innocent person suffering because of his youthful mistake. Of course, youthful mistakes didn't come much bigger than getting involved with a character like Rocky Montanna.

We heard the distant slam of a car door. While Malo kept his gun on us, Montanna peered out a half-open window.

"Made it in half an hour! Good news for you two. Now, as long as Bardot doesn't pull any crap"—he turned to me—"you'll be able to go home to your sweetie, and Callahan can go do... whatever the hell he usually does."

I still had a hard time believing Montanna would release us that easily, but I could certainly hope.

We heard the heavy front door below us grind open and bang shut. Two sets of footsteps jogged up the steps, as if Alan was hurrying and *Rogue Male* journalist Dan Fox was trying to keep him in his sights.

Even before they reached our floor, I felt the air change.

I'm sure Alan believed he had obeyed Rocky's orders and come alone. But something had followed him, anyway.

CHAPTER 34

When Bardot stepped into the huge, shadowy space, the atmosphere took on a different vibration, in more ways than one.

The first was the same kind of formless threat I had felt twice before—during the photo shoot at the jail and just before the tree limb fell on my house.

But I also picked up on a more mundane shift, in Montanna's attitude. He dropped some of the wise-guy stance, stopped waving his gun around and turned his full attention to Bardot. God knows, I had no special psychic connection with the pornographer, but an insight struck me like a lightning bolt.

This whole business—the harassing notes, the sabotage, the blackmail threats, even grabbing up Barry and me—had been mainly to capture Alan's attention. Montanna might really want money, but even more, he'd wanted this.

For Alan to agree to meet with him one more time, face to face.

Bardot, for his part, looked troubled and angry to see Barry and me trussed up in the corner. He wore ripped jeans and a faded old Doors T-shirt, having been rousted from a quiet evening at his apartment. He also carried a navy blue duffle, lumpy with the weight of its contents.

His temporary chauffeur held him at gunpoint. I supposed carrying out errands for Montanna paid a lot better than writing for a gay porn e-zine. This side job might explain how Fox could afford his cashmere V-neck and designer jeans.

Noticing his short, glossy black hair, I realized who Tony must have seen parked in the black SUV outside my house.

The idea that these guys had also been stalking *me* sent a fresh shudder down my spine.

"Mr. Bardot," Montanna crooned, "so kind of you to join us."

If looks could kill, Alan would have struck the guy dead on the spot. He tossed the duffle to the floor a few feet in front of him. It landed with a solid thunk.

"Here's the cash, Montanna. Count it if you want, then let them go."

The older man waved a dismissive hand. "Alan, Alan, this is about more than money. I can see why you'd misunderstand—I did resort to extreme tactics to get you to come here tonight. But you're in show business. You know sometimes you have to make a big, dramatic gesture to get your point across."

In a tight voice, Alan asked him, "And just what is your point?"

"That you and your band need better security! Look how easily Malo and I were able to overwhelm your two…associates. It wouldn't have been much harder to snatch a member of your band. And from what I understand, you've also had a string of accidents lately that the police have termed 'suspicious.'"

"Guess *you* wouldn't know anything about those."

"What I know is you need more protection, and that's what I'm offering." Montanna pulled a long business envelope from his shirt pocket. "With my connections on both coasts, you'll never have to worry about sabotage or stalkers again."

With a cynical smile, Alan shook his head. "Your connections are all in your mind, Rocky. The actual mob wouldn't put up with a joker like you for five minutes." Still, he sent another nervous glance in our direction, which Montanna noticed.

"Yes, I'm sure this has been upsetting for Ms. Matthews and Mr. Callahan, but they'll be released safe and sound. And I'm sure they'll keep their mouths shut, if not out of concern for you, then certainly for themselves. After all, if we got 'em once, we can always get 'em again." He underscored this threat with a wink at Barry and me.

When Montanna slapped the envelope down on the drafting table, I could feel the waves of Alan's banked fury. He clearly meant to do whatever it took, though, to defuse the situation and get us all out alive. He removed the papers from the envelope—apparently, two copies of the contract—and flattened them on the table.

Meanwhile, Rocky studied him closely. I had a sudden vision of him sitting in the audience at one of Mad Love's concerts, hidden in darkness and watching Alan perform. Slipping into Montanna's psyche, I felt the same hot waves of jealousy and resentment that I'd picked up from the printouts of his emails.

This punk not only stopped taking my calls, he crossed a damned continent to get away from me! Who the hell does he think he is?

Did that scene ever take place? Did Rocky ever think those exact words? I had no idea. But I did sense that, through all these years, he'd stayed fixated on Bardot, maybe just as the cute young kid who'd made a clean getaway. It had driven him nuts when Alan resurfaced again as a rising rock star, and Montanna had no piece of that success. This blackmail gambit was his desperate attempt to make his "protégé" pay for spurning him, one way or another.

Alan scanned the contract with the taut posture of someone trying to decide whether to dive off a high cliff. Finally, though, he scrawled his name on the bottom of both copies.

Rocky smiled widely between the drooping ends of his faux-biker moustache.

"Malo, Dan, you're our witnesses." He waited while they signed, also. Then he refolded one copy of the contract and held the other out to Alan. "Smart decision, Bardot. You won't regret it."

"I'm sure I will." Alan folded the paper, stuffed it into the back pocket of his jeans and drew himself up, a couple of inches short of Rocky's height. "Okay, you've got what you wanted. Now put away the guns and untie my friends."

"Oh, is Callahan your friend again? I thought you two hadn't spoken since you fired his ass." Making no move to free either of us, Montanna slouched against the big, wheeled scaffold, not too far from where I sat. "Y'know, a few months back, Dan approached him about messing up some stuff on your tour. Barry turned the gig down, but he never did tell you guys about that, did he? Never even warned you."

Callahan squirmed against his bindings. "I would've, Alan, honest, but they threatened me!"

My own bound arms now ached all the way up to the shoulders. I twisted my hands back and forth a little to relieve the pain, and noticed something promising. My nervous sweat had begun to make the thick cables slippery. That gave me a little more leeway, though still not enough to get free.

Blinking back tears, I wondered if this psycho ever intended to let us go. Our only chance might be if Alan kept acting as though he fully accepted Montanna's terms.

I tuned back into that deeper darkness lurking in the shadows around us.

Once, sitting outdoors just before a thunderstorm, I felt the air around me thicken with ozone until it got hard to breathe. This was the same kind of sensation.

Something was gathering power.

Watching. Waiting.

For what?

Meanwhile, Bardot didn't seem afraid for himself. Probably, he figured Montanna needed him alive for this sick plan to work. In a measured tone, he said, "I noticed your contract didn't include any mention of the video."

"Right, the video! How could I forget?" Montanna glanced at his two hostages. "Callahan probably doesn't even know about that. Does *she?*" Then he smirked at me. "'Course you do, honey—you're psychic!"

Bardot would not be sidetracked. "I want your word that as long as I cooperate and Mad Love makes the payments, that footage will never be released."

"Sure, Alan. After all, you guys are just starting to make it big, and the video"—he chuckled —"that's pretty hot stuff! I'm sure you wouldn't want it to go up on the Internet, so all your fans could see their idol—"

Bardot glowered at his tormentor, and I could feel him fighting again to control his temper. Though I had no reason to think it would work, I tried to send him a telepathic warning.

Stay cool, Alan. He's just baiting you. Play along, if you have to, until we all get out of here!

In disgust, Bardot kicked the duffle through the sawdust on the floor toward Montanna. "Look, none of this shit has anything to do with Barry or Quinn. I kept my part of the deal, so let them go—now."

The older man left his spot by the scaffold and stooped to open the bag. Alan's gaze slid sideways, as if he might make a grab for Rocky's gun. But he hesitated, for good reason—Malo and Dan still had us all covered.

Satisfied, Montanna zipped up the duffle again. "Looks like it's all there. You gotta admit, kid, I'm only asking for my due. After all, I gave you your start! I showed you around L.A., introduced you to people—"

"Oh, yeah, I have *so* much to thank you for! Twelve years ago, you got me totally wasted at a party. Then you not only talked me into a group scene with some people I hardly knew, but made a video of it without even telling me!"

Rocky shrugged. "It was a screen test. You passed with flying colors. Not my fault you never took me up on my offer."

Alan's tight control finally began to unravel. "Then let's fast forward to the present. You practically admit that you sabotaged our plane last fall and wrecked our equipment bus..."

"Like I said, just to show you the gaps in your security. Nobody in your band got hurt."

"The bus driver ended up in the hospital! And when you screwed with the stage at the Rialto, a big chunk of shit fell and *killed* a guy. I know you had to be aiming for me or Jeff—"

Montanna raised his hands to block this last charge. "Hey, listen, I never—"

"Y'know what? Do whatever you want with that video. There's no way you could prove it was me, more than ten years ago. I can just say you got a look-alike and gave him the same tattoo. My word against yours. Who're they gonna believe?"

Montanna's eyes slitted at this insult—Alan's suggestion that a successful young rock star would have more credibility than an aging, on-the-skids pornographer. While I could understand Bardot's anger, I wished he'd go back to his low-key, fake-cooperative approach. If the two of them kept going at it like this, I didn't want to imagine the outcome.

I tried to head him off. "Alan, please—"

"Besides, Rocky, I can tell everybody you got me to do it by lying to me and drugging me. I was even underage at the time! You shot it after the New Year's Eve party, right? I didn't turn eighteen 'til February. But I hear you do that a lot, use kids—even younger ones. The way I see it, that video could make a hell of a lot more trouble for you than me!"

Montanna dropped his oily, ingratiating act, and his face darkened with fury. I sensed it was not just because Alan had called his bluff and hinted about ratting him out to the authorities. He'd held out some ridiculous hope that once he got Bardot's attention, the singer really would treat him as an old friend—the way Rocky had signed his emails—and would willingly help him out of his financial difficulties.

For a minute he fell quiet, which scared me more than when he'd been yakking it up. I worked my slippery wrists back and forth against the cushioned cables. I happen to have long, slim hands, and maybe Malo wasn't used to tying up women. Whatever the reason, I felt something start to give.

"So that's it, huh?" Montanna asked, finally. "That's your real plan?"

Bardot flinched, realizing he'd screwed up. His eyes darted toward Barry and me again, this time in apology.

Secretly, I wriggled the joint of my right thumb out of the cables, which was the hardest part. One good yank now would free both my arms.

"Y'know," Montanna went on, "I really thought you'd have *some* loyalty, *some* appreciation, for the guy who gave you your start. But you're just another arrogant punk who thinks he can step on people while he climbs to the top." He shot a look in Callahan's direction. "Am I right, Barry?"

The former guitarist sat too paralyzed with fear to say a word. His eyes just kept tracking the automatic Rocky waved around so dramatically.

I sat closer than Barry to the drawing board, though still a couple of yards away. But I only suspected he might have a gun stashed there, which I probably wouldn't know how to shoot. If I tried to get to it, or even let on my bindings were loose, Montanna would nail me first.

A movement up by the ceiling caught my eye. First I thought it was a bird, since there were plenty of half-open windows. But it didn't flutter.

It congealed into a stealthy, man-like shadow and crept along the rafters.

Just like at the Rialto. The perspiration went clammy on my skin.

Whether anyone else would have seen the apparition if they'd looked up, I have no idea. At any rate, they all remained too embroiled in their conflicts down below.

Maybe it was my physical helplessness that made me fall back on Gail's advice. For a moment, I managed to tune out the drama around me. I half-closed my eyes for a second and surrounded myself with the imaginary cocoon of protective white light. It became more of a web, though, as I stretched it to also envelope Barry and Alan.

I prayed silently, *Keep us safe from harm!*

A new tremor in Alan's voice snapped my attention back to the crisis in front of me.

"C'mon Rocky," he said, "I'm not gonna sell you out. I'm just saying, the best thing for both of us is to let the past be the past. You got a lot of green in there"—he nodded toward the duffle—"and you've got the signed contract, so there'll be more coming. Just as long as you leave me and the band alone and let us go back to making music!"

But Montanna's face remained hard, and the smile that finally slithered across it was just as cruel. "I was wrong about you, Bardot. Even by my standards, you'd make a terrible actor. No, the stuff you said a few minutes ago about taking your story to the cops, *that's* the part you meant." He sighed in stone-cold resignation, and his gaze swept the dim expanse of the factory space. "What the hell, might as well get rid of all three of you right here and now." He thought aloud. "You and the girl came out here to talk to Barry, for God knows what reason. Bad area, though. Some gangbangers broke in, robbed and shot you."

Montanna glanced at his two gunmen, and they both

shrugged agreeably. He told Fox, who stood nearest to Alan, "Waste him!"

I'm sure Dan would have, except for a long-drawn, metallic squeal above our heads. Before the sharp-dressed henchman could even glance up, a heavy steam pipe crashed down, knocking him to the floor.

While the dust settled, Bardot tried to sprint toward me and Barry, but stopped short when Montanna leveled his automatic. Rocky's wild stare swept over all three of us, as he tried to figure out who had pulled this trick.

Malo tried a more reasonable explanation. "Somebody's up there!" He fired into the rafters a couple of times. The echoing shots hurt my ears, but had no effect on his unseen enemy.

A movement toward the front of the room made the gunman pivot around. One of the big, caged utility lights hanging above our heads had grown dim and began to swing slowly back and forth, all on its own.

Montanna's mouth fell open. To my horror, he spun toward me. "You! Are you doing that?"

The shock almost made me tip my hand—literally—but I remembered to keep them both behind my back. "No!"

Alan also chimed in to defend me. "Of course not, Rocky. Are you nuts?"

I appreciated the gesture, but this only made the pornographer turn back to Bardot. "Then it's...*you*. It is, isn't it? I thought all that Goth crap was just an act, but you really are...some kind of *freak*."

Startled, Alan choked off a laugh. I read it as disbelief—*What is this guy smoking?* But Montanna seemed to take it as an admission that the singer was, indeed, using some kind of supernatural power to swing the fixture.

At first, the mustached man looked too scared to even retaliate. Then he aimed his own gun at Alan with a deadly determination.

A thunderous rumble, like an oncoming freight train, made us all look to the one side. Alan leaped out of the way, and Malo fired another wild shot, but Montanna stood frozen.

In the half-light, something huge roared across my vision...

Sweeping Rocky along with it.

CHAPTER 35

A gigantic crash shook the whole space around us.

In the ringing silence that followed, the overhead light flickered back to full brightness.

I saw the huge red pipe scaffold rammed hard up against the factory's brick wall. A few chips of reddish masonry dusted the floor around it. Montanna had to be pinned behind it somewhere.

More good news—his weapon had landed on the floor not far from my feet.

I ripped free of my cables and dove for it. Held it in front of me stiff-armed, the way I'd seen cops do on TV, and shouted at Malo, "Drop it, and kick it away!"

To my astonishment, he actually did so.

From the doorway, I heard a familiar voice bark, "You, too!"

Fox had staggered back to his feet, still armed, but he obeyed this command. Tony reached around him, from behind, to pick up the gun from the floor.

Alan wiped his brow and grinned at us. "Way to go, Quinn and Tony. Whatta team!"

I appreciated the vote of confidence, but didn't know how long I could hold Malo. My finger had found the trigger, but my arms spasmed at the idea of pulling it and possibly killing someone. I breathed easier at the mournful wail of a siren outside, headed in our direction.

"About damn time," muttered Tony.

I cut the police some slack, figuring there might actually be other crimes going on around town.

The first two cops to reach our floor ordered Tony and me

to freeze, since we now held the firearms. One barked at us to drop our guns and put our hands up, which we did only too gladly. Taking in the fallen ceiling pipe and the one man still tied up, the cop burst out, "What the hell is going on here?"

Alan tried to convince them Malo and Dan were the real villains. "And there's another guy pinned behind that big scaffold."

Though the second cop discovered this to be true, it only confused the two of them more. They frisked me and Tony and found our press IDs. But even though trussed-up Barry also vouched for us, we remained under suspicion until the real cavalry came tramping up the stairs—half-a-dozen guys in FBI flak jackets with automatic rifles. Stern and Jeff brought up the rear.

These new arrivals quickly helped the local police sort out the good guys from the bad guys.

The danger over, Tony put his arms around me, and I sagged against him. I wiped away tears against his faded Rutgers T-shirt as the nightmarish quality of the whole evening started to sink in.

He was shaking, too. But he stroked my hair and kept repeating, "It's all right now," until I finally believed it really was.

While the FBI guys dealt with Rocky and his henchmen and untied Barry, I told the local cops in more detail what had gone down. I also fetched my magic recording pen from the drafting table and handed it over.

"If you plug this into a computer," I said, "you should have all the evidence you need."

Alan grabbed Jeff in a warm hug, ignoring the sideways glances from the Harrison cops. Once Tony and I had finished answering questions, we joined them in a round of mutual congratulations.

"That bastard Zack, the fake bodyguard, had a gun on you," Bardot reminded Randall. "He made you hand over your phone. How'd you get away?"

Jeff grinned. "He couldn't let me out of his sight, so when he wanted a beer, he told me to get it. I dropped some of my pain pills in the bottle." The guitarist shrugged at the simplicity of the trick. "After he caught on, he tried to come after me, but I belted him—lucky I still got a good right hook! Then I turned him over to your building's security and called Stern."

"Awesome, Randall! When did you turn into Vin Diesel?" Alan ribbed him. "But how'd you even find us?"

"Stern already was waiting for Montanna across the river with the feds. They just tracked your cell phone."

Tony, his arm still around my waist, would not let my contribution go unheralded. "How about this lady, with her *Charlie's Angels* routine?"

Jeff snapped his fingers. "I knew she reminded me of somebody. One of those actresses, on the old show..." He groped for a name.

"The smart one." It was one of our inside jokes, but Tony's delivery turned it into high praise. He beamed at me, and I felt surer than I had in a long time that I was with the right partner. "Seriously, Quinn, would you really have shot that guy?"

"I'll be asking myself that question to my dying day," I admitted. "How the heck did you get Fox to drop his gun?"

Tony pulled out his ballpoint and poked it firmly between my shoulder blades. "The pen is mightier than the pistol."

The cops hustled Fox and Malo out the door, but needed an ambulance and a triage team for Montanna. Amazingly, the open pipework of the scaffold had not killed him outright, but seemed to have done a lot of damage. It had taken the police a few minutes even to rescue him from behind the heavy contraption.

Jeff noticed, too. "How did you guys ever push that thing onto him?"

"We didn't." Barry still looked seriously spooked, but groped for rational explanations. "The wheels should've been locked! On the other hand, these floors aren't completely level. Maybe when Camo Guy fired at the ceiling, a bullet ricocheted and jarred something."

Alan nodded. "He probably hit some wiring, too. Man, the look on Montanna's face when the lights went dim!"

We all laughed, and for the first time, I realized the sense of oppression throughout the factory space had lifted. This wasn't the time or place, I thought, to tell any of them about the apparition. Maybe later I'd at least confide in Tony.

Stern, who'd been pacing near the windows and talking on his cell, finally hung up and joined us. He looked so grim, Alan elbowed him.

"Hey, man, chill! We're all in one piece and the bad guys are going bye-bye. We should celebrate!"

I picked up on something, though. "Bad news?"

The manager nodded. "That was Lark, at the hospital. Her sister is…gone." I thought he meant she'd run away until he added, "Melissa died. About half an hour ago."

That last piece of news dampened any high we might have felt over surviving our harrowing ordeal. More somberly, we all split up and went our respective ways.

I accepted Tony's invitation to sleep at his apartment in Union. He heated a frozen pizza for basic sustenance, and we shared a decent Cabernet. While he filed a bare-bones version of the news story on his laptop for the *Sentinel's* website and early edition, I showered away some of the terror of the evening. By the time we fell into bed, we both were too exhausted to make love, but it was comforting just to sleep in his arms again.

We cashed that rain check early the next morning, then he was off to the *Sentinel* to flesh out his report. We both hoped that, aside from Tony's byline, our names could be kept out of story as far as possible.

Left alone, I sat in one of his long shirts at the little table in his kitchenette. I savored my second cup of coffee, the memory of Tony's kisses and the bright sun that filtered through the wooden blinds, and my nerves finally began to settle.

The cell phone in my purse rang, with a number I didn't recognize.

Lark's voice had a stuffy, underwater sound, as if she'd been doing a lot of crying. She thanked me for stopping by the hospital the day before to see her sister. "That was so nice of you, Quinn, after…what she tried to do."

Privately, I'd been hoping my stiff lecture had not stressed

Melissa to the breaking point. "When I saw talked to her, she was getting treatment, and I didn't think she seemed so terribly ill. Did the doctors say what happened?"

"They're still not completely sure." Lark drew a long, shaky breath. "The nurse said after you left, Melissa even ate a little of her supper. But then she got back into bed and...slipped into some kind of coma."

"Coma?" I echoed

"The doctor tried to explain it to me, but I could hardly focus—" Lark sounded so choked, tears crept into my eyes, too. "I guess anorexics can go into something called a hyper... hypoglycemic coma. The doctor said usually the treatment prevents that. But her poor body was so messed up, who knows?"

The phone went silent for a moment, and I told Lark how sorry I was. I would not have pressed her for more details, but she went on—as if it was hard for her discuss her sister's final moments, yet on another level she needed to tell someone.

"They said she was like that for almost an hour. When I got to her room, the doctors were working on her, and I thought she was coming out of it."

I tried in vain to think of something comforting. "At least you were with her at the end. I'm sure, on some level, she knew."

Lark sounded taken aback. "Funny you'd say that. I couldn't get too close because of the doctors, but I tried to talk to her, and maybe she did hear me. At the end, she almost seemed to wake up. She never opened her eyes, but she actually smiled to herself. She said just one word—'Good!' Then...she was gone."

After I got off the phone, I washed up the breakfast things in Tony's kitchen and pondered Melissa's death. Though I could never tell Lark, I had my own theories about what had happened to her sister.

What if the psychic effort of creating the servitor had taken a steep toll on Melissa's mind and body, weakening her even beyond the effects of her self-starvation?

She had told me Alan was in danger and needed her help. I suspected that, stuck in the hospital, she'd put herself into a trance and summoned the entity, by sheer force of will, to follow Bardot to the factory.

The effort of protecting him from Montanna might have sapped what little was left of Melissa's own life. But, from her last word, it sounded like she thought the tradeoff was worth it.

At home that afternoon, I called Gail, who agreed with my assessment.

She recapped, "At first, Melissa created the servitor using her home altar, with festishes and rituals, but after a while, it almost took on a life of its own. From then on, she probably could conjure it from anywhere."

"That must have been the case," I said. "After all, she was sitting right next to me at the Rialto when it knocked loose that chunk of plaster."

"She targeted Jeff and tried to injure him during the video shoot and at the jail," Gail went on. "But once you talked to her, she must have finally realized her passion for Alan was hopeless. At that point, knowing he was in danger, she sent the servitor to save him."

I badly needed my mentor's advice on one point. "Gail, I haven't mentioned the servitor idea to anybody associated with the band. I let them all think the apparition I saw at the theater was just some kind of psychic warning. For a while, I thought that really might be the case. Last night, though, it definitely acted like an independent...being...that could harm people."

"Yes," she murmured. "The things it did at the factory... very disturbing."

Even when Gail claimed to be disturbed, I thought, she always sounded serene.

"Everybody else assumes now that Montanna and his thugs were behind the tour sabotage and the Rialto incident, Melissa sent the threatening notes and the poisoned food, and anything else was just an accident or a coincidence. It would be easier for me to let them all go on thinking those things. Since poor Melissa has died, no one's going to believe, or want to hear, that she conjured up some ectoplasmic hit man."

"You're probably right," Gail admitted. "And, after all, it's not as if you could ever prove it."

"But on the other hand, what you said about the servitor taking on a life of its own...you don't think there's any chance it might still be around?"

A worrisome pause on the line. "There have been legends about Tibetan *tulpas* escaping the control of their masters and acting on their own, but I've never heard of one actually outliving its creator. Besides, it accomplished its last task, didn't it, by saving Alan's life? No, Quinn, I think we can be pretty confident Melissa's 'servant' died along with her."

I sure hoped so. The trace of doubt in Gail's statement still worried me long after I'd hung up the phone.

Had Melissa been the only thing keeping the vengeful entity alive...or the only thing keeping it under control?

CHAPTER 36

A basically true but sanitized report of what went down at the Harrison factory appeared in the Sentinel and the wider media. Montanna had threatened to release an embarrassing video from Alan's past; the two had arranged to meet at Barry's construction site to make a payoff, where the FBI had sprung a trap and taken Montanna into custody.

That Friday night, when Tony and I went out to a favorite Indian restaurant in my neighborhood, he told me the feds had tracked down Barry's former employee. When they offered the guy a deal, he'd confessed to sabotaging Mad Love's bus and plane on Montanna's orders.

"Funny thing is," Tony added, "the worker claimed he had nothing to do with what happened at the Rialto. And he had a solid alibi—in another state—for that night."

I decided to finally come clean. Tony already knew about the vision I'd had at the theater, but I admitted to also seeing the figure just before several other incidents. I even dared to tell him about Gail's thought-form theory.

A year or so earlier, he might have referred me to a good therapist. But since then, Tony had suffered through the haunting at my house and experienced a few things that seriously dented his natural skepticism. From his head shake now, I knew he had difficulty believing my story, but couldn't come up with any better explanation.

"I can see why you hesitated to tell Stern or the band guys about this," he said, "but don't you think they should know? If this…this entity really pushed a scaffolding onto Montanna…"

I took a calming swallow of my white wine. "I've wondered

the same thing, but I don't really think the band has anything to fear. After fall, the servitor's last act was to *protect* Alan."

"Maybe. But before that, it went after Jeff...and you."

At his reminder, I almost hallucinated a cold shadow flitting across the restaurant table between us. "Gail is the best authority I have on this, and she seems pretty sure it was laid to rest with its creator."

Tony speared another piece of chicken tandoori. "Let's hope to hell she's right!"

True to his word, Alan did set up the gig for me with *Celebrity Homes* magazine. The editor insisted on seeing samples of my writing, but apparently I made the grade. Or maybe she just couldn't resist the scoop, now that Mad Love had become such hot news.

The magazine assigned its own photographer, but I spent a full day chatting with Alan, Jeff and designer-to-the-stars Dara Smithson about the apartment's colorful and imaginative decor. At first, I fought off occasional flashbacks to the grim conversations I'd had with the band members while surrounded by all of those ghoulish, grinning faces. After I finally relaxed, though, I had a ball.

My story practically wrote itself. With a little tweaking, it was accepted by the magazine and scheduled for the October issue. Just in time for Halloween.

By summer, Alan and Jeff were openly sharing the condo and admitted their relationship to anyone who cared to ask. Tony tried to get a comment about this, without success, from Mayor Randall. If the guy had any heart at all, he must have been mortified that his secret deal with Reverend Willis almost got his son killed. And after hearing about the devotion Alan and Jeff had shown to each other during the recent crises, he might even have worried that, one of these days, his stand against same-sex marriage might be sorely tested.

Mad Love's new album included a romantic ballad—of which the band had recorded very few—that sounded as if Alan had written it for Jeff. Called "I'm for You," it included the chorus,

"Let them know
Yeah, let them see
We're together, and we're free."

It got major play on not only hard rock but more mainstream stations, too. Alan told me the whole album was selling briskly, on track to top sales of their previous CD. So, if being fronted by a same-sex couple might have lost the band some fans, as Stern always had feared, it probably also gained them some new ones.

By now, the Rialto had been cleared of any negligence in the death of the cameraman, and the suits and countersuits had been dropped. Since all the legal wrangling had held up the theater's restoration, to make amends, Mad Love decided to kick off its rescheduled tour with a fundraising performance at the theater. They offered Tony and me third-row seats. I was happy they wanted to support the struggling venue and dispel any concerns it might be unsafe.

I just hoped nothing happened to undermine their effort. Were they tempting fate by returning to the scene of the crime?

The evening had to be scaled down from the full tour show because the Rialto stage couldn't handle the same kind of set and effects as an arena. That made things easier on my friend Nancy's sensitive ears; because her husband Rob worked with the theater throughout its difficulties, they also got tickets to the show.

When I first settled in my seat, my gaze kept straying to the shadowy proscenium arch. Seated so close to the stage tonight, I really had to crane my neck to accomplish that and couldn't see the area above it at all.

If by any chance I did spot a smoky silhouette lurking around the stage tonight, what could I do? Jump up, wave my arms and scream? The guys probably would think I was just enjoying the show!

Once they took to the stage, though, I got far too caught up to indulge in any morbid thoughts.

Though I'd gotten to know the band members so well, I'd

only seen them perform live when they did the "Vampire" song for the video shoot and then in rehearsal at Pat's place. Their full-scale, hour-and-a-half show blew me away.

Alan matched his terrific vocal range with high-energy stage presence, whether stalking and swaggering to a hard rock number or delivering a moody ballad standing still beneath a blue spotlight. Jeff flashed some sexy moves of his own and sang along on a few numbers, but mostly let his Stratocaster do the howling and growling. The other three guys performed to the same superstar standard—Pat doing some backup vocals and switching nimbly between electric keyboards and a baby grand, with Jack's bass and Donny's drums driving the whole show.

After a while, I even caught my rock-a-phobic friend Nancy bopping along with a grin.

The set drew heavily from the band's latest album. When we called them back for an encore, though, Alan introduced a new song they hadn't recorded yet.

"You're hearing it first tonight," he said, quietly. "It's dedicated to a young lady who's no longer with us."

Pat began a trademark Mad Love minor-key riff on the electronic keyboard, and the guitars laid down a similar melancholy background. Alan's lyrics about someone "flying by night, losing the light" and "the bird who lost her way" raised a lump in my throat. Lark and her husband sat a few seats away from us, and I noticed her subtly wiping her eyes.

That gesture first drew my attention...

Then I looked past her and froze.

The show was sold out, and Lark had the last seat in our row. But someone sat next to her—*in* the aisle—and hovered at the same level. I should not have been able to see much of that person, yet somehow I could clearly make out the frizzy red-blonde hair, sharp nose and weak chin, and narrow, squared shoulders.

Melissa watched and listened to Alan's tribute to her...and smiled. In our three or four brief encounters, I had never seen such an expression on her face—of pure love. The wounded, jealous, grasping vibe had completely disappeared, and tonight she radiated only peace and joy.

I might have been the only person who saw her. Certainly no one else—not in our group and not in the band onstage—gave any sign of it. Even my vision lasted only about a minute before she disappeared.

Back to wherever she'd come from. I believed now, more than ever before, it had to be a much better place.

During the after-show party backstage, Nancy and Rob met the band members, and Lalita thanked me for my efforts in clearing the theater's reputation. While the Sabatinos chatted on with her about the Rialto's future, Tony and I got the chance to ask Alan about the song he'd written for Melissa.

"I just wanted to do something, y'know?" Bardot said, looking half embarrassed.

I told him, "I'm sure, in some way, Melissa heard it and appreciated it."

"You really think so?" He tilted his head at me, curious. "Maybe it sounds weird, after all the trouble she caused, but I have to feel sorry for her."

"Sounds like she had a lot of problems," Tony said.

Alan nodded. "Her shrink said it's a real mental illness—fixating on somebody you can't have and convincing yourself that person also wants to be with you, but the people around him are keeping you apart. It's called erotomania."

"Not nearly as much fun as it sounds." Jeff joined the conversation. "And no, *Erotomania* will not be the name of our next album."

We'd all been drinking champagne, and Alan had had enough to make him wax philosophical. "It's such a weird trip, this celebrity stuff. Starting out, you just want to get your songs heard. And when you start to make it, it's great to stand backstage and hear people screaming for you…and when you're performing and they all sing along." He sighed. "But it's also creepy when fans literally *idolize* you. Plaster their walls with pictures of you, find out everything they can about you, even stalk you! I usually try not to think too much about that part, but this stuff with Melissa really brought it all home." Shaking off his gloom, he draped one arm over his partner's shoulders.

"That's why I'm sticking with this guy. He has *no* illusions about me, but he puts up with me, anyway!"

Randall laughed. "Speaking of the price of fame, man, I need to drag you away. They want photos of us with the Rialto folks."

Bardot hoisted his champagne glass to Tony and me. "You ever want tickets to a show, for yourselves or your friends, just let us know. Anywhere, anytime. You two saved our butts—you rock!" Then he and Jeff slipped off into the party crowd.

I faced Tony with a grin. "Hear that? Alan Bardot said *we* rock."

"I've always known that." He hugged me around the waist, but also squinted suspiciously. "But I don't know about this 'anywhere, anytime' business. Better not take him up on that invitation unless I'm along! I think you've still got a crush on the guy."

I leaned against Tony and savored his reliably masculine appeal. "Maybe I did, but that's all it ever was. Alan's not the one who bluffed his way into that factory, practically through a hail of gunfire, and saved my life." I caught his hand and squeezed it. "Don't worry. You're everything I could even want in a man... Well, almost."

Tony pulled back, stricken. "Almost?"

I gave him an appraising once-over, then played with his dark forelock. "Ever think about maybe...dyeing this purple?"

About the Author

Eileen F. Watkins specializes in mystery and suspense fiction. She originally published *Dark Music*, as one of eight novels—mostly paranormal—through Amber Quill Press. *Dark Music* won the David G. Sasher Award at the 2014 Deadly Ink Mystery Conference. Watkins' second Quinn Matthews Haunting Mystery, *Hex, Death & Rock 'n' Roll*, was a Mystery finalist for the 2014 Next Generation EBook Awards. In 2017 she launched the Cat Groomer Mysteries though Kensington Publishing. The series began with *The Persian Always Meows Twice*, which won the David G. Sasher Award for Best Mystery of 2017 at the Deadly Ink Mystery Conference, and received a 2017 Certificate of Excellence from the Cat Writers' Association, Inc. It was followed in 2018 by *The Bengal Identity* and *Feral Attraction*.

Watkins is a member of Mystery Writers of America, the Liberty States Fiction Writers and Sisters in Crime. She serves as publicist for Sisters in Crime Central Jersey and for the annual Deadly Ink Mystery Conference. Watkins comes from a journalism background, having covered art, architecture, interior design and home improvement for New Jersey's two largest daily newspapers. She also has freelanced on those subjects for major magazines. In addition, as is apparent in her fiction, Watkins has strong interests in the paranormal and spirituality as well as in animal training and rescue. Visit her web site at www.efwatkins.com.

ALSO BY THIS AUTHOR

As E. F. Watkins

The Quinn Matthews Haunting Mysteries
Dark Music
Hex, Death, and Rock 'n' Roll

As Eileen Watkins

The Cat Groomer Mysteries (Kensington Publishing)
The Persian Always Meows Twice
The Bengal Identity
Feral Attraction

Curious about other Crossroad Press books?
Stop by our site:
http://www.crossroadpress.com
We offer quality writing
in digital, audio, and print formats.